About the Author

Anthony Kopelakis is a husband and father of two. Born and raised in Brooklyn, New York, he enjoyed the art of writing from the young age of nine. As his works transformed from seven page child adventures in old spiral notebooks to three hundred page thrillers on his laptop, his passion only grew. As someone who aspired to be a published author his entire life, Anthony's goal is for his work to inspire others to follow their own dream.

D.A.R.C: Inauguration

Anthony Kopelakis

D.A.R.C: Inauguration

Olympia Publishers
London

www.olympiapublishers.com
OLYMPIA PAPERBACK EDITION

Copyright © Anthony Kopelakis 2023

The right of Anthony Kopelakis to be identified as author of
this work has been asserted in accordance with sections 77 and 78 of
the Copyright, Designs and Patents Act 1988.

All Rights Reserved

No reproduction, copy or transmission of this publication
may be made without written permission.
No paragraph of this publication may be reproduced,
copied or transmitted save with the written permission of the publisher,
or in accordance with the provisions
of the Copyright Act 1956 (as amended).

Any person who commits any unauthorised act in relation to
this publication may be liable to criminal
prosecution and civil claims for damage.

A CIP catalogue record for this title is
available from the British Library.

ISBN: 978-1-80439-503-5

This is a work of fiction.
Names, characters, places and incidents originate from the writer's
imagination. Any resemblance to actual persons, living or dead, is
purely coincidental.

First Published in 2023

Olympia Publishers
Tallis House
2 Tallis Street
London
EC4Y 0AB

Printed in Great Britain

Dedication

I dedicate this book to my wife, Elizabeth, and my two daughters, Diana and Alexandra. They are my inspiration.

Acknowledgements

Thank you to my friends and family who listened to me talk on and on about my writing.

Chapter 1

Fighter

The sun had just crept up over the city skyline when a cellphone alarm's blaring tone rang out throughout the apartment.

"It is six thirty a.m.. on Monday, April 19th, 2021. It is currently fifty-four degrees and partly cloudy in New York City," the computerized voice on the phone announced before the blaring alarm commenced.

Austin turned over and slammed his hand down on his phone with disgust. Before getting out of bed, he looked up at the ceiling and pondered for a moment.

"Another fight," he groaned.

Austin threw himself out of bed and grabbed his clothes to prepare himself for the day. He tossed on his running outfit and shoes and stepped into the bathroom, quickly running gel through his thick, black hair. As he washed his hands, he stared at himself in the mirror, his chestnut brown eyes staring back at him.

"Another fight."

As he walked into the kitchen and grabbed a box of cereal from the cabinet, his cellphone rang.

"Hello."

"Good morning, roommate-to-be. What's up?" the voice on the other end said through a mouthful of food.

"Come on, Christian, did you purposely wait till your mouth was full to call me? You couldn't do it before?" Austin asked as he poured the cereal.

"No way. Mom made pancakes for breakfast. Nothing comes before them. You should consider yourself lucky that I hold you to the same level as Mom's pancakes. If I waited till after, that would just be rude," Christian joked.

"Oh, how kind of you but listen, don't get so happy about Mom's pancakes because once you move in, the breakfast menu is going to be a consistent bowl of cereal for… well forever," Austin replied as he closed the milk carton and placed it back in the fridge.

"I can't believe you willingly moved out and away from Mom's breakfast just so you could have cereal every day. I'm disappointed in you," Christian antagonized.

"But aren't you doing the same thing once June rolls around?"

"Yeah but not voluntarily. Apparently, because you moved out at eighteen, I have to do the same thing. And once Mom heard that Nick moved in across the hall with Josh and you had a vacancy, forget it. She jumped on the opportunity to have her two boys live together."

Austin laughed. "Oh, shut up. It'll be fun living together again. It's been five years since I moved out."

"Oh, believe me, I know exactly how long it's been. That's the day I got your room. Best gift you ever gave me."

"Well this chat has been great but I have to hurry up and finish eating. I have to get my run in."

"Okay, enjoy," Christian responded and hung up the phone.

As Austin finished his cereal and put the bowl in the sink, his phone rang again.

"Hello."

"Hey, Austin, you ready to go?"

"Hey, Nick, yeah, I'm leaving in five minutes but you do know you can just walk three feet and knock on my door, right?" Austin asked sarcastically.

"Listen, I spent the last four years sitting across from you for breakfast. I didn't have to go anywhere to make sure you were ready. And now you want me to walk across the hall and knock on your door? You must be crazy. I've only lived here for three weeks. It's gonna take some time for me to break through that laziness," Nick explained.

"Of course, what was I thinking." Austin chuckled. "Josh is ready too?"

"Yeah, he's just throwing his shoes on," Nick answered, digging his hand into his loose brown hair as he leaned his head on it in wait.

"All right, meet in the hall in five," Austin ordered and ended the phone call.

Austin closed his apartment door behind him and locked it. When he turned around, Nick was already leaning against the wall in wait.

"I thought you said Josh was ready," Austin stated.

"He was but now he's filling up his water bottle. Said he couldn't afford to forget it again."

Just then, the door opened and Josh walked out with his water bottle in hand and a miserable expression on his face.

"I hate fight-morning jogs," he admitted frustratingly.

"Come on, they're not *that* bad. You only threw up twice last week," Austin said while sharing a smile with Nick.

"Yeah, laugh it up, you two. If it happens again today, I'm just gonna start driving behind you," Josh exclaimed.

The three young men walked out of the apartment building and began their jog. Josh passed the time complaining about collapsed lungs and side stitches while Nick remained solidly focused on his jog through his headphones playing the latest episode of his favorite podcast. Austin's inspiration was similar.

As the jog began, Austin put his headphones comfortably into his ears and began to listen to his playlist of instrumentals. The lyrics to a song were always important but it was the beat and melody behind those lyrics that always enticed Austin. As the instrumental played, Austin felt himself slipping into the perfect zone where nothing could break his stride or focus, except for one person.

Jogging toward them from the opposite direction was a woman dressed in her usual combination of a sports tank and running tights. Austin was almost immediately snapped out of his jogging trance as he caught sight of her, her bright emerald eyes shining happily at him through strands of jet black hair. As she jogged past, a quick glance and slight smile was all it took for Austin to become entranced. Austin's gaze followed her as she continued down the block.

"Eyes in front, Romeo!" Nick shouted, pulling Austin back into reality. "Last time you did that, you busted your head on the stop sign on the corner."

"Oh, man, that would have been embarrassing," Austin replied.

"Again," Nick added.

Austin looked at Nick annoyingly. "Again."

"Instead of staring like a creep, why don't you just ask for her name and number?" Nick inquired.

"Despite what Rom-Coms might lead you to believe, I'm pretty sure a stranger stopping you on your jog to get your number would be just as creepy."

"She obviously notices you too. She's definitely not sending that little smile my way." Nick playfully nudged Austin.

"Yeah... maybe next time."

Josh slowly caught up with a limp, half-hearted jog.

"I hate... you two... so much," he complained through short bursts of air as his lungs struggled to refill with oxygen.

"Come on, drink your water and let's keep moving." Austin chuckled and darted off in a sprint.

"Oh, we're burning it up already?" Nick exclaimed and sprinted off to catch Austin.

"Freaks... you're both... freaks." Josh wheezed and quickly guzzled his water before continuing his half-hearted jog.

Footage of the three runners played on a large projector screen in a barely lit room with only two men as the audience.

"Tapped into the traffic cam; there he is." One man leaned back away from his computer keyboard.

"I don't know, Mike. What makes you think this guy is a good candidate?" the other asked as he stood up from his chair.

"Do we have much of a choice, Grant? One of our top agents couldn't even stop the project," Mike shot back.

"I know but I think I finally realize why that is. I think we made a mistake sending Agent Lancer in undercover." Grant paced back and forth in thought.

"Agent Lancer was one of our best operatives, especially in undercover operations. He was the best candidate for the mission."

Grant turned to him and replied, "Yes, but this mission is different. We don't need someone undercover; we need a mole, someone actually on the inside. Someone who has legitimate ties to this guy. I think that's the only way we're going to be able to take him down."

"And that's why I think this kid would make a good

candidate," Mike continued.

"I understand that but we already have Agent O'Neal being briefed on the mission. Why do you think we need to bring in some nobody as his partner?" Grant asked, confused.

"Look, I know Lancer's intel is what led us to discover that O'Neal's father worked security detail for the project but, personally, I don't think that's enough of an 'in'. The entire project is kept very close to the chest and honestly, I don't know if O'Neal has enough going for him to come off genuine," Mike explained as he sifted through a file.

"And you're telling me this guy somehow has a better 'in' than that?" Grant continued with unamused shock.

"Yes, I do," Mike replied with a smile and tossed the open file he was holding onto the table, pushing it toward Grant with two fingers. "Look at his bio page."

Grant picked up the file and began to look it over, reading it aloud.

"Austin Michaels, age twenty-three, six feet, two inches. Blah, blah… younger brother, dad is out of the picture, yada, yada."

Suddenly, Grant paused and read the next fact to himself.

"Are you shitting me?" he asked.

"Nope, I did some recon on this guy before bringing it up to you. Turns out he's involved in the same fight club as our guy. Street name for it is Reign. Now you know if we try to take him down because of the club, he'll just weasel his way out and we'll be left with our dicks in our hands but if we use Austin, we'll have him. I'm telling you, this connection beats O'Neal's any day of the week. He's our ticket," Mike answered.

"Yeah, except he has no experience. We have a trained agent with a weak connection and the only stronger connection we can get belongs to some nobody street fighter. This is perfect!" Grant shouted angrily as he tossed the file back on the table in disgust.

"Grant, we're running out of options and time. I say we bring him in and see where it goes and I don't think Hardwick would have any rebuttals on the matter," Mike persuaded.

Grant exhaled heavily. "All right, make the arrangements."

As nightfall came, Austin prepared to leave his apartment. He walked past the mirror hanging on the wall and caught a glance of his reflection, examining it for a moment. His attire, basketball shorts on top of compression pants and a gray muscle tee. His accessories, a large duffle bag packed with everything he would need for the night and his grappling gloves latched around the bag's handle. Austin let out a heavy sigh.

"Another fight."

His moment of self-reflection was interrupted by his cell phone ringing.

"Yea."

"Hey, you ready for your fight, champ?" Nick asked.

"Yeah, wonder what Damien's got for me this time," Austin proclaimed.

"Yeah, me too. Demi called me and said I was booked against some guy named Butch. Whose name is actually Butch?"

"Hey, names don't matter. What goes on inside that ring does. Stay focused."

"Yes, Sensei!" Nick joked.

"Josh is still alive from our run, right? He's still coming?" Austin asked as he grabbed his keys.

"Yeah, of course."

"All right, good. I'm ready to go," Austin said as he opened his door.

"Us too," Nick replied opening theirs.

"So, who you got tonight?" Josh inquired as they walked down the hall, the strands of his shoulder-length, sandy brown hair bouncing with each step, the rest up in a topknot.

"I don't know. I guess keeping it a secret from me will make things more interesting."

"But wouldn't not being prepared for your opponent give you a bigger chance of losing?" Josh asked.

"Yeah, but that's Damien's point. We should always be prepared whether we know of our opponent or not. Complaining that we need to know who our opponent is would just show how weak we are and that's the last thing you want inside Reign," Austin proclaimed.

When they arrived at the club, two men stood at a staircase leading down to the entrance.

"Austin, what's up, my man?" one of the men asked as they gave Austin a fist bump.

"Nothin' man, same shit, you know? Looking forward to kicking some ass when I get inside." Austin laughed.

"Be careful, I heard Damien thought really hard about your square up tonight," the other added.

They walked through the entrance door and down another two flights of barely lit stairs, the black-painted walls lined with graffiti. As they stepped through the club's door at the bottom, the stench of stale blood and sweat invaded their senses. The club stretched out in every direction, further than the building above should have allowed.

Throughout the large floor were five octagonal rings surrounded by steel caging, and surrounding the rings were swarms of fans biting at the bit for bloodshed. In the very middle of the club floor was the sixth and center ring, the champion's ring, which was the only ring surrounded by an additional barricade to keep fans away from the cage walls. The three men pushed and wormed their way through the thick crowd towards the center ring. A mix of bass-bumping instrumentals and thunderous roars from the crowd created a consistent vibration in Austin's ears. As they passed the barricade, a girl ran up to Austin and hugged him.

"How are you, Austin?" she inquired as she squeezed him tight.

"Not bad, Demi, I'm still a little sore from last week's fight but I'm more than ready."

"That's good because Damien has a guy for you tonight that even shocked me."

"How shocked are we talking?" Nick chimed in.

"Believe me, shocked enough."

"Austin, you sure you want to do this?" asked Josh as he handed Austin his wrist tape.

"Come on Josh, do you know me to back out of anything?" Austin retorted.

As Austin was taping his hands, a large, intimidating figure walked past him, completely ignoring Austin's small gathering near the steps.

"Looks like we found your opponent," Josh stated but Austin was already staring at him intently.

"I know that look. This one's not gonna be an easy night," Nick interjected.

"Austin, it's not too late to back out, no one would blame you," Demi pleaded.

"I'm not backing out, I'm gonna fight and I'm gonna win," Austin remarked as he jumped to his feet.

"All right, well I have to go kick some ass of my own so I'll catch up with you guys afterwards. Austin, good luck," Nick said as he turned toward his designated ring.

"You too, Nick."

"Hold on, wait for me!" Demi shouted as she followed Nick through the crowd.

The fighter in the ring never took his steely gaze off of Austin as he made his way up the three small steps to the mat. The official entered the ring with another official padlocking the door behind him.

"Ladies and gentlemen!" a voice shouted from above.

The crowds turned and saw a man standing at a large, open window above the fight floor with a microphone in hand. At the sight of him, the crowd quickly died down to a still murmur.

"Thank you all for coming out tonight. For the loyal fans, thank you for making us your Monday night routine and for those of you in the crowd that are new faces, congratulations on finding the place. I know it wasn't easy." The man chuckled. "But on to a more serious note, for those of you who don't know exactly who I am, my name is Damien Church and I own and run this lovely business you see before you."

"Church! Church! Church! Church!" the crowd began to chant repeatedly.

"All right, all right, settle down." Damien's smile never left his face. "When I started Reign, I envisioned two fighters battling it out, putting everything on the line. And it wasn't for the fame and glory, it wasn't for the giant paychecks or raging endorsements. It was to find out, without a shadow of a doubt, who was the best of the best. And not too long after the inception, I found the best! Austin Michaels!"

The crowd erupted in cheers and chants as Austin's gaze circled the room.

"But tonight, he is challenged with a greater obstacle than

ever before. I searched long and hard for someone who could give you a fight, Austin, and I think I finally found him. Six foot five with a seven foot wingspan. A hulking two hundred and eighty-two pounds of muscle. Would you believe I found him in Scotland? Ayr of all places! So without further ado, ladies and gentlemen, get ready to see something magical." Damien extended his hand to the center ring. "Official! You know what to do!"

The official finished putting on his black latex gloves and stood in the center of the two combatants.

"Austin, ready?"

Austin nodded; his stare fixated on his opponent.

"Rick, ready?"

Rick just turned to him and nodded. "Fight!"

Rick charged at Austin and quickly brought him to the mat, Austin's back smacking with a thud. Immediately, the two were struggling with everything they had to gain the top advantage. Austin latched his legs around Rick's waist, throwing his weight to the side.

Austin began to bombard Rick with powerful punches but before the damage was too great, Rick tossed Austin off of him. Even just the small shove was enough to thrust Austin's body away as if he were as light as a feather. As both men got to their feet, Austin ran at Rick and tackled him into the cage wall, his body bouncing off the steel but no later did he thrust a stiff elbow down into Austin's back.

Austin dropped to the mat as Rick immediately pounced like a lion on its prey. Solid strikes and stiff elbows quicky opened Austin's skin, the white mat turning to a deep crimson. Austin clawed onto the cage wall, pulling himself up to a vertical base.

"Austin, should I throw in the towel?" Josh inquired.

"You throw that towel and I'll drag you in here next," Austin replied sternly, his eyes still hard locked onto his opponent.

Rick charged at Austin once more and threw all his weight into a straight punch. Austin dodged the punch while wrapping his arms around Rick's neck. Rick flailed around the ring like a caged beast with Austin holding tightly onto his back. Rick threw his body backwards and slammed himself into the cage wall, crushing Austin between his solid frame and the unforgiving steel. A second time and a third, Rick continued to smash his body back into the wall until the force was too great. The cage wall snapped from its supports and crashed down onto the barricade.

The crowd erupted as they began to push their way closer, itching to envelop themselves in the action. Austin never loosened his grip for a moment and, as the blood dripped from his head, Austin wrung his arms tighter around Rick's neck until his eyes reluctantly closed. The official wasted no time calling the match and awarding Austin the victory. Again, the crowd exploded with cheers as Austin pushed himself to his feet and had his hand raised.

"Once again, your winner, Austin Michaels!" Damien announced with a broad smile. "Austin, you never cease to amaze me. Here I was thinking I provided a worthwhile opponent for you tonight. I guess that just means I didn't search hard enough. Congratulations, Austin."

Josh rushed into the ring to Austin's side.

"I hate when Demi is Nick's corner woman. I have to deal with watching anxiety like this," Josh complained with widened, stunned eyes.

"Didn't mean to worry you," Austin joked, giving Josh a timid punch in the arm.

He turned across the ring, hoping to show good sportsmanship to his opponent but when he did, Rick was gone. Austin looked closely at the background; in the back corner of the floor, two men were dragging an unconscious Rick through a wide metal door.

"You had me worried!" Demi yelled as she latched on to Austin's body, snapping him back to reality. "Don't think I didn't see what was going on over here."

"I'm sorry, it'll never happen again." Austin giggled.

"I know I say it all the time but when I first saw you walk through those doors, I didn't think you had what it took to survive down here. An innocent eighteen year old just following Old Man Church wherever he went." Demi chuckled. "But ever since that first night, you prove me wrong over and over again."

Demi quickly turned to Josh, her smile replaced with an angry stare.

"Why didn't you throw in the towel! He could have died!" Demi shouted as she slapped Josh repeatedly.

"Ow, ow, stop it! He said not to!" Josh argued back.

"I guess I missed a good fight!" Nick interjected.

"Then maybe you should finish yours sooner," Austin teased, sitting back down on his prep bench.

Nick gave Austin a look, raising his eyebrow as if already waiting for a prepared response. "What do I always say?"

Austin groaned.

"I'd rather finish the match later and have my hand raised than finish early and take a nap," Austin and Nick recited in unison, Austin looking bored from the repetition.

"Hold still, this'll sting," Demi warned and began to clean Austin's multiple wounds.

"I haven't seen you this messed up in a long time," Nick

admitted.

"Does it ever matter how — ow!" Austin flinched from Demi pressing the cold eye iron against his head.

"Stop being such a baby or I'll dump the ice bucket on you again," Demi threatened, giving Austin a no-nonsense glare.

As she continued to treat Austin, he proceeded, "Does it ever matter how bad the winner looks? I won't lie, Rick was a tough son of a bitch but nothing I couldn't handle."

"Can you hurry up and go say goodbye to Damien? I'm starving," Josh complained.

"Yeah, I could eat. How about the burger stand on the corner?" Nick asked.

"Ew, no way. He keeps ripping down his health grade from the window," Josh replied, contorting his mouth in disgust.

"Count me out for tonight," Austin chimed in.

"Aw come on, then who's gonna cover the bill?" Josh whined.

Nick sent a confused look Josh's way.

"What are you talking about? When Austin doesn't come, I cover it."

"Yeah, but you actually ask for the money back, Austin doesn't," Josh answered with a matter of fact tone as if it were common knowledge already.

"Sorry, guys, not really feeling up to a trek to the diner after this fight."

"Aw, is someone sore?" Nick mocked in a baby voice.

"No, Austin's right. I can deal with the cuts but he should get some rest or else he'll wake up extra sore tomorrow," Demi interjected.

"I'll meet you guys outside." Austin hooked his duffle bag around his shoulder.

Austin made his way across the floor and to a staircase. At the top of the stairs was a single door and through that door was Damien's office, the same room that overlooked the fight floor.

"Congratulations on your win tonight. Some exciting match, huh?" Damien asked.

"It was all right. Kind of expected more from such a grand introduction," Austin joked.

"Hey, I hear you. The lack of change is bad for business."

The two chuckled and Damien extended his hand.

"Seriously though, congratulations."

"Damien, you don't have to congratulate me every fight," Austin replied as he shook his hand.

"Yes, I do. You've come a long way and, even though this isn't the best line of work out there, I'm proud of what you've accomplished. Not many people can come from your nurtured upbringing and thrive down here the way you have. You have a lot of heart and discipline and I couldn't be prouder."

"Thanks, Damien, that means a lot. I would have probably ruined my life three times over if it weren't for you. I was so lost and I…" Austin paused. "That means a lot coming from you."

Damien smiled and simply embraced Austin.

"I don't know what was going through your father's mind when he left but he missed out on raising one hell of a young man. Anyone would be proud to call you their son."

"Thanks, Damien. I really try to make you proud."

Damien pulled away from the hug and held Austin's shoulders at arm's length. "Believe me, I feel nothing but pride every time I look at you."

Damien handed Austin a white envelope.

"I believe these winnings belong to you."

Austin opened the envelope and quickly glanced inside but

that glance was enough to tip him off.

"Damien, I don't need extra. The base winnings are fine."

"Oh, cut it out. You've earned every cent of it. And besides, there's only so long the base winnings would be able to pay for that apartment. A bonus here and there is a good thing."

Austin chuckled.

"Thank you, Damien."

"Enough with the thank you. Here, take Nick's winnings and get out of here. Enjoy your night."

Damien shoved another envelope into Austin's hands and pushed him out the door.

"Here's yours for the night," Austin said as he handed Nick his envelope outside.

"I *love* payday." Nick beamed.

"Damien give you the same old 'dad' talk?" Josh asked as the group lingered outside the club.

"Yeah, same as usual. Still, it's nice to hear sometimes."

"Hey, I don't blame you. It was a blessing in disguise to cross paths with Damien when you did. If not, things could have been a lot different," Josh included.

"A lot worse," Nick added.

"What? Bludgeoning people half to death in an illegal fight club isn't bad enough?" Demi asked sarcastically.

Austin laughed. "Enjoy dinner, guys, I'll see you around."

Austin split off from the group and began walking home in the opposite direction, stuffing his envelope of cash deep into his duffle bag. During his jogs, Austin loved getting lost in the instrumentals playing in his ears but during his long walks home after a fight, he loved getting enveloped by the pure silence of the still night.

The clear sound of each footstep hitting the concrete

sidewalk, the unmistakable whoosh of cars driving by, even the sound of crickets piercing through the silence. All of it put Austin at peace as he walked and tonight was no different until the abrupt sound of police sirens broke Austin's trance. He turned around and saw a police car pull up next to him. Without a word, two officers stepped out of the car and approached Austin.

"Something I can help you with, officers?" Austin asked, confused.

Suddenly, one officer pushed Austin up against the wall while the other began to search him.

"What the hell are you doing? You can't search me without cause!" Austin asked as he was pressed harder against the wall, the officer now dropping to one knee to pat down Austin's legs.

"We got our cause right here," the officer said as he stood back on his feet holding a small bag of white powder.

Austin's eyes widened.

"Wait, that's not mine!"

"We hear the same thing from every lowlife we bust. Let's go," the other officer exclaimed.

Austin continued to argue as the second officer handcuffed him and escorted him into the back of the police car.

For the entire drive and up until he was put into his cell, Austin tried to piece together what happened.

"Why would they plant drugs on me? It seemed too planned out to be a random stop. I need to use my phone call to call Mom. She'll be able to lawyer me out of this before it even makes it to trial."

Austin began to silently debate with himself.

"Wait, can lawyers defend their own kids? Whatever, she'll get someone else to help me. This is illegal and I have to bite back before I'm officially charged with anything."

Hours went by and Austin was left with nothing but his own racing thoughts to keep him company. As he laid in the uncomfortable bed trying to fall asleep, his cell door clanged open.

"Michaels, you have visitors. You must be important to get someone here in the middle of the night," the officer announced, his low, gravelly voice echoing through the hall.

"Visitors? But I didn't even get my phone call yet. No one even knows I'm here," Austin asked.

"Well somebody must know. Now let's go," the officer barked.

Austin was escorted into a windowless room where two men in suits sat across the table from him. Two officers were standing on either side of the door, one closing and locking it as Austin sat down slowly, still handcuffed.

"So, are you guys my public defenders or something?" Austin wondered.

"Or something," Grant replied.

"We're sorry this happened to you but we had no other choice. We had to meet with you in the most natural yet covert way possible. Outright abduction was a little too harsh for my taste but, nevertheless, we needed you to come to us," Mike added.

"What are you talking about? I don't—" Austin's eyes enlarged as the realization dawned on him. "Wait, you guys are the reason I was arrested?"

Grant leaned forward and whispered sternly, "We know who you are, Austin. We need to talk."

Chapter 2

A Whole New World

"You planted drugs on me just to talk to me?" Austin questioned already furious at the thought.

"Well *we* didn't. That would be Agents Danvers and Adams behind you," Mike responded as he walked over to Austin holding a set of keys.

Austin turned and recognized the two men as the officers who arrested him.

"Sorry about that." Danvers smirked.

"I'm sure," Austin replied, mocking Danvers' expression. He turned back to the table. "Who are you guys?"

"Name's Grant Walker, former U.S. Army Ranger and C.I.A."

Grant had an overall sternness to him and his demeanor alone denoted a military background. Even just introducing himself, the stare from his piercing brown eyes provoked a standoffish reaction.

"Mike Hall, former Marine and F.B.I."

Mike seemed more laid back compared to the all-too-serious atmosphere Grant unwillingly gave off. Mike's dull blue eyes seemed to show gentler intentions than Grant though, again, it wasn't hard to see the military background in Mike based on the composed and unflustered manner he carried.

"We are Elite Special Agents of a covert government

organization known as the Division Against Radical Criminals," Grant proclaimed.

"Or D.A.R.C. for short," Mike included.

"Wait, did you guys just tell me you're secret agents?" Austin asked, his eyes lighting up with childish wonder.

"And we're done here," Grant snapped.

"Grant, please," Mike begged. "Austin, please focus. This is extremely important. We don't have time to waste."

"This is wild. Is this real? Like you guys are actual secret agents? You work for a secret government agency?" Austin inquired, a playful smile permanently glued to his face.

"D.A.R.C. has stopped some of the world's most dangerous criminal masterminds and all while shrouded in secrecy; this is no different. What we have already told you and everything you hear from this point on is completely and utterly classified. If after tonight, you spill one word of any of this and believe me, we will know, you won't simply be arrested, you'll disappear from society and be thrown into the deepest, darkest hole I can find. Everyone you know will have to live on without you and life as you know it will be over. Do I make myself clear?" Grant threatened.

Austin paused for a moment and replied, "Just for future reference, not the best opening point when you're trying to sell something."

"Excuse me? Do you think this is a joke?" Grant shouted in anger, the sweat already glistening on his dark skin.

"Grant, cool it!" Mike cut in again. "Okay, admittingly, that's not the best way he could have opened but, all threats and jokes aside, this serious matter might need your input," he proceeded. "For the better half of four years now, we've been tracking the actions of an individual and his organization, though he's clearly been running it for much longer than that. In all this time, we've been able to collect enough intel to at least know of his plan," Mike explained.

"He is planning on creating a unique chemical compound which can genetically enhance the human body," Grant added.

"Am I crazy for only thinking about comic book super soldiers right now?" Austin asked.

"Austin please, this is serious," Mike pleaded.

"The operation is known as Project: Hercules and based on what we've gathered, he's getting close to perfecting the formula. If that happens, there's no telling what devastation he can cause in this world," Grant explained. "We sent one agent in undercover as one of his security detail. His alias file was perfectly solid, nothing to suspect that it was a false identity but, somehow, he was discovered and he lost his life because of it."

"This man is extremely dangerous and the longer we wait to strike, the more capable his formula becomes," Mike continued.

Austin turned to Grant and asked, "But why did you guys seek me out? Are secret agents big on roping in civilians?"

Grant exhaled with frustration as Mike answered the question. "We are preparing to send in another one of our agents to stop the operation but ourselves and our boss, Director Hardwick, feel it wise to send him in with a partner."

"You didn't answer my question. Why me? Why not another trained agent?"

"This mission is unique and delicate. We don't need someone to go in undercover; we need someone to be a double agent. We need someone to go in as themselves; someone who has an actual connection with this man; someone who can be trusted." Grant explained.

"Wait, are you telling me I know this guy?" Austin asked

with a mixed expression of shock and confusion.

"That's exactly what we're telling you. You want to see the true face of evil? Austin, meet the man behind Project: Hercules," Grant exclaimed as Mike handed Austin another file.

Austin grabbed the file but alternated glances of doubt between Mike and Grant. Finally, he slowly opened the file and there it was. The very first picture inside the folder was of the man they were talking about. The jolt of shock caused Austin's heart to race, his eyes stretching involuntarily. Grant leaned forward, pressing his open palms against the table.

"We know him as the bastard behind Project: Hercules; you know him as Damien Church."

"No — no way. You — you got this all wrong," Austin stammered. "Damien may not be anything close to a model citizen but to do what you're accusing him of, no way. The worst thing he does is run the fight club."

"We now believe he is using the fighters from the club as his test subjects for his serum," Mike stated.

"So what? He's just making people disappear and no one notices?" Austin questioned rhetorically.

"Are you going to tell me in all your years at that club, you never noticed anything off color?" Grant asked, his volume already on the rise.

Austin pondered for a moment.

"Tonight, I saw Rick, my opponent, I saw him being dragged through a backdoor. I — I don't know where it led," Austin admitted but wasted no time jumping to Damien's defense. "But this is ridiculous. There's no way Damien is guilty of this stuff. You got the wrong guy."

"Austin, we're not wrong. We know he is behind it. We just can't seem to stop him," Mike assured.

"I just saw him a few hours ago, I mean it's not like he keeps himself hidden. What's stopping you from taking him down if you think he's so guilty?" Austin posed.

"Project: Hercules is bigger than just Damien. Despite how dangerous he can be on his own, his formula is worse. Sure, we could pop his head like a balloon with a .50 caliber sniper rifle as he exits the club but stopping him won't stop his research. We need to get close enough to make sure his entire operation is wiped out. Simply killing the man won't accomplish that," Grant explained further.

Austin slowly slid the file back across the table towards the two agents.

"I've known Damien for seven years. He's helped me in ways I can't even describe and it's not a stretch to say he saved my life. Like I said, he's not a saint but he's also not the person in this file. I'm sorry but there's nothing I can do for you."

"I know this is a lot to absorb but please don't dismiss this. We know he's our guy, that's how we connected you in the first place. If we don't get someone on the inside to break down his operation, we could be looking at a new world order. If he goes unchecked and is able to perfect his formula, there's no telling what the damage could be. He could create his own army or sell the formula to the highest bidder. Imagine our enemies with an army of enhanced individuals. The world would have to bow to their power," Mike explained in his usual gentle tone.

"This is ridiculous," Grant stated having lost his patience. "Do you think we wanted to come to some twenty-three-year-old street punk on our hands and knees? The only way to stop this bastard is to put someone on the inside who knows him. The agent we are sending in has his own connection to Church but no one is closer to him than you. That is the only, and I mean the *only* reason we would stoop low enough to come to you begging for your help," Grant explained.

"I don't care how close I am to him; I'm not going to help you hunt someone who's been like a father to me! And besides, I wouldn't want you to have to grovel to a street punk like me!" Austin rebutted with an angry attitude.

"Austin, he didn't mean it that way." Mike defended Grant once more but his statement went unnoticed as the tension only grew.

"You're right, that's the last thing I want but unfortunately for both of us, this is bigger than either of our wishes!" Grant shot back matching Austin's tone.

"Enough, Grant!" Mike shouted at his partner before looking at Austin and continuing, "Look, I know this is all a lot to process and I know you don't have any reason to truly believe us but we wouldn't be here if we weren't sure. There is no doubt that Church is our guy. We're risking our entire organization's identity just to have this meeting but, unfortunately, we've grown desperate. We'd rather swallow our pride and complete this mission than let Damien get away with this and hurt any more innocent people."

Austin exhaled slowly. "Listen, guys, even if, and this is a huge 'if', you're right about Damien, I still can't help you. When I was fourteen, my father left. No reason, no warning, just up and left us one day. I don't know why but for some reason, I took it the worst. I lashed out at anyone who tried to get close to me. I was angry all the time. I hated my father for leaving, I hated the world for letting it happen, and I hated everyone else for acting like they knew how I felt. I spent the next two years with that outlook but, eventually, it got me into trouble. That's when I met Damien. He taught me to not just erupt erratically with my emotions but channel them into something that could breed results. He introduced me to his fight club and taught me everything I needed to know. Focus, discipline, drive, I learned it all from him. Because of that, I was able to direct all my emotions towards the fight and the rest of my life benefited from it. He's the one who helped me get my life back on track and, over the last seven years, he's become like a father to me. So even if you're right, I can't help you go against him."

"Do you think a lot about your father?" Grant chimed in.

"Excuse me?" Austin asked, his insides already beginning to burn with rage.

"I'm sure it still eats away at you that you still have no explanation all these years later."

"Grant!" Mike shouted knowing Grant was about to go too far.

"What did you just say to me?" Austin asked, the anger building fast.

"I did a little extra digging on my own and found something very interesting in your mother's computer. You would like her, Mike, Debbie is very organized," Grant admitted, pulling a piece of paper out from the inside of his suit jacket.

"You were in her home?" Austin erupted from his chair but Danvers and Adams quickly overpowered him and forced him back down.

Mike was stunned. "Grant, what is this?"

"I knew we were going to need more leverage and you wouldn't have had the heart to go through with it. So I did it without your help."

"You went behind my back? Does Hardwick know about this?"

"Hardwick doesn't need to know how we recruited Austin,

just that we got it done." Grant turned to Austin and continued, "She must've uploaded it for posterity. I have here a copy of the note your father left your family." Grant began to read the letter aloud. "To my wife, Debbie, and my two sons, Austin and Christian, I know this will be shocking to hear but I cannot live this life any longer. I find my only option is to leave and do what I must for myself. You may find it selfish of me but if I don't, I would only be lying to all of you. We will all be happier once we are living separate paths. Thomas Michaels."

Even while being held down by the agents, Austin stared a hole into Grant through tears that were now swelling in his eyes.

"I'm sorry I had to go so far but that is how important this mission is."

"Go fuck yourself." Austin's voice shook.

"I'm sure I've deserved more than my fair share of those in my life but, right now, I don't give a damn about your feelings. We need your help."

"And reading my father's letter was supposed to do what, convince me?"

"I'm wondering the same thing," Mike added in an angered tone.

Grant slowly sat down in his chair and looked at Austin. "Here is my proposition. It's no secret that this letter from your father is pretty open-ended. If you assist in completing this mission and Project: Hercules is shut down, we will find your father and you can finally get the closure you've always wanted."

"You'll find my father? Just like that?" Austin asked in disbelief.

"We have access to every database and surveillance in the country, and our worldly connections are anything but limited. If he's breathing, we'll find him and, if he's not, we'll show you his tombstone."

Austin paused again, his eyes wandering into a thousand-yard stare as he contemplated.

"It's been almost ten years since he left us. I never thought closure was an option."

"Austin, we're not asking you to put a bullet into the man, we just need your help stopping his operation. If we're wrong, then there would be nothing to do against Damien and nothing about your relationship with him changes. But if we're right, you'd be helping to save countless lives and ensuring that this world we live in remains intact," Mike consoled.

"Did anyone ever tell you you're the nicer one?" Austin asked.

"All the time." Mike gently smiled.

Austin glanced over to Grant. "And did anyone ever tell you you're a dick?"

"All the time," he admitted.

Austin pondered once again, countless thoughts racing through his head. The unbelievable truths, the outrageous accusations, and the promise of something previously thought out of reach.

"We need an answer," Grant demanded.

"I—" Austin stopped immediately as if already retracting the decision he was about to make.

The room was still and silent as the anticipation of Austin's answer just grew.

"Austin, please, we need your answer," Mike pleaded.

Austin shook his head subtly. "I honestly don't know."

The atmosphere deflated in failure.

"I don't agree with any of your findings. I don't think Damien is your guy and I would never want to betray someone who did so much for me. But being able to talk to my father and finally find out why he left us, that's something I'd be stupid to pass up."

"What if we took things slow?" Mike asked.

"Mike, if we go any slower, we'll be going backwards!" Grant barked angrily.

"How slow?" Austin questioned.

"We won't demand your loyalty at this table. All that I'm asking is that you give this whole thing a chance. Now that you know what we know, you can take your time and see things with a fresh perspective. If you still think that nothing is wrong, then we'll bow out gracefully. But if you feel like things aren't what you thought they were, then you help us take Damien down."

Austin stared at Mike intently for a moment. Mike could practically see the gears turning in Austin's head as he considered the offer.

"I can do that."

"Perfect." Mike smiled widely.

"Ridiculous," Grant murmured with anger.

"So what about my arrest?" Austin asked.

"What arrest?" Mike gently banged his paperwork on the table to get it organized. "It's such a shame when central booking loses a suspect's fingerprints."

Mike traded looks with Danvers and Adams and gave them a reassuring nod. Without a word, they lifted Austin from the chair.

"Sorry for the misunderstanding, Sir, we'll escort you to the exit as soon as possible." Adams gave a fake, exaggerated smile.

"So you guys like playing dress up?" Austin mocked as they escorted him out of the room.

As soon as the door closed, Grant verbally pounced on Mike.

"Are you kidding me? Why would you offer him something so absurd? I don't know if you've noticed but we don't exactly have the luxury of time!"

"And we also don't have a lot going for us in this mission. O'Neal is working on half a prayer. We both know Austin is our best shot at taking Damien down so if that means giving him some breathing room and having a little bit of patience, then I'll take it. I'd rather earn Austin's trust than demand his loyalty."

"When Damien succeeds, it'll be because of your soft heart." Grant poked Mike aggressively in the chest.

Mike responded with a slight smile. "If you didn't think my method was going to be productive, you would've shut it down before Austin left the room. Don't try to pull your tough guy shit with me, Grant. I know you better than that so I think the words you were actually looking for were 'good idea'."

Grant remained silent, letting his angry stare do all the talking. Without a single response, Grant stormed out of the room in a huff.

As promised, Austin was escorted out through the parking lot entrance of the precinct.

"Thanks for the night, fellas, but I don't think I want a second date," Austin said annoyingly.

"Don't act cute. You have no idea what's riding on this mission," Danvers fired back. "In my entire career in D.A.R.C., I've never seen a civilian get brought in on a mission briefing. Everything about this mission is unprecedented. That should speak volumes as to the importance."

Adams handed Austin a small phone.

"Hold on to this. Unable to be traced, hacked, or tapped. If Mike and Grant want to get in contact with you, it'll be on this. There's one number in the contact list in case you decide to take them up on their offer sooner."

"I'll keep that in mind," Austin replied, putting the phone in his back pocket.

Austin walked into his apartment, his feet sliding across the floor in exhaustion. He flopped onto his bed but, before closing his eyes, he reached into his back pocket and pulled out the phone he was given. He stared at it for a moment, mentally retracing everything he was told and what he was offered.

Austin opened his eyes and saw his bedroom bathed in the yellow glow of the sun.

"I must've dozed off. ATOM, what time is it?" Austin asked his virtual assistant device that sat at the corner of his nightstand.

"Good afternoon, it is currently 12.37 p.m..," ATOM announced.

Austin shuffled into the kitchen and opened the refrigerator door. After a quick glance, he closed it.

"Great, late start and I'm out of eggs," he groaned.

Austin threw on the first outfit he could reach and prepared to leave. As he zipped up his hoodie, he caught sight of the phone still sitting on his bed, half buried in the comforter. After a brief pause of debate, Austin scooped up the phone and put it in his pocket.

He stepped out of the apartment building and headed down the block, walking for several minutes before coming to a corner diner. A "grand opening" sign hung across the side with plastic streamers dangling from the long awning. "Shaw's" was written across the awning in beautiful calligraphy.

"Might as well try this place, the day's weird enough anyway." Austin convinced himself and opened the front door.

"Welcome to Shaw's. How may I help you today?" A woman approached with an inviting smile.

"Table for one, please." Austin smiled back.

"Of course, right this way." The hostess placed a single menu under her arm and directed Austin across the dining floor.

Finally, she stopped at an empty booth and placed the menu on the table.

"Alyssa will be your waitress today and if there's anything else you need, don't hesitate to ask," the hostess informed.

"Thank you very much."

The hostess stepped away and, a moment later, the waitress walked up to the table. Austin was already laser focused on the menu, scanning for which dish would be a decent substitute for the usual breakfast he would make himself.

"Well, if it isn't my jogging stalker," the waitress announced, her voice playful and inviting.

Austin's head quickly snapped up from the menu in shock but then his eyes caught who the words came from.

"I don't believe it,." he confessed.

After countless mornings of jogging past each other and exchanging tiny, barely noticeable smiles, the woman who always pulled Austin from his jogging trances was now standing two feet in front of him.

She laughed playfully. "I'm sorry, this is my first day but I couldn't pass up that kind of opportunity."

"I would have never imagined meeting you here of all places," Austin continued.

"I would have never imagined you ever talking to me."

Austin immediately felt his body drain of all confidence.

"That was cold," he admitted humorously.

"Oh come on, I'm kidding. We've jogged past each other for months and you never said a word. I was beginning to think I read the whole thing wrong."

"I was afraid of coming off creepy if I stopped your jog to talk but, apparently, I only came off as a mute." Austin laughed.

Alyssa sat down on the other side of the booth and tugged on the nametag on her shirt. "Well, you know my name, do I get to know yours?"

"Austin. Austin Michaels."

"Oof, you missed a perfect chance to hit me with a suave James Bond intro like this." Alyssa raised her eyebrow and deepened her voice. "The name's Moore, Alyssa Moore."

Austin laughed and said, "I am clearly very unprepared for this meeting."

"That's okay. I had time to prepare. I saw you when you first walked in," Alyssa confessed.

The two laughed and stared at each other for a moment.

"I'm sorry, I should really do my job." Alyssa jumped up from the booth.

"No, no, it's totally okay. I'm really glad we were able to finally meet."

"Me too. And who knows, maybe one day we could go on that jog together." Alyssa smiled.

Austin smiled back. "That would be great."

Alyssa walked away still wearing her smile while Austin tried his hardest to refocus on the menu. Suddenly, Alyssa darted back over in embarrassment.

"I should probably take your order before I go." She blushed.

"I'll just have the eggs," Austin stated as he handed Alyssa the menu.

"No problem, I'll make sure they just do the egg whites. I'm sure you only want the healthiest." She winked.

"You read my mind." Austin gleamed.

When Austin finished his late breakfast, he headed towards

the exit but saw Alyssa standing by one of the diner's podiums. After contemplating for a moment, Austin made his way over to her.

"I don't want this to come off weird or pushy but I was wondering—"

"Yes," Alyssa cut in.

"Yes?" Austin questioned confused.

"I would love to go out, sometime," she admitted. "They told me my schedule would be pretty consistent so I'll be out of here every night by eight. So just let me know when."

Austin was speechless as his stunned, widened eyes remained locked on Alyssa.

"Okay, sounds good," he finally got out.

"Great," she replied with a smile before turning back to the podium screen.

That night, as Austin was putting away the last of the groceries he had recently bought, he heard a phone ring. He quickly peeked over at his cell phone which laid silent on the table. The phone rang again. This time, Austin knew where to look. He moved several items on the table and uncovered the agency phone he was given.

It rang again. Austin stared at it, the bright, active screen revealing "Restricted" as the caller. The phone rang again, this time in Austin's hand as he lifted it from the table. He tapped the screen and put the phone to his ear.

"Hello?"

"Look outside your living room window," Mike directed.

Austin walked over to the appropriate window and pushed the blinds apart with his index and middle fingers.

"Across the street is a black van. That's your ride."

"Ride to where?" Austin asked but the call abruptly ended.

Austin exited his apartment building, looking cautiously at his surroundings before making his way across the street. As Austin crept closer to the van, the side door slid open.

"Mr. Michaels. We're here to escort you to the testing grounds."

"Danvers! Did you miss me that much?" Austin teased. "Is Adams driving?"

The driver side window lowered.

"Evening, Mr. Michaels," Adams greeted.

"Guys, what is this? You were there when the deal was made. I thought you were giving me my space to decide this for myself," Austin claimed.

"Agent Hall has all intentions of adhering to the agreement but, in the meantime, Agent Walker deemed it necessary to test your limitations before any mission work was to be done." Danvers gestured with his arm for Austin to enter.

"So you just let me think I had a choice, was that it?"

"Not at all, Mr. Michaels. But if you happen to accept the offer, D.A.R.C. has to make sure you are fit for active field duty. If not, then there is no point in this outrageous plan," Danvers continued, again gesturing for Austin to enter the van.

Austin exhaled heavily and reluctantly entered the van. From within the back of the van, it was impossible to see where it was headed. When the van stopped and Danvers opened the door, Austin stepped out and saw a large warehouse in front of him.

"Right this way, Mr. Michaels."

"Just call me Austin. You guys arrested me; I feel like we're closer than that," Austin jested once more.

Danvers and Adams escorted Austin into the warehouse and through a single door and, suddenly, Austin found himself in a dark room. The lights turned on and Austin saw that he was standing across from Mike, Grant, and two other unknown men.

"Welcome to stage one of your inauguration," Mike stated.

"Before we begin, I would like to introduce you to our superior agent, Director Theodore Hardwick. Director, this is Austin Michaels," Grant introduced as Austin and Hardwick shook hands.

"Pleasure to meet you, son."

Hardwick was older in years, his wrinkled skin already beginning to weigh down. His pure white hair was only overpowered by his even whiter veneers which showed through his thin, aged lips. His bushy yet trimmed eyebrows rose with excitement as he smiled.

"I just want to thank you for even considering such a service. I know all of this seems surreal and I'll be the first to admit that the feeling is mutual on our side as well. We have never needed the help of a civilian to this extent. Believe me when I say we are not taking any of your actions or motives for granted."

"I appreciate that, thank you. But like I told Mike and Grant, this whole thing is still up in the air for me. I'm not committing to anything," Austin replied.

"I understand that completely. We know that none of this should have to fall on you and we are willing to be patient with your decision," Hardwick continued.

"So what did you call this? Inauguration?" Austin questioned.

"We'll get to that, but first, we would like you to meet the agent that you will be partnering with. This is Agent Jeffrey O'Neal." Mike waved his arm to the agent as if revealing a game show prize.

"Jeff's fine. And I gotta say, I don't know much about the backstage politics of this division but I know this mission must be pretty damn important to warrant bringing a civilian on board." Jeff chuckled as he shook Austin's hand, his grip strong and firm.

If seen in any other environment, Austin would pass Jeff up as any normal civilian. His lightly stubbled beard and long ponytail didn't exactly scream covert operative but Austin wondered if that was maybe the point.

"Apparently you have a connection to Church just like I do," Austin responded.

"Yep, though I hear your connection is quite a doozie. This inauguration should be interesting." Jeff smirked.

"Austin, are you ready to begin?" Grant asked.

"Sure, but what am I doing?"

Grant turned away from Austin and while looking back from the corner of his eye, he answered, "You'll see."

Chapter 3

Inauguration

The group stepped through a nearby door into another room that looked very similar to the local gym Austin was familiar with.

"You brought me here to work out?" Austin asked with a playful smile.

"Not quite," Mike replied simply. "It goes without saying that we could never send a civilian into the field, no matter how dire the mission is."

"That's why by the time we're done with you, you won't be a civilian any more. When we're through with you, you'll be conditioned enough to be considered a partial agent. At least good enough to not be a hindrance to O'Neal," Grant added.

"So, how does this conditioning work?" Austin asked.

Mike stared at Austin with a giddy smile.

Austin leaned over to Grant. "Why is he staring at me like that?"

Grant shook his head and said, "Mike loves conditioning potential agents."

Austin was given a change of clothes, something he would be more comfortable working out in. When he returned after changing, Mike was the only one left in the gym, standing impatiently by the treadmill.

"So what's first?" Austin asked, looking around at the numerous machines spread about the room.

"First thing I like to do is a benchmark test. We're gonna stick you on this bad boy and see not only how much you can push yourself, but how your body reacts to being pushed to the limit." Mike patted the treadmill's console like a proud father.

Two agents hooked Austin up to the treadmill, putting EKG electrodes on his chest and a clamp on his index finger. Mike stepped into the connecting room where the other three agents were waiting. Austin readied himself on the treadmill, his eyes staring directly at a reflection of himself in the two-way mirror imbedded in the wall.

"Are you ready to begin?" Mike spoke into an intercom while holding the button down.

"Guess so," Austin answered nonchalantly.

Grant shoved his way over to the intercom.

"I wanna hear more resolve in your voice. Not a single ounce of this entire ordeal is a game so start taking it seriously."

Austin stared furiously at the mirror hoping his gaze would connect with Grant's.

"You wanna see serious? I'll show you serious."

The treadmill whirred to life as the rubber treading began to move. Austin started the test at a leisurely pace but it didn't take long for the speed to pick up. The four agents watched intently from behind the mirror but Director Hardwick broke the silence.

"I still can't believe this is what this agency has come to. In all my years, I never thought I'd see the day where we rely on a civilian."

"Sir, you know we wouldn't be doing this if we had any other choice but Austin is like a son to Church. If we can recruit Austin, we have a real chance of stopping Project: Hercules," Mike rebutted.

"Guess he blows my connection out of the water then. Just

send him in, Church won't hurt his precious boy and I can take my vacation days," Jeff exclaimed, his arms folded tightly.

"You know it's not that simple, O'Neal. Austin is the connection to the heart of Project: Hercules but you are the heart attack that kills it," Grant responded.

The treadmill's speed increased again and the slope elevated, Austin now having to fully run to keep up. With every passing minute, the test became more grueling but Austin continued to push himself furiously. The monotony of his rubber soles pounding against the sleek tread was enough to drive someone mad but Austin pushed onward regardless, mostly to spite Grant's overwhelming negativity towards him.

"Mike, how are his readings?" Hardwick wondered.

"Stable, Sir. His vitals are still within an adequate range. His body seems to be handling the test fine." Mike handed the tablet over to Hardwick.

Hardwick squinted slightly at the screen in disbelief. "This is quite impressive. We don't have many agents with these kinds of readings."

"Turn it up again," Grant interjected from the back of the small room.

"More? Why? What would that prove? This already tells us that he passed the first test," Mike questioned in confusion.

"Just do it," Grant said simply, the frustration hiding just beneath the surface of his words.

Mike glanced over to Hardwick who was already handing the tablet back to him. Mike dragged his finger across the screen and, just like that, the treadmill kicked into an entirely different gear. Immediately, Austin felt the difference in intensity under him and began to run as fast as he could, hoping to keep up with the blur of rubber beneath his feet.

Mike looked at Grant with an air of arrogance. "Satisfied?"

Grant stayed silent for a moment as he stared at Austin through the window. "Move on to the next test."

"You did fantastic, Austin. We're moving on," Mike stated through the intercom, a smile stretched across his face.

For the next several hours, Austin was tested in a wide range of exercises and activities. Strength, endurance, agility, flexibility, speed, and power. Austin was systematically assessed in all six traits and he impressed without question. All the while, Hardwick watched on with admiration, Grant watched on with irritation, and Mike simply stared at Grant with a smug smile. Finally, the benchmarks were over.

"That's it, Austin. You completed each benchmark with very impressive numbers," Mike stated still staring at the information on the tablet.

Austin was wiping the abundance of sweat off his face and chest. "Huh, maybe next time I should take it less seriously."

His eyes locked on tight with Grant's. Grant said nothing and simply walked away.

"So what now?" Austin asked.

"Now that we know you can handle it, we're going to be pushing the limits you set for yourself today. In addition, we're going to be focusing on combat training as well as firearms training," Hardwick explained.

"So you're pretty much training me like an agent even though I'm not one."

"That's the only choice we have if we want to feel confident sending you out in the field with Agent O'Neal. O'Neal is a great agent but he needs to know he can count on you to have his back. He isn't going to play babysitter," Mike continued.

"I understand."

"If you head straight through that door, the van is waiting for you outside. We'll be in touch." Mike smiled with a nod.

Austin did as he was told and headed through the exit but instead of the van, he saw Jeff standing across from him.

"Hey," Austin greeted.

"Heard you did pretty well tonight. That only bodes well for our mission."

"It was pretty much one long workout session and I'm pretty good at those." Austin laughed. "I was told the van would be here to bring me home."

"Sorry, that's my fault. I sent them away already. I figured we could go grab a bite to eat and talk a little. It'd be nice to know the guy that's gonna be my partner." O'Neal smiled.

"Honestly, I still haven't decided anything about the mission but yeah, I could go for a bite to eat, couldn't hurt."

Austin followed Jeff to his car at the end of the warehouse parking lot. Jeff drove to a walkup burger shop nearby. Jeff grabbed the two trays of food and walked over to Austin who was already sitting at one of the tables.

"All right, so question of the night. Why were you chosen by the suits?" Jeff asked as he sat across from Austin, shoving a fry into his mouth.

"Well, turns out the guy they're after, Damien Church, runs the fight club I'm in."

Jeff chuckled. "Wait a minute, you're in a fight club? Like a real fight club? Cages and everything?"

"Yeah, pay per view quality, not pay per view endorsements." Austin chuckled as he wrapped his hands around his burger.

"That's wicked! So, they want you to take him down from the inside using your fight club connection?"

"Yeah, seems that way. They know how close we are which is why I said I still had to think about it. I've known Damien for seven years and I don't think he's capable of doing the things you guys say he did. But at the same time, if I could use this opportunity to prove his innocence, then I'll do it. So I'm still on the fence about the whole thing." Austin latched his teeth onto his burger and ripped off a big bite. "How about you? What connection do you have?" he asked with a mouthful of food.

"Okay, here it is. My father always worked private security: CEO's, tech firms, high interest assets, whoever flashed the cash. About four years ago, my father starts working for this client but he won't tell us anything about him. Not a name, not a location, wouldn't even send a postcard. When it began, my mom would tell me that my father was doing it for us, bringing in more money for our family, but he was never around. I would have given up every cent if it meant having him around, not so much for me but for my mom but he was never there. If we were lucky, we would see him twice a year and only for a day at a time. After a while I just accepted the fact that I pretty much just didn't have a father any more."

"That's rough, man. I know what it's like to not have a father. I know it isn't easy," Austin acknowledged.

"Yeah but, in hindsight, I would have embraced that fact with open arms if it meant not dealing with what happened next. About three years ago, my mother was diagnosed with A.L.S. Her condition was rapidly declining and there was nothing the doctors could do to help her. For some reason or another, her condition was rare and almost impossible to treat. The symptoms were constantly getting worse and it didn't take long for her to go from a hundred percent to zero. I spent every day taking care of her, trying to help her any way that I could. I would do anything to take her mind off the inevitable but it was never enough. The money my father was sending home began to not be enough either. The hospital bills were staggering and the money could only pay for so much. We had no other family so there was no one else to take care of her. Even when I got in contact with my father and told him, he said his boss wouldn't allow him to leave. He never even asked. He just assumed that because of the magnitude of his post, he would never be allowed to come home. I had to watch my mother deteriorate into nothing and, finally, she died in my arms."

"Jeff... I'm so sorry," Austin stated, not knowing how else to respond to such a tragic story.

"I never forgave my father for not being there but, after my mother passed away, I lost contact with my father completely. It was like he no longer had a reason to communicate with me: like my mom was the only thing linking us. I was twenty-two, my mother was dead and my father might as well be; I had nowhere else to go so that's when I joined D.A.R.C. I came in under their I.R.P."

"Their what?"

"Initiate Recruit Program. It gave younger people like me a chance to join the agency directly instead of going through the channels of becoming an F.B.I. or C.I.A. agent or some type of military first. Of course they never advertised that it was for a covert government division but if you were good enough to pass, you were told everything. It's sort of what you're doing except your case is a lot more unique. I immediately loved what I did and it gave me a sense of purpose again. Whenever I'm on a mission, I think of my mother and that gets me through it all. Fast forward three years and we get back Agent Lancer's intel. Turns out Church has been my father's client all this time. My father is a member of the security board for Church's entire operation so I was an obvious choice to go in after Lancer's death, but then they found you and your direct connection to Damien supersedes mine."

"Yeah, but it won't matter if I turn down the offer," Austin stated.

Jeff slammed his fist down on the table, the clanging of the metal echoing out loud enough to draw the attention of the other tables nearby. Austin gave a quick scan around the environment, all eyes suddenly pinned to them.

"You have been given a golden opportunity, something anyone else would kill for and you're still saying you have to think about it? I am not going to let this chance slip away from me. I am going to put a bullet in Church's head whether you like it or not and you aren't going to do a damn thing to fuck up this mission. Do you understand me?" Jeff's tone became angry and sinister with an expression to match.

Austin could feel his fist clenching, a rebuttal at the edge of his tongue, begging to barge through his tightly sealed lips.

"I bet you want to hit me, don't you?" Jeff antagonized with a sly grin.

"You have no idea."

"Let's get one thing straight. We might have to work together but I do not like you nor do I respect you. You disrespect every single agent of this division just by being here, especially when you're still thinking of siding with the enemy. I worked my ass off to get to where I am and you're only here because that son of a bitch is the father you never had. I hate the fact that Hardwick agreed to this joke of a task. I was perfectly fine getting in close and ending Church's whole project. But now I'm forced to sit back and wait to play babysitter to a guy who might stab me in the back when it matters most. And even if you decide to be on the right side of this thing, I will never see you as my peer. I'll act civilized and professional in front of the suits but, make no mistake about it, you will never be anywhere but below me."

Jeff abruptly stood up and walked away from the table, leaving Austin alone at the table with nothing but rage to accompany him.

The next night, Austin found himself right back at the warehouse preparing to take on the next challenge. Immediately, Austin and Jeff locked eyes, the raging tension already building between them.

"Good evening, Austin. Thank you for being so prompt," Mike welcomed.

"The van's outside my apartment, kind of hard to be late."

"Today, we'll do one cycle of every exercise you did last night and end it with combat training," Grant stated.

"I don't think I'll have much trouble with that." Austin smiled confidently.

"Save it till we're through."

Austin went through everything he did the night before, running a fitness circuit on an extreme level. Instead of cataloguing Austin's limitations, they pushed him to shatter those limitations. By the end of the fitness portion, Austin could feel the effects on his body. His limbs felt heavy, his muscles tensed up and he winced in pain with every breath. Austin sat on the floor in a pool of his own sweat trying desperately to catch any ounce of air he could.

"Are you ready for the combat training?" Grant asked arrogantly.

Austin just looked up at Grant without a response, still trying to catch his breath. Austin was escorted into another room of the warehouse, this one with a six-foot wide circle in the center.

"You may be the champion of that pissant excuse for a fight club but let's see what you can do against some of our specially trained agents," Grant announced.

"Step in the circle, please," Mike requested.

Austin did as he was asked and stepped into the circle, waiting patiently for his training. Mike began to point out the various cameras surrounding the room. "These cameras will record your entire training from every angle. It'll give us a chance to see where any errors occurred and what we could help you improve on in the future."

"Plus, we get to watch you get your ass kicked on demand." Grant smirked.

"Let's just get this over with," Austin snapped.

The door opened and Agent Danvers stepped into the room.

"I believe you know Agent Danvers," Hardwick spoke.

"Danvers! And here I thought you were just one of the wheel men," Austin joked with a light chuckle.

"Don't underestimate me, Mr. Michaels. You've never seen me in the field before."

Danvers stepped into the circle and prepared himself.

Mike clicked a button on his tablet and said, "Begin!"

Danvers instantly went on the offensive, swinging violently at Austin but Austin calmly deflected every swing as if rehearsing a choreographed dance. His calmness and lack of erratic movement made it seem like he knew exactly what Danvers was going to do.

Without warning, in the blink of an eye, Austin countered one of Danvers' punches and entangled his arm, flipping him effortlessly to the mat. He wrenched his arm until Danvers let out a helpless yelp, indicating the end of the fight. Austin dropped

Danvers' arm while burning a hole into Grant.

"Anything else you wanna say about my pissant fight club?"

Grant's lip quivered in anger. "Danvers, get your sorry ass out of here! Send in Adams!"

Danvers left wearing a cloak of embarrassment over him, not even lifting his eyes to look at Adams who was walking in.

"My turn already?" Adams smiled and stepped into the circle.

"Ready, begin."

Adams instinctively went for Austin's legs, something he wasn't expecting, and took him straight to the mat.

"That's it." Grant beamed.

The moment Austin hit the mat, he wriggled unpredictably until he was able to escape Adams' grasp, twisting his body and putting Adams on his back. Austin plunged his fist down into Adams' face, forcing a geyser of blood from his nose. Austin pulled his fist back, ready to land another punch.

"Enough!" Grant shouted.

Austin got to his feet, extending a hand to help Adams up.

"Nothing personal," he said.

"Thanks." Adams grabbed Austin's hand and pulled himself up.

"Adams, get out," Grant ordered, the anger bubbling in his throat.

Mike tossed a towel to Adams, the agent pressing it firmly against the bottom of his nose to quell the bleeding.

"Grant, we expected as much from his background," Hardwick chimed in.

"With all due respect, Sir, I didn't expect D.A.R.C. agents to look like fools against a civilian."

"Let me have a go," Jeff interjected as he took his jacket off.

Austin immediately knew what Jeff's true motive was in volunteering.

"We didn't expect you to spar with Austin, are you sure, Agent O'Neal?" Mike asked.

"Yeah, positive. I think it'll be fun to really push him. No offense to Danvers or Adams but they really don't have what it takes to dance with guys like us." Jeff smiled, all the while looking at Austin.

"Floor's all yours," Austin invited with a gesture.

Jeff stood across from Austin, stretching out his wrists in preparation.

"Ready, begin."

Jeff erupted, attacking Austin without remorse. Austin began to block the punches but, even blocking, Austin could tell there was malice behind Jeff's attacks. One of Jeff's punches managed to sneak its way through Austin's defenses and made contact with his face. He dropped to one knee from the force and Jeff instantly capitalized, sending a horrific right hook into Austin's mouth. The second punch was enough to send Austin straight to the floor, blood already dripping from his split lip. Jeff grabbed a handful of Austin's hair, stretching him backwards.

He wrapped his arm around Austin's neck, squeezing as tight as he could. Blood pooled onto Jeff's arm from Austin's mouth as he tried desperately to breathe but Jeff left no opening in his vice grip. Like an ironic parallel to his fight with Rick, Austin got to his feet and flew backwards, slamming Jeff into the nearby column. The very moment Jeff loosened his grasp, Austin turned around and paid him back with a right hook of his own.

Jeff dropped to one knee until a second punch from Austin put him to the floor. Jeff quickly retreated in order to get back to his feet and, once again, the two continued their fight.

"O'Neal is really fighting Austin," Mike said, worried.

"Good, maybe that's just the thing Austin needed. It'll be good to knock him down a few pegs. Maybe Austin won't act so arrogant when he sees how low on the ladder he really is," Grant exclaimed.

"That's enough!" Hardwick shouted, surprising the two Elite Special Agents.

Austin and Jeff turned to Hardwick, both bloodied.

"This was supposed to be a training session, sparring to see Austin's combat limitations. All I see is two men trying to beat the hell out of each other!"

"Director Hardwick, I—"

"No, Grant!" Hardwick barked. "This is not benefitting Austin in any way and if his skills aren't improving and progressing, then this is all worthless! Get those two on the same page and get your head out of your ass."

Hardwick stormed out of the room, slamming the door behind him. The room went silent, thick with tension.

"Go get cleaned up, you two, now," Mike said, his usual positive tone replaced with a stern, serious one.

Mike and Grant walked out of the room, Grant hoping to have a minute to talk to Hardwick. In the bathroom, Austin finished cleaning off the blood from his hands, looking in the mirror at his clean reflection.

"You got some fight; I'll give you that," Jeff said as he walked in already drying his hands with a towel.

"That means less than nothing coming from you," Austin snarled.

"I meant what I said last night. I won't let you ruin this mission for me just because you have daddy issues."

Austin shut the water off and turned to Jeff. "From what you told me, sounds like I'm not the only one with daddy issues."

Without warning, Jeff's fist imbedded itself deep into Austin's gut. Austin dropped to his knees, gasping and coughing desperately for air.

"Don't ever talk about my father. As far as I'm concerned, you're just as guilty as Church is and the more you defend him, the more I want you buried next to him. Just do us both a favor and decline Mike and Grant's offer now. At least then I don't have to feel bad when I give you a bullet to match Church's."

Jeff tossed his towel onto an agonized Austin. Austin barely had the strength to reach his hand out, attempting to grab at Jeff before he left. The door closed and Austin toppled over onto his side, clenching his sternum.

The next night was more of the same. Austin was pushed to his physical limits in the circuit and then was pushed into the connecting room to train in hand to hand combat, though Jeff was not allowed to be his partner. Jeff stood by with a permanent look of disdain on his face and Hardwick was inexplicably absent from the session.

When Austin first started his conditioning, what pushed him the most was disproving Grant's opinion of him. The more Austin succeeded, the more it angered Grant, but tonight was different. Tonight, Austin only had Jeff on his mind. His comments, his actions, all of it filled with malicious intent. The more Austin pondered over it, the more he resented Jeff and the less he saw him as an agent. Austin finished his combat session against agents he had never met before and was quickly rushed into yet another door.

"Welcome to your firearms training," Grant announced.

Before Austin was a large shooting range. Targeted cutouts were moving on predetermined tracks, weaving periodically through walls used as cover. Austin stepped up to the shooting counter and looked out at the range in front of him.

"Have you ever shot a gun before?" Mike asked as he stood next to Austin.

He prepared a Beretta M9 pistol on the counter, slotting in the magazine, the hammer snapping into the readied position. With a quick flip, Mike handed the pistol to Austin with his hand on the barrel. Austin grabbed the pistol and examined it for a moment.

"So I'm guessing that's a no." Mike chuckled.

"Is it that obvious?"

"Don't worry, that's why we're here. By the time your conditioning is over, you'll be confident in any situation, though let's hope you never find yourself in one."

Mike spent some time going over the different parts of the pistol, how to reload and unload safely, as well as how to aim and, of course, shoot.

"Now, of course, this is just one of many sidearms, not to mention all the other weaponry we have at our disposal, but, for now, this is the best place to start. So whenever you're ready, you can take your first shot," Mike announced.

Austin placed the protective headphones over his ears and planted his feet firmly in a comfortable stance, steadying his hands. As the pistol came up to eye level, Austin took a deep breath and calmed his breathing. He squeezed his index finger and pulled the trigger for the first time. Immediately, the jolt of recoil surged through Austin's arms, the bullet firing wildly off target from any cutouts and smashing into the upper half of the back wall.

"It's okay, just take your time. You'll get used to it," Mike continued.

"This isn't little league practice," Grant snapped. "He needs to be field ready and, right now, your little pep-talks aren't helping."

"Give him time, Grant. He excelled at everything else we threw at him, the least we can do is be patient with firearms training."

Austin readied himself once more. He pulled the gun up to eye level and focused on which target he wanted to hit. With another deep breath, Austin pulled the trigger, the bullet smacking into the cutout though out of the targeted space.

"I did it!" he proclaimed, a burst of excitement uncontrollably erupting from his mouth.

"Good! Now keep practicing. The more you shoot, the better your aim will be." Mike smiled proudly.

The next several hours were all the same, Austin firing countless rounds into the shooting range with the M9.

"I think I've seen enough. I'm gonna head out for the night," Jeff stated and quickly took his leave.

"Do you think we should address the fight they had last night?" Mike asked, leaning over to Grant's ear.

"No, leave it alone. If it was that bad, Austin would have come forward. He's a civilian, he wouldn't keep quiet about a government agent assaulting him," Grant replied.

"I'm sorry, are we talking about the same Austin? He's the top fighter of an illegal fight club. He was literally raised to keep his mouth shut and fight through. He wouldn't say a word to us."

Grant's eyes peeked at Mike and then back at Austin.

"I'm not starting something that, for all we know, could already be finished. Unless someone comes forward, I'm not going to address it."

"If you say so," Mike agreed reluctantly.

As Austin pulled the trigger once more, the hammer snapped back signifying that the gun was empty. Austin put the gun down, the vibration still humming in his palms.

"So? How'd I do?" Austin asked as he took off his protective headphones.

Mike and Grant stepped over to Austin and examined all the targets in the range. Most of them were struck outside the targeted zones but for some, the bullets hit with deadly accuracy.

"You've already improved tremendously in just a few hours. Great job," Mike complimented.

Austin turned to Grant, waiting for his response with a smile.

"I'm not saying 'great' anything until you hit every single target dead on." Grant pointed to all the cutouts that weren't hit in the targeted zones.

"Why did I expect anything different?" Austin groaned.

"For the most part, the first stage of your conditioning is complete. Now we'll just work on improving on everything you've learned. And once you master the M9, we can move on to other weaponry. You're coming along great, Austin." Mike patted Austin on the back.

Austin smiled but then paused for a moment.

"Look, guys, I don't want you to get the wrong impression. I'm still holding to what we agreed upon. If and when I make my decision, if I choose to pass on your offer, then I won't be helping O'Neal."

Grant's expression already changed to that of disgust and annoyance.

"We know that's still a very strong possibility but we'd rather be safe than sorry. Yes, if you decide to pass on our offer, then all this time would have been wasted on a civilian. Is it pointless? Yes. Is it embarrassing? Honestly, yeah it is. But if you decide to accept the offer, then we already conditioned you to be field ready and we could finally proceed with our mission. It's a big gamble but one that we're willing to take on you," Mike explained sincerely.

Austin nodded. "Okay, I get it."

Austin was escorted out of the warehouse but, once again, Jeff was waiting for him.

"What do you want, Jeff?" Austin asked in a disgusted tone.

"Just thought I'd stick around and say good job. That was impressive work you did in there."

"Had we not had that lovely conversation last night, I might actually believe you." Austin walked past Jeff and towards the van.

Jeff followed behind Austin. "I meant every word that I said last night but I'm also telling the truth now. If you end up joining, at least I know you're a decent shot."

"And if I choose differently?" Austin asked angrily as he turned back to Jeff, the two now face to face.

Jeff smiled arrogantly. "Well, then at least I'll know killing you might actually be a little challenging."

Austin stared at Jeff intently but, soon, he simply chuckled in relief.

"You know, Jeff, I'm glad you showed your true colors. If it wasn't for trying to prove you wrong, I might have not been able to do what I did today and that is just going to keep happening. I'm going to keep shattering records and impressing and succeeding until you look like nothing more than an incapable fool."

"Watch your tone, Austin," Jeff threatened.

"No, I don't think I will. You see, you made a very good point. We should stay civilized in front of Hardwick, Mike, and

Grant. It looks really bad otherwise. But right now, none of them are around."

Without warning, Austin threw his head forward and smashed it into Jeff's face. The force sent Jeff straight to the ground as he grabbed his nose in pain. Austin paid no mind and simply opened the door to the van and stepped inside.

Austin slowly opened the door to his empty apartment and stepped inside making sure not to make any unnecessary noise. He dropped his keys into the dish on the nearby table and sluggishly made his way toward his bedroom. As he reached for the doorknob, his ears perked to the sound of the floor slightly creaking. He slowly turned his head and scanned his apartment.

Austin gently moved his hand away from the doorknob and made his way over to the kitchen, his steps broad and soft. Upon reaching the kitchen, he grabbed a knife from the knife block on the counter. As he gripped the handle tight and made it back into the living room, a masked figure grabbed him from behind.

Austin tried to wrestle free but his arms were trapped inside the man's hold. He backed up into the wall causing the man to loosen his grip and the moment he could move his arms, he plunged the knife into the man's thigh. He screamed in agony as he dropped to the floor but before Austin could react, two more men ambushed him. It wasn't long before Austin was rendered unconscious and dragged out of his apartment, the rest of the residents being none the wiser to what had just transpired.

Chapter 4

The Final Test

Austin opened his eyes slowly, his vision blurry and distorted. When his vision adjusted, he could see his surroundings clearly for the first time. A windowless room, grimy and dimly lit. Silence except for the subtle repetitive sound of a drop of water plunging onto the floor from a loosened pipe on the ceiling.

Austin's breath was shallow and quick, his anxiety building as the realization hit him. He was abducted. By whom, he didn't know. For what? Also a mystery. He tried to break free from the zip ties his wrists were bound to the chair arms with but it was no use. When he tried to move his legs, he realized they were shackled to the floor.

Suddenly, Austin heard footsteps walking outside the door. Several clangs echoed out as the various locks were undone. The door screeched open as two masked men walked in.

"What do you want?" Austin quickly asked, hoping with all his being that they would answer.

The men stayed silent as one unshackled Austin's ankles and the other cut the zip ties. The moment Austin's hands were free, he erupted off the chair, taking one of the men down with ease. As his body slumped to the floor, Austin was already on top of the second, throwing him to the floor and sending his fist into his face.

Austin darted to the door but was stopped in his tracks at the sight of a gun, the barrel aiming right between his eyes. Austin froze, his limbs petrified with fear. Without a word, the man struck Austin in the head with his pistol.

Austin opened his eyes again and immediately looked around in a panic. His hands were shackled together, the connecting chain strung up over a hook in the ceiling just high enough so his toes couldn't reach the floor. As he dangled helplessly, he looked around at his new environment. Solid concrete walls enclosed a smooth, concrete floor with a drain in the center, the gold-plated drain cover tainted with dried blood.

Again, the door opened and two masked men walked inside. One man walked up to Austin wielding a pair of scissors.

"Wh-what are you doing with those?" Austin asked, fearfully trying to wriggle his body away.

The man grabbed Austin and steadied him. Austin watched panic stricken as the man wrapped the scissor's blades around the bottom of his shirt. He shredded Austin's shirt in half, revealing his bare sternum underneath.

"What are you guys doing?"

Instead of an answer, one man thrust his fist into Austin's ribs unexpectedly. Austin involuntarily coughed from the blow, trying his best to catch his breath again.

"We have some questions for you and it would be in your best interest to answer," the assaulter uttered.

"Questions? About what?" Austin asked perplexed.

The mystery man holding the scissors twiddled with them in his hands. "Damien Church and your connection to D.A.R.C."

Austin's heart stopped; his lungs closed up and his eyes practically exploded from his head.

"What are you talking about?" He hoped his shock didn't show through his voice.

"Mr. Church knows that you've been disloyal to him. He knows you've been communicating with D.A.R.C. but, because of your history, he's willing to give you the chance to redeem yourself. Tell us everything you know about D.A.R.C. and the people who work for it."

Austin had mere seconds to think of the words that were going to come out of his mouth.

"What the hell are you guys talking about? I don't even know what a 'dark' is! There's no way Damien told you guys to do this. He would never do this to me."

"Mr. Church only takes care of those he can trust. Once you break that trust, you're only seen as a problem. So make it easier on yourself and tell us what we want to know."

"Guys, I'm telling you, I don't know what you're talking about," Austin continued.

Again, he was punched in the sternum.

"This is how it's gonna go." The man finally tossed the scissors aside and walked up close to Austin. "Every time you lie, we beat you. We beat you and beat you and beat you until you either decide to be honest or die. Those are your two options."

"I am being honest. I don't know what you're talking about. I can't tell you what I don't know. Tell Damien to come in here, I'll tell him myself," Austin pleaded.

This time, both men took turns beating into Austin's body. Austin coughed heavily as he waited for the initial pain to subside.

"Is D.A.R.C. using you? Are you working for them?"

"Who's dark?" Austin cringed.

Again, Austin's body was used as a punching bag for both assailants, one of them even sending a right hook into Austin's mouth. As the beating continued and the punches landed on top of already bruised and tender skin, the pain grew more and more excruciating.

"How much do they know about Mr. Church's operation?"

Austin spit out a glob of blood onto the floor as he panted heavily, desperately trying to catch his breath.

"I don't know what the fuck you're talking about!" Austin screamed angrily. "I don't know what a 'dark' is! I don't even know what operation you're talking about! What the fuck is Damien doing that I don't know about?"

The man presumably in charge of the interrogation exhaled heavily in disappointment.

"Do we really have to resort to this? Do we really have to go this far? Beating you isn't enough?" the man questioned, pacing back and forth in annoyance. "What about your friends, hm? Do we have to pay them a visit too? Or how about Debbie and Christian? I'm sure your mother and brother would love to know the answers to our questions as well."

Austin's expression immediately changed to one of pure rage. Without a retort, Austin used whatever strength he had left in his core to lift his legs into the air just to send a kick into the man's chest. He stumbled backwards but remained standing.

"That's it, isn't it?" he snarled. "Your friends and family. That's what's most important to you. You'll sit here and take a beating all night but what will you do when everyone else is in danger? Last chance, Austin. Tell us what we want to know or I leave this room and I come back with your mother's head in my hand."

The room went quiet as Austin stared deep into the man's eyes, still the only part of his face showing through the mask.

"I'm waiting," the man antagonized.

The air stood still, everyone holding their breath for Austin's response. Finally, he answered.

"I don't know where you got your information from, but it was wrong. I swear, I don't know anything about any 'dark' or anything that Damien is doing. I've known Damien for seven God damn years, he's family to me. If this is how easily that bond is broken, then I guess I never really knew him at all. But I swear, if you go near anyone I love, I will rip you to fucking pieces!"

Tears formed in Austin's bloodshot eyes as he erupted. His voice cracked as he spoke with assurance but there was one thing that both men heard underneath the words, sincerity.

"You really don't know anything, huh?"

"Not a fucking thing," Austin exclaimed, still staring a hole into the man.

The man stared back but only for a brief moment until it was replaced with a hardy laugh. Austin was taken aback by the man's reaction, the other man now joining in the hysterics.

"Wh-what the fuck is this?" Austin asked, somehow more worried than before.

"You did good, man, very fucking good." The man laughed and finally ripped the mask off his head.

The other man did the same as the door to the room opened once more. Austin couldn't understand what he was seeing. The pieces of the puzzle were sprawled out in front of him but even so, he couldn't manage to piece them all together.

"I'm impressed. Really impressed, actually." Grant smirked.

"I never doubted it for a second." Mike beamed with pride.

"What the fuck are you guys doing here? What the fuck is going on?" Austin shouted.

"If it hasn't dawned on you yet, you can rest easy. This was all just a test. Your assailants were Agents Diaz and Loro," Grant answered.

"Rest easy? How the fuck am I going to rest easy?" Austin wriggled his body again, still hung up by the chain.

"Let him down," Grant ordered. "With field work comes the risk of being captured and tortured for information. Our enemies will show no mercy on you and Damien Church is no different. No matter how strong your bond, if he finds out you are working against him, he will make you pay. We had to ensure that you could handle at least the most basic of torture techniques."

"Beating the shit out of me is basic?"

Austin was brought down from the hook and his shackles were finally removed.

"Well we can't exactly practice ripping off your fingernails or poking your eyeball with a pin, now can we?" Grant asked as he leaned in close to Austin.

Austin began to rub his wrists as if trying to magically rub away the scabbed irritation from the shackles.

"So this entire thing was a fucking test?"

"As much as we're trying to prepare you for field duty, at the end of the day, you are still a civilian. A civilian who owes us and this organization nothing. If you were going to give up our information, we wanted to make sure it was to our own people. Better to find out how weak you are when the fate of the world isn't truly on the line," Grant explained, examining Austin's numerous wounds.

"I don't believe this." Austin was astonished by the revelation.

"Please believe us, we didn't mean to deceive you. We just had to make sure," Mike chimed in.

"If it really came down to it and you had your back against the wall, you would have no reason to lie for us and yet you did.

As much as I hate to admit it, I didn't expect it," Grant admitted.

Mike placed a chair down, gesturing for Austin to sit.

"By the way, don't think we don't know how you handled yourself in your apartment. That was pretty good intuition to realize you weren't alone."

Austin's eyes widened as another epiphany hit him.

"Wait, then who did I stab?"

Grant and Mike answered in unison, "Danvers."

"But don't worry, after a few weeks of desk duty, he'll be back on his feet and good as new," Mike added.

"So what now?" Austin asked.

"Now you take tonight and you internalize it. Understand why we did what we did. Understand the motive and the purpose. Take away as much as you can from it," Grant replied, his chest proudly expanded. "We all feel pain. The thing that separates agents from civilians isn't if we feel pain but rather if we can endure it. An agent's mind is an impenetrable steel vault that houses this organization and this country's deepest secrets. You must ensure that under no circumstance will your body become the skeleton key that opens it." Grant leaned in close and stared into Austin's eyes. "Never break to pain."

After Grant's stern speech, Austin was whisked away to be examined for his injuries and to be escorted home safely. Mike and Grant were left alone in the concrete room.

"Grant, I know I'm the last person to bring this up since I'm the one constantly in Austin's corner but what are we gonna do if he decides to decline the offer? We put so much time and resources into him," Mike questioned.

"Nothing has changed since the last time this was discussed. If he declines, then yes, this will have all been for nothing but the gamble is worth it if he says yes. He needs to be ready. We *need* him to be ready. We're all sailing uncharted waters with this mission so we just have to keep doing what we think is the right move. We have to be smart and strategic and know when to be risky. In Austin's case, risky is all we have," Grant admitted with honesty.

"You know, it's nice to see stone-cold Grant so vulnerable. We should have missions like this more often," Mike teased.

Once again, Grant's expression became rigid. "Get out."

Mike exited the room as ordered, laughing the whole way out. Before following behind, Grant took a moment for himself in the silence of the empty room.

"Damn it, Austin, don't screw us on this one."

Chapter 5

Catching Up

Austin opened his eyes to the beaming rays of the sun breaking through his curtains. He pushed himself out of bed slowly, cringing from the abrupt pain his body suffered the night before. The hot, steamy water of the shower helped sooth Austin's sore body as he stood motionless under the showerhead. As he stepped out of the shower and wiped the foggy condensation off the mirror, he stared at his reflection.

It was the first time in what seemed like forever that he was able to take a close, hard look at himself. The longer he stared, the more imperfections he could find. A busted lip, a swollen left eye, dried-up blood around his nostril from a nosebleed that was beaten out of him. Austin's hand was still pressed against the mirror. He glanced over to it and saw the light bruising on his wrist from the shackles.

"I don't know if I've ever looked this bad, and I fight for a living." Austin couldn't help but think of the obvious. "Am I crazy for even considering this? Since I started, I've been pushed to the point of exhaustion, beaten half to death, and I have one of their agents dying to pull the trigger on me. And all because I'm their best chance to succeed."

Austin stepped back into his bedroom and grabbed his clothes for the day.

"They're using me, that much is obvious. Mike seems

genuine but as far as the rest of them are concerned, I'm nothing but a tool. They just want to use me to stop Damien and whether they're right about that much is still up in the air."

Austin finished getting dressed and dropped backwards onto the bed to sit at the edge. He rubbed his hands vigorously through his hair as if trying to brush the chaotic thoughts out.

"Just keep going." He finally decided. "Keep pushing through the bullshit until a clear answer shows itself. Eventually, I'm gonna know exactly what to do and, once I do, I'll be able to get my life back to normal."

Austin stepped out of his apartment building ready for his jog and instantly caught sight of Alyssa making her way down his block.

"Care for some company?" He smiled as she got closer.

Alyssa's face lit up. "I would love some but I have to warn you, if you're jogging with me, there's no headphones. I like to talk when I run with a partner."

Austin pretended to think hard about the decision before giving her the answer he had already chosen to begin with.

"I'm good with that."

"Great, try to keep up!" Alyssa yelled as she jogged away.

Austin wasted no time catching up to her and the two began to jog side by side.

"I haven't seen you out jogging the last couple days. Where have you been?" Alyssa asked.

"I've been around, things just got busy so I haven't had the time."

"Do those busy things have anything to do with why your face looks like that?"

Austin wasn't surprised that Alyssa noticed his injuries, they were obvious, but still, hearing her ask such a blunt question caught him off guard.

"Well, to be honest, they do but it's nothing bad. I don't want—"

"Relax, Austin, I'm kidding." Alyssa chuckled, cutting off Austin's ramblings.

"If I thought you were a bad person, I wouldn't have bothered talking to you, let alone agreed to jog with you." Alyssa gave Austin a quick smirk from the side of her mouth.

They continued to jog and Austin didn't want to waste the chance to get to know Alyssa better.

"So I've seen you jogging this route for a few months now, did you just move to the neighborhood?"

"Something like that. I've always lived around here but my dad is very over protective and a little bit paranoid. I used to just jog around the block of my house a bunch of times but after I got my college degree last semester, I told him that wasn't gonna work any more. I always wanted to jog around the city and just take in the life I was running by. He finally agreed and that's when I started running around here."

"Well, I'm glad you were able to convince him." Austin smiled.

"So what about you? How long have you lived here?" Alyssa questioned back.

"I've been here for five years. I moved out of my parents' house when I was eighteen."

"Wow, that's pretty young. How could you afford it?"

"I…"

Again, Austin paused for a moment but finally answered.

"I made sure I always had a steady income."

"Oh yeah? Maybe more of that busyness you were talking about?" Alyssa giggled with a mocking smile.

"Something like that." Austin chuckled.

"What made you move out so young?"

"Well, what made you stay home so old?"

Alyssa's eyes expanded as she was taken aback by Austin's sudden question.

Austin smiled. "See, we can both play that game."

"Don't be a jerk." Alyssa laughed playfully as she impishly shoved Austin away. "But you know the answer already. I told you, my dad's always been over protective and paranoid. It was always very important to him for his family to stay together. It's always just been my parents, me, and my brother Sean."

"No cousins or grandparents?" Austin questioned further.

"Nope, just the four of us. That's the way it's been for as long as I can remember," Alyssa answered but added, "But don't think I forgot about my question. What made you move out so young?"

The two continued to jog as Austin stayed silent, unwilling to answer. "Look, if it's something personal, you don't need to tell me. I just thought we were getting to know each other."

"No, no, it's fine," Austin quickly replied, not wanting Alyssa to think he was pushing her away already. "Growing up, my parents and my younger brother were the most important things to me and I always looked up to my father especially. He was an investigative journalist but he would only handle the most sensitive cases. News companies would always offer him stories to look into but he turned down most of them. He wanted to really help people. He wanted to uncover deception and corruption so that no one had to live in uncertainty."

"He sounds like an amazing man," Alyssa chimed in.

"He was. Growing up, he always told me that no one in this world should ever live in obscurity, that there should always be someone who cast the brightest lights into the darkest corners. And that's what he did with his stories. He used to call himself the Gracey Burnes of the modern era."

"Who?" Alyssa asked with complete confusion.

Austin laughed. "Gracey Burnes was the main character of these really old detective novels my father loved to read. People would throw money at him to solve cases for them but he worked exclusively for people who *couldn't* pay him. He didn't do it for the money, he did it to help the people who were truly less fortunate and needed him most. My father always felt like he was somewhat doing the same thing."

"I don't mean to sound insensitive but this doesn't sound like any reason to move out." Alyssa chuckled lightly.

"When I was fourteen, my father left us."

"Left? Like left, left?" Alyssa questioned with surprise.

"Yeah, he left an extremely vague note and left and I haven't seen him since. One day, he just up and abandoned our family."

Alyssa stopped running and turned to Austin.

"Austin, I'm so sorry. I didn't mean to make you spill something like that. It wasn't—"

"No!" Austin stopped her. "You did nothing wrong. And it's okay, I'm pretty far removed from that fourteen-year-old kid."

"So that's why you left home?" Alyssa asked.

"I kept my father on such a high pedestal because of the work he did and the values he had so, when he abandoned us, it was like everything I was taught my whole life was a lie. After that I wasn't the best kid growing up but I started turning it around at sixteen and, by eighteen, I had enough money saved up to move. I knew it was the right thing for me to do. Ever since he left, I had an itch to get out and make a life for myself. It was like I needed to become my own person as fast as I could so I could prove to myself that his deception didn't ruin me."

"You know, when I asked that question, I really didn't expect such a heavy answer but, for what it's worth, I think you've already proven so much more than you know." Alyssa smiled.

Austin smiled back and the two found themselves staring into each other's eyes.

"Would you like to have breakfast with me?" Austin asked unexpectedly.

"I know a place nearby that makes the best breakfast burritos but don't worry, they're super healthy," she replied.

"Sounds great."

"Great! Race you! First one there gets to pay!" Alyssa shouted and darted off down the block.

"Wait! That's not fair! I don't know where we're going!" Austin yelled back as he raced after her.

Austin finally made it to the restaurant, Alyssa already leaning against the wall in wait.

"Took you long enough." She grinned.

Austin simply stared at her with a disapproving glare.

"I'll remember that," he warned.

"Good, you can keep track of how many times I beat you." Alyssa gently poked Austin in the chest as she turned and walked inside.

As the two sat down to eat, Alyssa stared at Austin who was busy opening his burrito. His eyes glanced up for a moment and caught her stare.

"What?" he asked with a shy smile.

Alyssa leaned her head into her hand. "Tell me more about your dad."

"What more is there to tell?"

"Why didn't you ever look for him? I mean you moved out at eighteen, 'cause you had 'a steady income'." Alyssa bent her fingers in the air creating air quotes for Austin's phrase. "Why didn't you ever bother looking for him. Didn't you want him to answer for what he did?"

"I thought about it, I thought about it a lot actually. But in the end, I decided I wasn't going to chase him. I wasn't going to waste my time, money, or resources hunting down a guy who wanted nothing to do with me."

"Do you think you'll ever change your mind?" Alyssa asked, intrigued by Austin's story.

"Honestly, yeah. Just recently I met someone who might be able to help me find him and it wasn't until then that I thought about it again."

"Oh my God, that's great! So are you gonna do it?" Alyssa asked with glee.

"Maybe. I haven't decided yet."

"Well, whatever you decide, it'll be the right choice. Only you know what's best for you." Alyssa smiled widely and took a bite of her burrito.

Austin just stared at her with a smile glued to his face.

"What? Did I get some on my face?" Alyssa asked, her mouth still filled with food.

"No." Austin continued to smile. "It's perfect."

Alyssa scoffed, her face turning red. "Shut up and eat your burrito."

Chapter 6

Mission Priority

The rest of the week was more of the same; Austin spent his nights being pushed to his absolute limits in the hopes that he would become the savior D.A.R.C. was hoping for. In the meantime, the tension with Jeff became worse with each passing day. Finally, it was Monday once again and Austin was preparing to leave for his fight. He stepped through his apartment doorway and caught Nick and Josh waiting for him.

"It's about time, we've been waiting. It's not like you to be running behind on fight night," Nick exclaimed.

"I know, just a weird day, I guess," Austin lied.

The truth was that Austin didn't have the same energy he had just a week prior. His body was sore, his muscles ached, and he spent more time treating his wounds now than he ever did in Reign.

"Where have you been? I feel like you've been a ghost lately," Josh asked as the three walked down the hall.

"I've just been busy with things, no big deal." Austin continued to rush through any chance of explaining.

It wasn't long until Austin found himself already taping his hands at ringside.

"You ready, boo?" Demi asked as she hung her arm around his shoulder.

"Aren't I always?" Austin asked back with a confident

smile.

"Good!" Demi gave Austin a quick peck on the cheek and jumped up, quickly heading over to Nick's ring.

"Huh, I don't know if Nick is oblivious, Demi's oblivious, or both," Josh chimed in, his arms folded in contemplation.

Austin and Josh looked at each other.

"Both," they said simultaneously.

One of the officials walked over and leaned down to Austin's ear.

"Mr. Michaels, we're ready to start," he informed.

"Good luck, champ." Josh gave Austin a playful punch on the arm as he stood up.

Austin turned and looked at the ring, his opponent already waiting inside. He took a deep breath and a familiar thought popped into his head.

"Another fight."

It didn't take long for Austin's hand to be raised as he made quick work of his random opponent for the week. Several strong boos cut through the sea of cheers, all from unhappy fans who wanted to see a longer fight. Austin readied himself to leave and noticed Nick's fight still going on.

"He's taking his sweet time, isn't he?" Austin asked as he zipped up his duffle bag.

"From what I can see, it looks like he's having a little trouble. I think it's a clash of styles," Josh replied.

Austin looked closely at the ongoing fight. "Is that guy using Aikido?"

"Yeah, but he's incorporating some strong strikes too. Looks like Nick is having trouble reading his blended style."

"Nick will be fine. Once he sees it enough, he'll find an opening. In the meantime, I'm gonna go have my usual speech with Damien so we can get out of here."

"Does that mean you're buying tonight?" Josh's face lit up with glee.

Austin laughed as he walked away. "We'll see."

Austin opened the office door and saw Damien still looking out the viewing window.

"Great fight, as usual." Damien turned around with a smile. "And as usual, here are your winnings."

Damien handed Austin his envelope full of cash.

"There isn't any extra this week, is there?" Austin asked suspiciously.

"No, no, not this week. I figured your opponent wasn't that much of a challenge. I'm not just gonna throw money at you, you know." Damien gave Austin a lighthearted smile.

"What about Nick's?" Austin asked.

"I don't know if you noticed but Nick hasn't won yet. I think he might actually lose to his guy," Damien replied as he turned back to the window.

Austin stood next to him and the two watched the remainder of Nick's fight. Almost immediately after they began watching, Nick found the opening Austin knew he would find and laid a right hook into his opponent's jaw, dropping him straight to the mat. The official raised Nick's hand in victory as the crowd erupted.

"About those winnings?" Austin smiled.

Damien chuckled and handed Austin another envelope. Just then, there was a knock at the door.

"Ah, I think that's our guest," Damien said excitedly.

"Guest?" Austin questioned.

"Come in!"

The door opened and someone walked in. It didn't take long

for the man to look less like a stranger to Austin, and more like someone he knew: more specifically, someone he hated.

"Austin, I'd like to introduce you to Jeff O'Neal." Damien smiled.

"Pleasure." Jeff extended his hand.

Austin stared at Jeff with a mix of shock and animosity but extended his hand as well.

"Nice to meet you."

"I just recently brought Jeff onto my staff," Damien informed.

"In what role?" Austin quickly asked, his heart racing a mile a minute.

Damien gestured his hands in the air as if debating between two things. "Let's call him my personal bodyguard."

"Bodyguard? Since when do you need a bodyguard?" Austin continued.

"It's not a matter of need, Austin. It's a matter of want. I've been searching in very unique places to find fighters worthy enough to go up against you. And sometimes, those places aren't the most desirable. Do I necessarily *need* the help? No. But I thought it would be good to have an extra pair of hands… or fists as it were."

"Mr. Church has already told me a lot about you." Jeff smiled.

"Has he now?"

"From what I hear, your fighting ability is quite impressive. Maybe one day we can have a session."

Jeff continued to look at Austin with a smug smile plastered on his face. Austin found himself clenching his fist tightly at his side. He wasn't sure what was worse. The fact that Jeff was already moving forward with the mission while his conditioning was still ongoing, or that he had to pretend not to know Jeff while he smiled superiorly at him.

"Yeah, maybe," Austin answered simply.

Another knock at the door broke up the subtle tension.

"Sorry to bother you, Mr. Church, but I had a few questions about next week," another official asked as they walked in.

"Of course." Damien began to walk towards the door. "Excuse me for a moment."

Damien walked out with the official, closing the door behind him and the moment the door creaked closed, Austin exploded.

"What the hell are you doing here?" Even his whisper had a tinge of anger to it.

"Mike and Grant felt it necessary to begin the first phase of our mission while you were still being inaugurated. So we pulled the trigger on my father's connection and got me this cushy little job."

Even while speaking in secrecy, Jeff still acted with an air of arrogance.

"And they didn't think to tell me?"

"What makes you think you're important enough to know? What makes you think you're important at all?" Jeff stepped closer to Austin. "I don't know if this past week has clouded your vision to what this whole situation is but let me make it perfectly clear to you. Whether you impress the suits during your inauguration or not, whether you decide to take the offer or not, you mean nothing to our organization. They don't owe you a single thing, especially an explanation. You're a means to an end, Austin, nothing more."

Even now, Jeff's sly, conceited grin made Austin's blood boil beneath his skin. Austin was fully prepared to soak his hands in Jeff's blood as he rained his fist down onto his face like a constant hailstorm of fury and rage.

"I bet you're itching to beat me half to death right now, aren't you?" Jeff antagonized.

"Only half?" Austin seethed.

Jeff chuckled with amusement. "I hate to admit it but no matter how we feel about each other, this goes beyond that. Planting me was mission priority, they weren't going to wait on you forever. And whenever you're done in the little leagues, if you make the choice they want, I'll see you on the inside."

"And what's stopping me from outing you to Damien right now? You're pretty trusting of a guy you threatened on multiple occasions," Austin asked with a little smugness of his own.

"And what's stopping me from putting two in your chest right now?" Jeff jammed his finger into Austin's chest twice, signifying the two bullets. "Damien, I don't know what happened? The second you left, he pulled out a knife and said he was gonna kill you," Jeff acted, playing out the scenario he would use. "It wouldn't be hard."

Austin had heard enough. His fist ached from clenching so tightly. Austin had lost all tolerance for Jeff long ago but this conversation whittled his patience down to nothing. He prepared to throw the first punch, fully aware of everything that would inevitably follow. Suddenly, the door creaked open once more, instantly deflating the tension in the room. Damien walked in with a smile on his face as he looked at Austin and Jeff.

"I hope you two had time to get acquainted." He beamed.

"Absolutely." Austin smiled in return.

"Listen, Austin, I hate to run but I have something I have to take care of and I'll need my new bodyguard to tag along. Next Monday then?"

"You got it, Damien. See you then."

Damien and Jeff exited the office but Austin stayed behind for a moment.

"A bodyguard and the rush to handle something this late at night? Has he always been this way and I just never noticed?" Austin began to ponder over his bond with Damien. "I'm starting to sound like them. It's only been a week and I'm already finding ways to distrust Damien. This is wrong."

Austin made his way back downstairs where his usual group was waiting for him.

"Come on, I'm starving," Josh groaned.

"You're always starving," Austin replied while handing Nick his envelope of cash.

He immediately noticed Demi hanging on Nick's back.

"What's with the piggy-back ride?" The confusion on Austin's face was obvious.

"I wore new boots tonight and my feet are killing me," Demi whined dramatically.

"So Nick is gonna carry you all the way to the diner?" Austin asked, his eyebrows raising in intrigue.

"Yeah, that's not a problem, is it, Nick?" Demi asked, double-checking with Nick.

"Not a problem, just get comfortable, it's a bit of a walk." Nick smiled.

Nick and Demi were the first to exit and Austin and Josh gave a gratifying glance to each other as they followed behind. Austin enjoyed the night with his friends and appreciated the fact that he didn't have to go through conditioning for the first time in a week.

Austin's Tuesday afternoon was more of the same routine he was used to but, when he prepared for his night of training, he peered out the window to see that the van wasn't in its usual spot.

"That's strange, it's usually here by now," Austin thought to himself. "Did they just decide to cancel my deal because they sent Jeff in?"

Before Austin could lose himself in speculation, there was a knock at his door. Austin walked over casually, expecting the ordinary but once he opened the door, he knew this moment was anything but. With a stern, yet fretted expression, Mike's slouched demeanor spoke volumes before he even opened his mouth.

"Austin, we need to talk."

Chapter 7

A Change of Plans

Austin stared at Mike for a moment with apprehension.

"Mike, what are you doing here?" he wondered in confusion.

"Can I come in?" Mike simply asked, ignoring Austin's question.

"Yeah, come in."

Mike stepped into the apartment and, before closing the door, Austin looked out into the hallway to make sure no one saw their quick exchange at the door.

"Mike, what's going on?"

Mike sat on one of Austin's couches, Austin impulsively sitting on the other.

"I thought this would be better done in person." Mike reached into his suit jacket and pulled out a folder. "Grant wanted to come as well but he lacks a certain finesse when it comes to conversations with you."

"If that's what you wanna call it," Austin uttered.

"As you are aware, we sent Agent O'Neal into Damien's operation as of yesterday morning. He acted as Damien's personal bodyguard which would have given him access to almost every facet of the operation. We would have learned everything we needed to know," Mike began.

"Why do you keep talking in past tense?" Austin sat up at attention as he immediately noticed the discrepancy in Mike's words.

Mike released a heavy sigh. "At 0300 this morning, we received a heavily encrypted file in our servers. People can't exactly just send D.A.R.C. spam mail so we knew whoever sent it was pretty technologically equipped. Once we opened it, we knew exactly who had sent it."

"What was it?" Austin questioned, completely immersed in the discussion.

"It was a series of images." Mike handed the folder over to Austin.

Austin took the folder from Mike's hands, unsure what he was now holding. He opened it slowly and saw the first image. An empty table with an identification card on it, dried, crusted blood covering the top left portion. The name in the center: Jeffrey O'Neal.

"Wh-what is this?" Austin had to ask but he had a feeling he already knew the answer.

"That's Jeff's D.A.R.C. I.D. When we're investigating, we carry a series of I.D.'s with us. F.B.I., C.I.A., N.S.A., anything that could gain us access into these other organizations. Nobody is aware of D.A.R.C.'s existence. But we use those cards to check in and out of our headquarters." Mike pointed to the bloody card in the photo.

"Why would he carry the one thing that could blow his cover?" Austin asked with a puzzled look.

"He wasn't, which means they found out where he lived and gained access to it," Mike replied swiftly.

"Doesn't that mean they could just find you guys now?"

"The moment we saw that photo, we wiped our entire security code and created a new one from the ground up. Every agent is getting a new I.D. by tomorrow morning, that card is useless now," Mike continued. "Keep going."

Austin looked back down at the pictures and cycled to the next one. Austin's eyes widened to an extreme degree as he saw the picture. Jeff tied to a chair, his face practically unrecognizable and hung low as if he were unconscious.

"Jesus," Austin managed to speak.

"We don't know how but Damien made him," Mike stated.

"Are they torturing him for information on you guys?" Austin questioned.

"We can only assume that was their intention."

"Are you guys gonna mount some kind of rescue mission? You guys follow the 'no soldier left behind' thing, right?"

Mike hesitated to respond for a moment.

"Flip to the next one."

Austin's head tilted slightly in confusion. He sorted to the third and last photo. Immediately, he tossed the entire folder onto the glass coffee table as he slouched back on the couch. His eyes closed shut and his hand covered his mouth in disbelief and disgust. Austin stayed frozen for a moment but even he didn't know why. He couldn't decide what was more of an overwhelming feeling, the shock of what the photo meant or the pure, nausea-inducing revulsion of what he saw.

The photos were now sprawled across the coffee table, the third photo sitting almost perfectly in front of Austin. A large cardboard box overflowing with thick, dark blood. A hand and forearm, a foot, and part of a thigh, all propped to the top of the box, presumably by the rest of the body parts underneath. Blood dripped down from the top into a small pool on one end and on the other, the blood had soaked through the cardboard, resulting in a leak that pooled almost onto the floor.

"Your reaction is understandable." Mike broke the silence.

"Understa—" Austin immediately stopped, swallowing the vomit that began to rise, back down his throat. "Understandable? The man's body parts are floating in a fucking box."

"I know," Mike said solemnly.

Austin wiped his hands down his face, dragging and stretching his skin to the bottom as he tried to process what he had just seen. The entire apartment was silent and the atmosphere was thick with dread.

"Austin, you do understand that Damien is responsible, right?" Mike asked for assurance.

Austin glanced at the pictures again but quickly recoiled.

"I don't really have a choice but to believe. I saw them leave together last night and a few hours later, Jeff looks like that. What else am I supposed to think?"

"I know you and Jeff didn't get along. Jeff was bugged last night; we heard your conversation with him. We weren't very pleased with the way he was speaking to you and I can only imagine how much worse the encounters were before that. Even so, I think we can agree that Jeff didn't deserve this."

"I wanted to beat some sense into him worse than anyone but no, he didn't deserve this." The thought suddenly clicked in Austin's head. "Wait, he was bugged? Doesn't that mean you have some evidence of how his cover was blown?"

Mike shook his head. "Once he left the club, the bug just picked up static. I assume Damien's transport has a frequency jammer in it. We lost Jeff's audio and his tracker in the alleyway of the club."

"So you don't even know where he went afterwards?" Austin asked and, again, Mike shook his head.

"We have no more leads, no more connections, and Damien has already killed two of our agents."

"I'm all that's left." The realization hit Austin like a freight train. "That's why you came here and told me all this."

"I know I offered you time and space to decide this for yourself. I know I said you can take your time to think and we would wait for your response." Mike leaned forward. "You have to believe that I had all intentions of holding to that promise but this..." Mike ripped the photo of the box off the table and held it up to Austin. "This changed everything."

Austin sprang up from the couch, now feeling suffocated by the situation.

"This is insane," he exclaimed as he paced across his living room floor.

"We need you, Austin. The offer to find your father is still on the table but we don't have the luxury of waiting for your decision. I need to know before I leave this apartment if you're in. Your inauguration will be finished, you'll be considered a partial agent, and we'll get to work on planting you inside Damien's organization," Mike explained.

"Yeah, the same way you planted Jeff? I'll be in a box just like that in twenty-four hours!" Austin shouted.

"No you won't! You're closer to Damien than Jeff ever could be. We knew Jeff's connection was weak but it was all we had. That's why we were counting on you joining him. We figured sending him in early wouldn't hurt the operation and you two would just work two different angles once you joined. We mapped out everything as much as we could. Something like this shouldn't have happened."

"But it did, Mike. You said it yourself, you lost two agents in this mission and now you wanna send in your last-ditch attempt. I'm not one of you, I'm not an agent," Austin argued as he walked away towards the kitchen.

Mike jumped up from the couch and followed him.

"But you are! In one week, you have excelled at every stage of inauguration. Your physical fitness and combat skill are second to none and you've already come a long way in firearm training. For all intents and purposes, you're better than half the new recruits we're gonna get from the Initiate Recruit Program this year. As far as miracles are concerned, we couldn't have asked for a better civilian to be caught in this situation with Damien. You have the connection to get close enough to ruin Damien and you have the skill to see it through. I've been doing this a long time, Austin. I know what I'm talking about."

The sincerity in Mike's voice was obvious and he didn't hesitate on a single word. Austin looked at him and then looked away again, still debating everything. Mike rested his hands on the half wall separating the kitchen from the rest of the apartment.

"Austin, please, I need an answer."

Austin turned to him once more, the mental and emotional pain enveloping his face. Without a word, Austin turned away again, leaning on the counter for reprieve. Austin's action was all Mike needed.

"Okay, I understand. I'm sorry to have brought this into your home." Mike began walking towards the door.

He reached for the handle and managed to wrap his hand around it before Austin stopped him.

"Mike, wait!"

Austin walked out from the kitchen and stared at Mike across the foyer.

"I'm in."

Chapter 8

Desperate Measures

The black sedan raced down the brightly lit streets, a driver silently steering the speeding blur. Mike sat in the back with Austin, who was still quite silent.

"I know this is all going to take some time to process and honestly, once we get to our destination, it'll probably be even worse," Mike admitted.

"Did you know I was gonna say yes?" Austin gave Mike an almost suspicious stare. "Did you show me those photos because you knew it would convince me to turn on Damien?"

"I'll be honest, Grant was ready to use every tactic in the book to get you on board but, like I told you earlier, I knew it would be better if I came to talk to you in person. I'm not in the business of manipulating people, especially as a first impression. I brought those pictures to you because I wanted you to know exactly what kind of man Damien Church is. You may have your own view of him and I'm sure he's genuinely been there for you like you said but that doesn't change the kind of man he is behind closed doors."

Austin leaned his arm against the door and rested his head in his hand.

"I can't believe all this time, Damien has been lying to me. He's been living a completely separate life and is doing such horrible things."

"I know it can't be easy seeing someone you care so much about in such a drastically different light but the important thing is that you know the truth before it was too late," Mike continued.

"What do you mean?" Austin questioned.

"What if Damien completed his formula without you having any idea what he was up to? You two are close and he knows he has your trust. If he really wanted to, he could use you for whatever twisted experiments he wanted. It wouldn't be hard to recruit you, whether voluntarily or involuntarily."

"Do you really think he would do that?" Austin's eyes enlarged with understanding.

"You know, a week ago, you would have never even questioned Damien's actions or purpose and now you're asking me if I think he would really use you," Mike scoffed innocently.

Austin looked out the window at the bright blurs of light darting past.

"A week ago, I didn't see firsthand that Damien was a murderer."

"We're going to stop him, Austin." Mike's gentle tone was replaced by a stern one to match the expression on his face.

The car finally pulled up in front of a large office building.

"We're here." Mike exited the car and gestured for Austin to follow.

Austin stepped out of the backseat and looked up at the building.

"This is it?" Austin asked, completely unamused by the sight. "This looks like every other building in the city."

"Exactly the point," Mike whispered as they walked towards the front doors. "Nobody knows we exist; we can't exactly throw our acronym on the front of the building."

Mike held the front door open and Austin walked in.

"Welcome to HQ."

Austin looked around the large lobby, trying to take in every detail he could. Everything covered in steel, chrome, and glass. A large front desk sat at the end of the lobby with multiple elevators on the back wall with their own row of card scanners. Doors lined both sides of the lobby leading to what Austin could only imagine. A staircase covered the back left corner leading to a second floor landing that overlooked the entire lobby, also with its own set of doors and elevators. Sitting atop the entire two floors was a large, ornate light fixture that basked the entire room in a bright, white glow. Even at the late hour that it was, people were walking about the lobby with purpose.

"What do you think?" Mike asked with a proud smile.

He swiped his card through a card scanner next to him causing a small green glow to emit.

"After you." Mike gestured.

"It looks pretty ordinary to be honest," Austin admitted as they walked past the scanners by the front doors.

"Like I said, that's the point. To the average citizen, we're just a normal business acquisition firm."

"Wait, your cover is that you buy out other businesses? Don't you get people coming in here to sell you their pitch?" Austin asked.

"Yeah, we have people come in here all the time but when they do, our staff takes care of it. They know exactly how to handle it and, in the meantime, we get to continue our work uninterrupted."

"How do normal people get past that scanner? Doesn't everyone have to swipe?" Austin questioned, looking back at the scanners for a brief moment.

"We always have an agent standing by at the door. If

someone unrecognizable steps through those doors, our agents immediately intervene and if they're legitimate, the agent allows them passage with their own card. Agents Dawson and Luder handle the day shift and Agents Chen and Madison handle the night shift.

"Mike!" Grant shouted from the top of the staircase.

Austin and Mike both turned and Grant waved his finger gesturing for them to join him. The two walked across the lobby and up the stairs where Grant was waiting impatiently.

"It's about damn time," he growled.

"What if I said no?" Austin asked.

Grant stared deep into Austin's eyes. "One way or another, that wasn't an option."

The three stood in front of a heavy, steel door. The look alone was enough to know the door was solid and durable, used to keep out unwanted guests. Next to the door was a circular scanner, a red light shining through a black glass dome. Mike leveled his eye with the scanner and leaned in close. The light scanned his eye for several seconds before turning green. Immediately, a loud hiss erupted from the door as it swung open revealing a large, dark room.

Grant and Mike walked in first, followed by Austin who was still trying to absorb it all.

"This is the Central Organizational Room: the C.O.R. All mission briefings and debriefings go through here. It is the brain of this agency," Grant explained as they walked up the center aisle towards the front. Hardwick was already standing at the front.

"Good to see you again, son, though I wish it was under better circumstances." Hardwick shook Austin's hand strongly.

"Same here, Director Hardwick."

"I assume you being here means you're on board with the operation?" Hardwick continued.

"It looks like you guys were right about Damien all along and I want to make sure he's stopped."

"That's good to hear and just know that the offer Mike and Grant gave you is still in play. We wouldn't expect all this from you without giving you back something in return."

"I appreciate that." Austin sat back in a nearby chair.

"Are we ready to get started?" Mike rubbed his hands together in anticipation.

Grant walked over and stood over Mike's shoulder as he sat down at a computer.

"Pull up everything we have. Let's get this briefing started."

Mike typed something into the computer and a video appeared on the large projector screen. "Before Agent O'Neal, we sent Agent Lancer in undercover. We created an airtight backstory for him, nothing that would raise any red flags if someone checked. Even an extensive background check should have been clear but, somehow, Damien found out. This was the last piece of intel we got from Agent Lancer before he was killed."

The video on the screen began to play. The footage came from a body cam Lancer had on his lapel. Lancer walked through a large, snow-covered compound as other guards patrolled nearby.

"Is this where Damien lives?" Austin asked.

"This is a compound in Russia, we know that much," Mike answered.

Grant quickly cut in, "Wait, you don't know where he lives?"

"No, I've never been to his house. We've always met in

public and he only came to my apartment a handful of times."

"And that never seemed off to you? This guy was like a father to you but never opened up his private life to you?"

"When you do what we do, private lives aren't really important. In case you didn't know, Reign is a pretty illegal operation," Austin answered Grant sarcastically.

"Guys! Pay attention," Mike yelled.

Everyone turned back to the video just as Lancer made it to a small building in the back right corner of the compound. He quickly snuck through the door and inside the small room was a single elevator on the opposite wall. After taking the elevator down, the doors opened up into an enormous lab, Lancer stepping out onto a catwalk.

"This is where they conduct all their experiments. Subjects are kept in incubation pods before and after injection although time inside the pods seems to vary," Lancer whispered, informing his superiors of what he had discovered.

Lancer began to walk up and down the multiple aisles of pods, scanning his camera along the rows of machinery. Unconscious men and woman occupied each pod, their bodies connected to it by electrode pads.

"My God," Austin said under his breath as he watched on.

"I attempted to discuss the serum with a lab technician several days ago but they didn't help on shedding any light on new information. I managed to catch a glimpse of one of the subjects, post pod, and the results seem to be unsatisfactory and inconsistent, though Damien's mood seems to allude to the fact that they are working through the problems and are getting closer to a final product."

As Lancer continued to record the facility, a gunshot rang out in the lab and Lancer's body dropped to the floor. His agonized breathing could still be heard over the feed as the camera recorded several guards walking up to Lancer's body.

One guard spoke into his communicator. "Sir, we found him. What should we do with him?" The guard stared off into the distance as he listened in to his new orders. "Understood," he responded with a sickening grin.

The guard knelt down to Lancer's body, Lancer still breathing erratically. He aimed his pistol at Lancer, pressing the barrel against his head and, suddenly, the camera feed ended, constant static now occupying the screen.

"What happened?" Austin asked anxiously.

"We lost the feed after that." Mike paused, his eyes full of regret. "We lost him."

"There was nothing we could have done, Michael. We never thought Church would be able to see through Lancer's background," Hardwick jumped in.

"We shouldn't have underestimated him. We knew the implications of his goal; we should have done more. We should have sent in someone with him."

"Why? So they could have died too?" Grant interjected.

"You guys are making me feel really good about saying yes." Austin leaned back in his chair. Instantly, he sprung back up. "Wait a minute, you said this compound is in Russia. You know where it is, why can't you just hit it with a missile strike or something?"

"I'm sorry, did I miss the part when the film crew came in here?" Grant looked around the room, pretending to search. "This isn't a movie!" he snapped at Austin. "We can't just pick up the phone and drop a bomb on the compound. Not only would that cause an international incident with Russia but it wouldn't bring us any closer to stopping Church!"

"He'd be dead and his compound would be destroyed, how would that not be closer?" Austin questioned.

Mike spun around in his computer chair, now facing Austin. "Judging off the size of that lab from Lancer's footage, this compound obviously goes deep underground. Any missile strike small enough to keep under the radar wouldn't reach the core of his research and experiments and anything that *could* reach that far down would pit the U.S. in a war with Russia within twenty-four hours. D.A.R.C. can't afford to start World War III because of Church."

"Not to mention that still wouldn't guarantee our success. We may know where Damien keeps his work and what he's working on but we have no idea how prepared he really is. For all we know, he could have safehouses all across the globe with backup files of all his research. As of now, we can't guarantee destroying this compound would destroy his entire operation. That's why we need someone on the inside, to find out all this pertinent information. Once we know every facet of his operation, we can decide how to strike," Hardwick added and sat down slowly in a nearby chair, an involuntary grunt seeping from his mouth.

"We don't just need to kill the man; we need to kill the legacy," Grant cut in.

"Then I'll get the information you need," Austin said confidently.

Hardwick leaned forward onto the table and folded his hands together near his mouth. "Good, but before that, there's something I need to know. If we're going to trust you on this mission, we need to know everything we can about your relationship with Church. You have the closest connection to Church and I want to know why."

Austin paused momentarily and looked down as if playing the events back in his head.

"It really all started when I was fourteen. My father left and I had a really tough time coping with that. I can confidently say I made some really bad decisions. I acted out against everybody I came in contact with and, sometimes, that meant putting a target on my back. When I was sixteen, things really got out of control. There were these kids I went to school with, they were part of a new street gang, wanted to make a name for themselves. They made everyone afraid of them, afraid of what they could do but me being the type of person I was back then, I didn't care. They expected me to step back but, instead, I stepped up." Austin looked up at Hardwick. "That was a mistake." He inhaled deeply and continued, "One night, I was about ready to turn in when I got a phone call. These kids had grabbed one of my closest friends, Nick, and threatened his life. They wanted me to meet them, exchange myself for Nick."

"And you did it?" Mike asked, enthralled in the story.

"Of course I did it. Nick was my best friend, he's still my best friend. I would never want something to happen to him because of me. So I met them where they told me to. This old trainyard downtown. Even seven years ago, the thing was practically abandoned."

"An old, abandoned trainyard," Grant scoffed in a snarky tone. "And you didn't think you were gonna die?"

"Looking back, yes, I was 100% going to be killed but, at the time, I was just focused on saving Nick." Austin leaned forward in his chair and leaned his arms against his knees. "When I got there, they had already roughed up Nick pretty badly. I gave myself up but they didn't stick to their deal."

"Because it was a fake deal!" Grant exclaimed.

"I know that now, Grant!" Austin snapped back.

"Grant, for Christ's sake, let him finish," Mike interposed.

Austin's eyes drifted into a thousand-yard stare as his mind took him back to that night once more.

"They beat me half to death. There were so many of them, I couldn't even try to defend myself. Their leader, the one I didn't back down to in school, he pulled a knife. He toyed with me, joked about stabbing me over and over again. He would get so damn close and then pull back and just laugh."

Austin's hands shook with anger as he recalled the event. His voice grew hoarse and his eyes filled with tears, just on the cusp of streaming down his face.

"They were going to kill me. They were going to kill Nick. All I kept thinking was that my mother was going to get a phone call that her son was found dead in the trainyard gravel. I kept thinking, how fucking pathetic and sad."

The room was silent and tense as the three agents listened to Austin's story. What started out as simple information became a retelling and reliving of the darkest moment in Austin's life.

"The kid finally got tired of joking and was ready to end it. But right before he did, a gunshot went off. I'll never forget the sound of it. It was loud, so loud. The echo bounced off the train cars for so long, it felt like it never ended. I remember the kid's body hit the ground so hard, like he was a bag of bricks."

"Damien killed a kid?" Mike asked.

"No, he just grazed his shoulder. But the kid dropped like he *had* been killed. He started crying and screaming but the bullet never even went into his body. I remember catching a glimpse of his arm. He was barely even bleeding."

"So for all his tough talk, that's all it ended up being, I guess," Grant stated.

"Damien walked up holding the gun and started going off. He threatened them so badly, so vividly, they were terrified. He started counting down from five and, by three, the whole gang was gone. Damien saved our lives that night."

"And that's when you started turning it all around," Hardwick said, coming to the conclusion on his own.

"Yeah, that night in that trainyard, my life changed forever. Facing my own mortality like that was enough to set me straight and it turned out Damien had the means to make sure it happened."

"Did your friend feel the same way? He was involved that night too?" Mike asked.

"No, Nick didn't cling to Damien like I did. When I eventually joined Reign, Nick came with me and our other close friend, Josh, came with us too as a cornerman but I was the only one to bond with Damien. He got me on track, my attitude changed, I was able to channel my emotions better, Damien did all that." Austin leaned back in his chair, releasing a heavy sigh of relief. "I haven't told that story in so long."

"Well thank you for sharing it with us," Mike replied.

"Yes, thank you," Hardwick added. "I can see why your bond with Church was so strong. I don't blame you for feeling the way you did."

"Seeing what I've been blind to for so long is surreal. I knew Damien was never a saint but this is on a whole other level. I would have never aligned myself with him if I knew this is who he really was," Austin admitted, gesturing to the screen where Lancer's video had played.

"Well, you're not that lost kid any more and you haven't needed Damien's help in a long time. It's time to show him the error of his ways," Grant said sternly.

Austin looked at Grant firmly. "Whatever it takes."

"Great, now we just have to come up with a way to get you on the inside of the operation," Mike uttered. "Reign's gotta be our best bet."

"I've been fighting in that club for over five years and I never knew any of this was going on behind the scenes. Clearly, he knows how to keep this separated. We won't get anywhere with Reign," Austin countered.

"That's not necessarily true." Grant jumped up from his chair, pacing as he worked through his thought. "What if we generate a scenario that forces this side of his life to come out? If we can somehow create a situation where you're physically in Church's presence when Project: Hercules is brought up, he'll have to tell you about it."

"Yeah or kill me," Austin responded.

"If you two are as close as you say you are, he wouldn't kill you simply because you overheard something. He'd be reluctant to reveal everything to you but he'd try to recruit you before killing you," Grant continued.

"So what do you propose?" Austin questioned.

"We could send in an agent," Mike chimed in. "Send someone in, stage it as if he's there simply to assassinate Church. He'll spout out something about Project: Hercules and go for the kill but then you can fight him off."

"It's a pretty juvenile plan but saving Church's life would put him in a vulnerable position. He might feel indebted to you and be more inclined to share information," Hardwick added.

"Are we ignoring the part where Austin has to fend off a D.A.R.C. agent? Whoever we send in can't hold back or it'll look staged. Would Damien believe Austin could take down one of our agents?" Grant inquired.

"Grant, I don't know what inauguration you've been sitting in on but Austin *has* been taking down D.A.R.C. agents during his combat sessions. It won't have to be heavily staged; Austin can hold his own against most of our field agents," Mike replied.

"But what do I do once I stop him? I can't kill him," Austin asked.

"Of course not, once you save Church's life, you can 'spare' the agent." Mike gestured air quotations with his fingers.

"You don't understand. Reign is more than just a fight club. It's a family, a sanctuary for the underground population. If someone threatens Damien's life, he won't leave that club alive, no matter what I say," Austin admitted.

Hardwick folded his hands on the table. "Well, Reign is your domain, what do you propose we do?"

"There is one thing we can do to make sure your agent gets out alive but you're not going to like it, Grant especially."

"I already don't like where this is going," Grant murmured.

"We're open to any ideas," Hardwick ensured.

"The only way I can guarantee your agent's safety is if I hand him off to someone else to be dealt with," Austin stated.

"How does that save his life? You're just making someone else kill him?" Grant asked, already annoyed by the idea.

Austin smirked slightly, the reaction happening involuntarily. Austin couldn't help but be slightly entertained by the thought of Grant exploding over the final reveal of his idea.

"Because that person will be filled in on all of this."

Grant's eyes snapped wide open.

"Absolutely not! That is completely out of the question!"

"I figured you'd say that." Austin chuckled.

"We have to be open to the idea," Hardwick stated.

"Sir, with all due respect, it's bad enough we were forced to fast-track a civilian into our ranks but now we're going to do it twice?" Grant argued.

"He won't be joining anything. He'll only know of D.A.R.C.'s existence and the plan against Damien. Not only can I personally vouch for him keeping your secret but I know he'll be more than willing to help once he finds out the truth about Damien," Austin explained further.

Hardwick exhaled from his nose, the sound of the rushing air somehow loud enough to be heard throughout the room.

"Who did you have in mind?"

"It's Nick, isn't it?" Mike cut in.

Austin smiled slightly. "Yeah, if I hand your agent off to him, he'll make sure no one gets their hands on him."

"I'm open to the idea," Mike admitted.

Grant stayed silent for a moment. "I don't like any of this. It seems like the more this mission progresses, the more D.A.R.C. loses itself." He turned to Hardwick. "Sir, the decision is ultimately yours."

Hardwick stayed silent for what felt like forever. He alternated glances between his agents and Austin, all of which were waiting impatiently. Finally, Hardwick's stare locked onto Mike.

"Bring in his friend."

"If you don't mind, I think it would be easier if I brought him in," Austin interrupted. He smiled. "I just need that car and driver we came here with."

Nick was putting the last bit of clean dishes back into the cabinet when his cell phone rang. With a quick peek, Nick caught Austin's name and picked up the phone.

"What's up, Austin?"

"Is Josh with you?" Austin quickly asked.

"No, he had a date tonight with a girl he met over the weekend, Rebecca," Nick explained.

"Okay, good, come outside."

"Outside like the hallway?" Nick leaned in to the peephole on the door.

"No, on the street."

Nick quickly made his way to the window and looked out, seeing Austin leaning against the black car. Austin was already looking up at the window and waved with a smile.

It didn't take long for Nick to walk through the front entrance of the building. "Austin, what is this?"

"Get in, I'll explain everything on the way." Austin opened the back door and gestured Nick inside.

Nick looked at Austin perplexedly. "On the way? On the way to where?"

"Just get in," Austin repeated.

During the drive, Austin explained everything to Nick, down to the last detail. His arrest, his meeting, his inauguration, his tension with Agent O'Neal, and of course, every revelation about Damien. The more Austin spoke, the more he felt like he couldn't stop. There was always more that Austin remembered and blurted out.

Although Austin had only become aware of this world a week ago, he felt as though he was carrying years' worth of secrets on his back. He described Mike and Grant and their opposite personalities. He explained as much as he could about Hardwick and D.A.R.C. overall. Nick listened intently but found it hard to focus on such outrageous claims and explanations.

"That is…" Nick sank into the backseat of the car and let out a big gust of air from his mouth as if deflating. "That is a lot to take in."

"I know and I'm sure there was a better way to explain all that to you instead of one big info dump but I couldn't help myself," Austin confessed.

"No, it's okay. I get it. That all must've been a lot to keep to yourself."

"You have no idea." Austin chuckled faintly.

The car went silent for a moment as both men stared out their respective windows.

"So Damien, huh?" Nick turned to Austin.

"Yeah," Austin replied simply, looking back at Nick.

The car pulled up in front of headquarters once more and the driver escorted them into the building. Nick looked around with the same awe that Austin did.

"Welcome back, Mr. Michaels," Agent Madison greeted, swiping his card through the scanner.

"Wow, Mr. Michaels. Guess you're all fancy now," Nick joked.

"Come on, this way."

Austin led Nick through the lobby and up the staircase; all the while, Nick still looking around astounded by it all.

"Is it weird that I'm amazed at how normal it looks?" Nick asked.

"Nope, same reaction I had." Austin chuckled.

Austin knocked on the door to the C.O.R. and a few moments later, it hissed open again.

"Welcome back, this must be Nicholas." Mike smiled with an extended hand.

"Uh, yeah, but Nick is fine. You must be Mike, right?" Nick replied.

"I see Austin gave you the rundown before you got here. Kid already can't keep his mouth shut," Grant growled.

"And you must be Grant." Nick grinned as he walked down the center aisle.

"Director Hardwick. Nice to meet you." Hardwick gripped Nick's hand firmly in a handshake.

"Nice to meet you too. Austin filled me in on mostly everything I think."

"Good, then let's begin," Hardwick replied.

Grant opened a folder in his hands and began to read from it aloud.

"Nicholas Dennison. Twenty-three years old, son to Mary and Franklin Dennison. No siblings. Born in—"

"Grant, enough with the dossiers!" Mike snatched the folder from Grant's hands.

"This is necessary, Mike! This is what we do! This is how we preserve our secret!" Grant barked.

"By blackmail?" Nick questioned.

Austin leaned over to Nick. "Don't take it personally, he threatened me too."

"That's enough! Let's get down to business," Hardwick ordered and, just like that, the room went still. "Has Austin filled you in on your role yet?"

"I'm responsible for getting your agent out alive, right?" Nick double-checked.

"Can you handle that? We don't need maybes, we need certainties," Grant asked.

"Yes, if you give him to me, I'll get him out alive," Nick replied, his demeanor becoming serious and focused.

"Good. As you can probably tell, we are all in uncharted waters at the moment. We've become desperate in our pursuit to stop Church," Hardwick claimed.

"Well, you know what they say about desperate times," Nick

said, leaning back in his chair.

"Yeah, and we seem to have hit the most desperate, lowest measure. I'm glad no other agency knows of our existence because they'd think we were pathetic." Grant sat down in his chair looking defeated.

"Grant, you have to stop looking at this like a sad failure and start looking at it like a working plan," Mike chimed in.

"Grant," Austin said firmly. "If this works and I get in close with Damien, I'll prove to you that this isn't a failure."

Grant scoffed, "I hope so."

Nick placed his hand on Austin's shoulder with a smile and said, "Let's get you into Project: Hercules."

After spending some time ironing out the last of the details, Austin and Nick were escorted back to the car out front. Upon making it back to their apartment, Nick stopped Austin by the front door.

"Austin, hold on."

"What is it?" Austin asked, pulling his hand away from the handle.

"When Damien saved us, we were young, we were scared. I never put any thought into it except that he saved our lives. But now that we know everything that we do, it makes me wonder." Nick gave a quick look around as if double-checking that no one was watching them. "What *was* Damien doing in the trainyard that night?"

Austin's eyes widened with realization as it dawned on him as well.

Nick continued, "He always claimed he was just walking by and heard the commotion—"

"But what if he was already there?" Austin finished Nick's statement.

"Exactly!" Nick exclaimed.

"We need to get into that trainyard," Austin stated.

Nick smiled widely. "You read my mind."

Chapter 9

A Past Revealed

The two wasted little time racing downtown to the trainyard. As old as it was when they were sixteen, it had aged tremendously in the seven years since. The decrepit, abandoned train cars sat on rusted rails. Overgrown foliage had claimed ownership to most of the yard and the city's wild life had become its inhabitants.

Austin parked his car in an empty parking lot across the street and the two snuck their way to the nearby wall.

"You first," Austin stated as he placed his right hand over his left, his palms facing upwards.

He bent slightly and prepared for Nick's ascent. Placing his foot in Austin's hands, Nick was propelled up onto the top of the wall. After adjusting himself, Nick reached down and helped Austin up. The two walked as slowly and silently as they could across the yard though they doubted the half-conscious night guard would catch wind of them.

"Look at this, two hours into the secret club and we're already on a mission together." Nick chuckled, turning on his flashlight.

"Do you really think Damien would have had something here?" Austin asked, turning on his as well.

"I don't know for sure but after hearing everything, I wouldn't be surprised if he did. We have to look at everything about Damien in a different light now," Nick answered.

They headed towards the south section of the yard, the same direction Damien had approached from that fateful night. As they continued to walk, the beam of Austin's flashlight swept across the ground and he stopped in his tracks.

"Austin, what is it?" Nick asked.

"This is where it happened." Austin's eyes never moved from the spot on the ground.

Austin could almost replay the entire event out in front of him. He still remembered how many people were there, where they were standing, and where he was hopelessly lying. It was as if he could see projections of everyone right there before him. As he continued to remember the moment, he panned his flashlight up into the distance.

"Damien came from that direction. If he had anything to hide, it would be down there."

The two continued through the yard, passing dilapidated train cars and old office huts. As they made it past the tracks, they saw two rows of old buildings. They were separated, each with their own rolling gate protecting them.

"What are these?" Nick inquired, sweeping his flashlight over the sight.

Austin walked over to the side of the nearest building and wiped his hand across it, the thick, blackened dirt wiping away to reveal what was hidden underneath. Just like that, Austin's heart sank as if he had already seen the evidence he came for. One word, practically shining from the wall like a distress signal: STORAGE.

"Any chance it's a coincidence?" Nick asked.

Austin wiped the excess dirt from his hand onto his pants. "Not a chance."

They began to walk down the row, trying to find a way to distinguish one storage building from another but, unfortunately, they were all identical.

"Are we really going to break into every single building until we find Damien's?" Nick questioned as he looked around at the many buildings, already seeing too many to count.

Austin stopped walking, a large smile spreading across his face.

"Nope, we just have to find the one that's different."

"But none of them are different. They all look exactly the same," Nick argued.

Austin pointed at the rolling gate.

"But not all of them are protected the same."

Nick's eyes met where Austin was pointing and saw that the lock was much different from the rest of the standard locks used. The lock was larger, sturdier, with a heavy bar locking it in place through the gate's security hole.

Nick took a moment to examine the lock. "How the hell are we gonna break through this?"

Austin didn't respond but, instead, began to look around on the ground. Finally, he jolted down and picked up a metal rod, half buried in the gravel.

"Like this." He smiled.

Austin set the metal rod in place, angled through the bar and lock of the contraption on the gate.

"Okay, push on three." Austin grabbed the pipe and prepared himself, Nick doing the same right behind him. "One, two, three!"

The two pushed as hard as they could, the pipe jamming itself diagonally through the mechanism and soon, they heard the loud, heavy snap of the lock breaking open. The heavy steel clanged onto the ground and Austin and Nick gave each other a look of approval. Austin threw the gate upwards, revealing a single door behind it. He slowly grabbed the doorknob but stopped before turning it.

"What are you waiting for? Let's go," Nick asserted and began to walk forward but Austin quickly grabbed his arm and pulled him back.

"What's wrong?" Nick wondered.

"If this storage unit really is Damien's, then he might have security measures in place," Austin whispered.

"Like what?" Nick asked.

"Like cameras, and they might be able to pick up audio."

Nick's mouth went agape.

"Good catch, I didn't even think of that," Nick murmured. "So if he does have cameras in there, how do we get in?"

Austin stayed silent, pondering what their next move could be. He pulled out the phone Mike had given him and quickly made the call.

"Austin? What's wrong?" Mike answered, already panicked.

"No, nothing, I was wondering if you could do me a favor."

"Why are you whispering?" Mike questioned.

"I can't explain, just hear me out. If I give you a roundabout location, can you remotely access the cameras in the area?"

"That's a pretty vague request and also extremely difficult. This isn't a movie; we can't just snap our fingers and have an entire database at our disposal. It takes coding, hacking, data dispersion and retrieval, not to mention swift typing skills. Some firewalls act on timers, if you're not fast enough, you can't make it through the door, no matter how good your hacking is. And then there's—"

"All right, all right, spare me the details, just tell me you can't do it," Austin groaned.

"No, I can do it."

"What?" Austin snapped over the phone.

"I just don't like that people assume it's so easy, especially coming from a partial agent like you," Mike admitted. "But I hope you know I'm not doing anything until you tell me what this is about. We sent you home, so I can only imagine this is to see the camera feed to your front lobby."

"No, Nick and I are in the trainyard I told you about."

"You're what?" Mike exclaimed. "Not only is Grant going to kill you when he finds out but I'm debating it myself! What the hell are you doing there?"

"There's no time to explain. I'll tell you everything after we're done here."

Mike sighed. "Every single detail. Now give me a location."

Austin scanned his surroundings for safe measure.

"South end of the trainyard near the Draco Avenue intersection. There's a bunch of old storage units here if that helps."

Mike checked his own surroundings as well, hoping Grant wouldn't pop up over his shoulder at any point during his search.

"Okay, my scan found three speeding cameras, one red light camera, and a ton of cameras linked to a security network. I'm guessing those are the storage units."

"So each unit *does* have its own camera," Austin reiterated.

"If you give me the unit number, it'll make this go a lot quicker," Mike informed.

Austin quickly looked at the building, trying to swiftly find the answer.

"Got it, it's unit number twenty-eight."

"Okay, I'm in. The camera is only facing the front entrance.

I can't even make out what's inside," Mike stated.

"That's why we're here."

"Okay, I implemented a loop sequence. Even if you walk by the camera, it will only see the untouched door."

Austin scrunched his brow in surprise.

"Wow, I thought that was only in the movies."

"I'm sure you'll be saying that a lot throughout this mission." Mike chuckled. "Now hurry up before Grant kills all of us."

Austin hung up and slowly opened the door. The two walked into the dingy storage unit, the smell of stale dust immediately invading their noses. A single light illuminated the front entrance but kept the rest of the unit shrouded in darkness. Before either could continue forward, a single red beam pierced through the black, laying perfectly in the center of Austin's chest.

Austin looked down, his breathing short and panicked.

"Austin," Nick uttered.

A large gun rolled out of the darkness; the light still trained directly on Austin's center mass.

"State authorization password," a robotic voice demanded.

"There's a fucking password?" Nick exclaimed in a low yet high pitched tone.

"State authorization password," it repeated.

Austin's heart was racing to the point of feeling as if there was no rhythm to it at all.

"Final warning, state authorization password."

Austin shut his eyes tight and said the only thing that came to mind.

"Project Hercules."

He held his breath, waiting for the gunshot, the last sound he would ever hear.

"Password accepted, welcome back, Mr. Church."

The aiming light turned off as the gun powered down and rolled back. Austin exhaled, his entire body deflating of all its anxiety.

"Holy shit, that was close," Nick admitted, his face still panic stricken.

Suddenly, several lights hummed to life, revealing the entirety of the unit, though the two men immediately wished it didn't. Their eyes saw what their minds couldn't believe. With astonished stares, they looked around the room.

Hanging from long rods throughout the unit were rows and rows of blood bags, each labeled and categorized. Rough sketches of the human body, something akin to Leonardo Da Vinci's human body illustrations, covered the back wall.

"Austin, what is all this?" Nick asked, his eyes bulging from his head.

Austin took another step forward and felt the difference in the floor beneath him. He looked down and saw that he was standing on a thick puddle of dried blood.

"I — I think this is ground zero," Austin replied.

"Ground zero? You mean this is where he first started this sick idea?" Nick questioned with disgust.

Austin gently combed through the blood bags with his hands. "The blood bags, the drawings, the dried blood, Damien used this unit as a research facility."

"This was here the whole time. When he saved us that day, this is where he had just come from," Nick explained, still astonished by the entire situation.

"Makes you feel a little sick, doesn't it?" Austin asked.

"Yeah, I mean that and everything else in this room," Nick admitted. "How are we going to show all this to your suit friends?

We can't exactly have them crowd this place; Damien will know."

Austin took out his phone. "Record everything in this room with your phone while I take pictures."

Nick did as he was asked and began to walk around the storage unit, recording every inch of the environment. Austin snapped countless pictures of everything he saw. The labeled blood bags, the wallpaper made of body sketches, the stale blood on the floor; Austin took pictures of all of it. If it was within the storage unit, it was being documented and nothing was being left to assumption or chance.

"Can we get out of here now?" Nick asked, putting his phone back in his pocket.

"Yeah, I think we got everything," Austin replied, giving the room another scan.

Austin and Nick quickly made their way out of the trainyard and back to Austin's car. Upon entering the safety of the car, a wave of relief washed over them, as if instantly escaping the horror they just witnessed.

"What now?" Nick asked.

"I guess I call Mike back."

Austin dialed the number in his secure phone but the moment he put it to his ear, Grant's shouting roared through the speaker.

"Get back to your apartment right now!" Grant shouted with rage.

The phone call ended abruptly and Austin and Nick shared a concerning look.

"We're in trouble," Nick moaned.

Austin did as he was ordered and drove home.

"So do we call them back?" Nick asked as they walked down

the hallway to their apartments, Austin fidgeting to find his key.

Austin plunged the key into the apartment door but when he opened it, he and Nick were immediately dragged inside, the door closing behind them. The door across the hall opened and Josh poked his head out.

"Damn, pizza's still not here," he groaned and closed himself back inside.

Austin and Nick stood in the foyer and stared at the sight in front of them. Mike was sitting on one of the couches with a laptop in front of him. Grant's eyes never moved off of the two men, his rage-filled stare burning a hole through both of them.

"Can I just say one thi—"

"Sit down!" Grant barked, cutting off Austin's plea.

Austin and Nick made their way to the living room area and plopped down on the adjacent couch from Mike.

"Guess he found out," Austin said.

"Well I definitely didn't tell him that our new partial agent and his friend went on an unauthorized intel grab," Mike scoffed.

Grant walked over slowly, his entire body emitting his anger.

"What the hell were you thinking?" he screamed.

"Grant, listen, we—"

"No, you listen!" Grant's eyes bulged from his head with wrath. "You are not a top agent who can act upon his own impulses! You are not part of a squad that has backup every time you're in the field! You are a partial agent! You're barely considered anything more than a civilian and you pull a stunt like this? You could have been killed! You could have derailed this entire mission and for what?"

Grant's shouting echoed through the apartment and bombarded Austin and Nick's ears.

"Grant, we don't need more people in this building knowing

about D.A.R.C., keep it down," Mike chimed in softly.

"Grant, I know you're pissed but please, just look at what we found. It'll be worth it," Austin pleaded.

Grant stared at Austin for a moment, his chest rising and falling as he attempted to control his unruly fury.

"This better be good," Grant spoke through his clenched teeth.

Austin and Nick handed Mike their phones and he quickly hooked them up to his laptop. Within moments, Nick's video was playing on Austin's T.V. screen. Mike and Grant looked at the footage intently.

"What the hell did you guys find?" Mike asked with surprise.

"The day Damien saved our lives, this is where he was coming from. He didn't just stumble onto the scene; he was already there. We think this is where he first started his twisted idea," Austin explained.

The footage showed everything they found and the longer it played, the more intrigued the agents were.

"He stored blood, most likely to test his serum on," Mike stated.

"Those drawings, it was like he was trying to see what enhancements he could make," Grant added.

"And he didn't just use drawings to figure that out," Austin interjected.

Mike switched to Austin's photos and everyone could see the more detailed evidence before them.

"Is that all blood?" Mike questioned.

Nick spoke up, "We think he worked on actual people in there too."

As Mike cycled through the countless photos, Grant's eye caught something and he immediately halted Mike.

"Go back two photos."

Mike obliged and everyone looked at the image, a list of chemicals and, at the bottom, a row of question marks.

"Austin, did you look at this closely?" Mike asked.

Austin looked at the image with just as much intrigue. "Honestly, no, I just kept snapping pictures. I guess I didn't even realize everything I was looking at."

"This is it," Grant muttered.

"Grant?" Mike questioned.

Grant continued, "This is his formula. You found his formula."

"If that's true, then it's incomplete. Clearly, he was missing an ingredient," Mike stated, addressing the row of question marks.

"He was but there's no telling if he still is. We can't be sure how long it's been since he last visited. If he has that final ingredient, then it won't be long until there's human weapons walking among us," Grant exclaimed.

"Still mad?" Austin sneered arrogantly.

"Don't get smart. What you two did was extremely reckless, irresponsible, and dangerous. You could have cost D.A.R.C. everything." Grant paused for a moment. "But I won't lie, this information was invaluable."

Austin cupped his hand around his ear dramatically. "I'm sorry, that sounded like a 'good job'."

"Don't push it," Grant bubbled.

"Austin, come Monday, there is no room for failure. You need to get in with Church's operation no matter what," Mike stated as he handed Austin's phone back to him.

"I know and I'm ready."

Mike closed the laptop and sprung up from the couch. "I moved everything over to my hard-drive. I'll give it to tech and see what else they can pull from the intel."

The two agents walked to the door but before leaving, Grant turned back.

"Austin, this doesn't mean you sit on your ass until Monday. Tomorrow night, expect a car to be here to pick you up. Your training isn't over."

Austin gave a faint smile to Grant. "I'd be disappointed if it was."

Grant scoffed and opened the door. The moment the two agents left, the air immediately felt thinner as if an enormous weight exited with them. Austin and Nick dropped onto their own couch and sunk in.

"Aren't you going to go home?" Austin asked.

"Nah, I think I'll just stay here for a bit. It's been a long night," Nick replied.

Mike and Grant headed down the hallway with quickened pace.

"Don't think I didn't notice that back there." Mike smirked.

"Notice what?" Grant questioned in his normal, stern tone.

"You like him."

"Mike, I don't have time for your nonsense tonight," Grant barked.

Mike giggled. "Just admit it, you like the kid. He's surprised you at every turn and now you've become a fan."

As they made it to the elevator, Grant pressed the down button and turned to Mike.

"Only you would see this as being someone's fan. You're one of two Elite Special Agents, you should start acting like it."

The elevator doors opened and the two stepped in.

"Yeah, you're right." Mike looked up at the floor number above the doors. "But you didn't disagree."

Grant didn't respond as a subtle smile crept onto his face though Mike's eyes never caught it.

Chapter 10

Mission Commence

Time seemed irrelevant as the week passed by and, before long, Austin found himself preparing to leave on Monday night. Austin prepped himself to leave but stared at his reflection for a moment: something he did quite frequently before a fight.

"Another fight." Austin continued to stare. "Probably the most important one of my life."

Greeting the bouncers, worming their way through the thick crowd, and congregating with Demi, everything repeated like it did every Monday but Austin and Nick knew this night was different. Although everyone around them was completely unaware of their true intentions, paranoia had set in and it seemed as if all eyes were on them.

Austin began to wrap his hands as Nick walked off towards his designated ring with Demi by his side.

"All right Austin, Agent Nash is in position. Once your fight is over, proceed to the skybox for your usual goodbye," Mike's voice reaffirmed through a pair of communicators lodged in Austin and Nick's ears.

"Sounds good," Austin whispered as he stood up and stared down his opponent who was already in the ring.

"Owen, ready?" the official asked and Austin's opponent nodded his head.

"Austin, ready?"

Austin nodded but, as soon as the match began, it ended. Austin wasted little time taking Owen to the mat and beating him into submission. The official raised Austin's hand as the crowd cheered like always.

"Great job, Austin," Josh complimented as Austin stepped out of the ring.

"Thanks," Austin answered simply, digging into his duffle bag for his change of clothes.

By the time he finished, Nick and Demi had regrouped as well, Nick smiling from his own victory.

"Another win for both of us?" Nick asked.

"Is it ever any different?" Austin chuckled.

"Austin, enough distractions. Get up to the skybox so Agent Nash can proceed with the plan," Grant cut in.

Austin passed a quick glance onto Nick, who obliged the gesture.

"I'm gonna say goodbye to Damien," Austin informed.

The moment he headed towards the staircase, Nick proceeded with his objective.

"Demi, could you grab a few more pairs of sparring gloves from the supply room?" Nick asked.

"Sure thing." Demi smiled happily. She grabbed Josh's arm and pulled him along. "Come on, you're helping."

"Oh come on! The supply room is huge and nothing is ever organized," Josh groaned as he was whisked away.

Austin opened the office door and saw Damien standing by the window as usual but the thoughts in Austin's head were anything but. It was the first time he had seen him since truly discovering what kind of person he was. Somehow, Damien looked just a little different to Austin now, his entire image bathed in a dark, sinister light.

"Remarkable as usual." Damien turned to Austin, already donning a smile.

"Thanks, I try," Austin joked, ignoring the feeling of deceit buzzing around his head.

Damien handed Austin the usual two envelopes. Austin took a quick look inside like he always did. It was important for him to act as normal as possible despite the overwhelming responsibility of the plan.

"Agent Nash has entered the building, keep stalling," Mike informed.

"Hey, where's that Jeff guy? We were wondering if he wanted to grab a bite to eat with us," Austin lied.

"Mr. O'Neal wasn't passionate about my role for him. He was expecting a more hands on approach," Damien replied.

"He quit?"

"Not exactly. I completely understood his point of view and made some phone calls to get him picked up by a private security firm. He'll have plenty of time in the field working for them." Damien shrugged.

"I'm sorry to hear that," Austin replied but those seemed to be the only words he could release from his mouth.

He was astonished, appalled at the fact that Damien could lie to him so effortlessly.

"Damien was responsible for a human being getting hacked to pieces and stuffed in a box but he created an entire lie to tell anyone who asked questions." The thought blared in Austin's head like a fire alarm.

It was only then that he realized that he had been staring at Damien the entire time.

"Austin, are you all right?" Damien asked worriedly.

"I'm almost in position," Nash's voice came through the

communicator.

Austin snapped back to reality. "Yeah, I'm fine. Just tired, I guess."

"Maybe you should skip a bite to eat and get some rest." Damien chuckled innocently.

Finally, Nash's voice gave the final word. "Breach."

The office door was kicked in and a single bullet was fired from Nash's pistol but instinctively, Damien grabbed Austin and dropped to the floor. Damien sprung to his feet, racing across the office as bullets smashed into the viewing window right on his trail. Damien dove behind his desk in the corner but Nash was already approaching. Nash stood over Damien with his pistol loaded and aimed.

"It's over, Church. Project: Hercules is finished."

This was it. Austin had to play his part and play it well. He lunged across the room and quickly knocked Nash's gun out of his hands, the gun flying across the room. Austin and Nash began to trade punches and blocks as they fought around the office, all the while, Damien watching on in astonishment. "He can hold his own against a D.A.R.C. agent. Very interesting." Damien thought with a devious smile.

Before long, Austin dropped Nash to the ground and jumped on top of him ready to slam his fist down into his face. The office was suddenly bombarded by several bouncers and Nick.

"Sir, is everything okay? We heard a commotion," one bouncer asked.

"Yes, everything is fine now, thank you. Austin just saved my life," Damien answered, brushing himself off.

Austin pulled Nash up from the floor and tossed him to Nick.

"Nick, take this guy outside and make sure he doesn't come back."

"Not a problem," Nick replied sternly and forcibly dragged Nash out of the office.

"You won't win, Church! You can kill me but we'll still hunt you!" Nash exclaimed in a panicked scream as he was pulled away.

"Are you sure you're all right, Mr. Church?" the bouncer asked again.

"Yes, I'm fine. Go back to your posts," Damien ordered.

As the room emptied and the door closed, Austin looked at Damien pull his chair close and sit down.

"Go for it, Austin," Mike whispered into Austin's earpiece.

"I didn't think Nicholas had it in him to do such a thing but if you trust it, then so do I." Damien laughed.

"Are we really about to pretend that didn't happen?" Austin asked in a firm tone.

"What do you mean? With the business I run, I'm not surprised someone came after me. Probably just a disgruntled fighter trying to blame me for his failures," Damien replied, brushing off the entire situation.

"Damien, that was no fighter," Austin barked. "He was trying to kill you, there's bullet holes in the room to prove it. And what the hell is Project: Hercules?"

"Austin, I honestly have no idea what he was going on about. Don't you find this whole thing just as crazy as I do?" Damien continued with a surprised yet entertained expression.

"Damn it, Damien, you said it yourself, I saved your life! And besides that, I thought we were closer than that. All this time, I thought I could trust you but how could I trust someone who's lying right to my face?" Austin's eyes began to swell up with tears.

Austin knew what he had to do to get through to Damien but

that didn't mean his feelings weren't sincere. Aside from the mission, Austin wanted answers for himself and this was his chance to speak to Damien as purely as possible. The tears were real, the feeling of betrayal was real, and Austin used every bit of it to his advantage.

"Austin, I didn't mean—"

"No! I thought I deserved better than to be lied to but I guess I was wrong. I guess I'm just not meant to have any kind of father in my life." Austin turned and headed for the door, not even waiting for Damien's response.

Before he could even grab the handle, he had won.

"Stop! Stop!" Damien yelled, springing up from his chair. "All right, fine, you win. You're right, you don't deserve to be lied to. I never want you to think you're not like a son to me because you are."

"Then tell me what the hell is going on," Austin pleaded as he retreated from the door.

Damien exhaled heavily, preparing to unload it all. "The truth is, I do so much more than run this club. Reign is just an extra source of income and resources."

"For what?" Austin asked innocently.

Damien walked over to his desk and grabbed the glass carafe from a silver tray that sat on top. He pulled off the cork as he picked up a glass. Damien blew into the glass, blasting away any debris that had fallen in and poured the dark, golden liquid into it.

"I secretly run a large organization dedicated to creating a chemical formula that, when administered into the human body, would grant the recipient untold strengths and physical abilities."

"Wait, what are you talking about?" Austin asked, trying to sound genuinely confused.

Damien poured a second glass and picked them both up.

"Do you know why I chose a business like Reign?" Damien asked as he handed one of the glasses to Austin. "I could have created anything for money and resources but I chose this and do you know why? Because it's my purest passion. Fighting, combat, the human body enthralled in merciless battle. It's what's deep in our cores, rooted in our very souls, the primordial need for violence." Damien clenched his fist tight and clamped his teeth as he spoke.

Austin could see that, despite the lunacy of Damien's idea, his passion was real.

"Before technology, before revolutions, and discoveries, and inventions, there was simply survival of the fittest. The strong survived and the weak perished. All my life, I've been fascinated by the idea of the human body and what it can do. But as I got older, I began to think, what if it could do so much more?"

"More? Like super humans?" Austin asked, still feigning confusion.

"That term always seemed so childish to me but pretty much. People became complacent as time went on. Our lives got easier; everything was done for us. I want to change that. The human race was at its best when it had to fend for itself out in the ruthless world. The world of today is nothing like that," Damien continued.

"And you want to make the world like it was back then?"

"No, of course not. It would be impossible to revert the world to that degree. The infrastructure of our society has become too strong, it's undying. So instead, I am going to create a new level of existence, one that towers over the common knowledge and norms of today. Once I do that, the hierarchy of the human race will change, people will change, society will change, and then the perfect world image will be realized," Damien announced with a sinister smile.

Austin leaned against the wall, his eyes locked in a thousand-yard stare.

"And all this time, you kept it from me. You never even seemed like you had other things going on in your life," Austin stated.

"To be honest, I didn't tell you because I was afraid of what you'd think," Damien admitted.

"What do you mean?" Austin asked as he walked closer to Damien, grabbing a chair on the way.

Austin sat down directly across from him.

"I'm not stupid, I know my idea sounds insane, I know what people would think if they heard it. I didn't want you to look at me like I was crazy or worse, like I was immoral. At my core, I do care about you and see you as a son. I've watched you grow and I feel genuine pride when I look at you and what you've accomplished. I was afraid all that would have been thrown away."

Austin was genuinely shocked. Despite everything, deep down, Damien truly cared and it was something Austin was not expecting.

"So that guy who barged in here, who was he?" Austin continued, trying his hardest to block out any sympathy.

"If I had to guess, he was a D.A.R.C. agent," Damien answered with a roll of his eyes.

"A what?" Austin asked.

"D.A.R.C. is a covert government organization, or at least they think they're a secret. Most of the time, if someone is a big enough threat for D.A.R.C. to go after, chances are, they know of them too. They've been a thorn in my side for a while now but

I've managed to keep them at bay. Judging by tonight's blatant attack, I'd say they're getting desperate," Damien explained.

"If a covert government agency that doesn't exist on paper is coming after you, don't you think that's a sign to stop?" Austin pushed.

Damien leapt from his seat. "Oh please, those government stooges are the last people who should judge what I'm doing."

Damien quickly turned back and sat back in his seat, leaning in close to Austin with intensity.

"Did you know the government uses over a billion dollars a year on soldier enhancers? They were running their own version of Project: Hercules years before I was. The only difference is that they wasted all their money on failures. They lack the vision for something this important."

Austin looked at Damien sternly. "That was Jeff's real role here, wasn't it? To protect you from them."

Damien nodded.

"You can never be too careful when you live in a world like mine. D.A.R.C. is going to keep trying so I have to make sure to stay one step ahead of them. I'm close, Austin, I'm so close to figuring everything out and realizing my dream."

Austin paused for a moment but then raised his glass towards Damien.

"Then let's make sure D.A.R.C. keeps losing." He smiled.

"What?" Damien asked confused.

"I'm in. I'll fill Jeff's role for you and protect you."

"Are you crazy? No! That's out of the question!" Damien exclaimed to Austin's surprise.

"What do you mean?" Austin questioned.

"Austin, what I'm doing, the enemies I'm making, my life is always going to be in peril. I would never put you in such a dangerous situation," Damien explained.

Austin was speechless. Damien sounded sincere, concerned but at the moment, his genuine concern for Austin's safety was jeopardizing the mission. Austin knew he had to keep pushing.

"I'm sorry, when was the last time our lives weren't dangerous?" Austin jested.

"Austin, the answer is no."

"Austin, you *need* to convince Damien to let you join or this entire operation is finished!" Grant barked through the communicator.

Austin had one card left to play and he prayed it would be enough. Austin stormed over to Damien.

"Hey!" he shouted.

Damien's eyes widened with surprise.

"You saved my life, damn it! I was two seconds away from bleeding out in that damn trainyard and you saved me. Even after all these years, you still continue to help me, look after me, push me forward. The least I can do is help you when you need it most. Please, Damien. This isn't impulsive and this isn't taken lightly. I want this."

Damien stared at Austin as he raised his glass once more.

"Come on, Damien, let your son help you," Austin continued.

Damien exhaled heavily, simply staring at Austin in debate. Finally, he answered.

"If you're serious about this offer, you need to know, there is no turning back. Once you join my world, your life will change forever."

"I joined your world a long time ago, Damien." Austin smirked.

Damien stared at Austin once more and, for a brief moment,

Austin feared that he somehow saw through his ruse. Did Austin say something wrong? Did he sound disingenuous? The mere seconds felt like an eternity as the two stared at each other, Austin still holding his glass and his smile. Finally, Damien smiled back.

"You can't imagine how happy it makes me to hear you say that."

Damien raised his glass to meet Austin's. The two glasses clanged in celebration.

"Austin, welcome to Project Hercules."

Chapter 11

Week One

Austin slowly opened his eyes, the sun's rays waking him just before his alarm. After a quick shower and breakfast, Austin was ready for his day, though a sudden phone call would change all that. Austin grabbed his phone and saw Damien's name across the screen. A sudden burst of anxiety surged through Austin's body. Despite the success the night before, he didn't expect to hear from Damien so soon after.

"Hey, Damien," Austin greeted as he put his empty cereal bowl in the sink.

"Good, I'm glad you're already up and about. I ran our little conversation by a couple of my advisors and they were just as hopeful. I'm ready to introduce you to the project," Damien stated with glee.

"Wow, that was fast," Austin said, though his tone didn't match his slightly frightened expression. "But that's great news."

"I need you at JFK within the next two hours. You will find a man at the entrance holding a sign for you, he'll take you right to my plane."

"You have your own plane?" Austin exclaimed.

Damien chuckled heartily. "You have no idea. See you when you arrive."

Damien hung up but, before he even put his phone down, Austin was picking up his secure phone with the other hand.

"Austin, what's the matter?" Mike asked immediately.

"Damien just called. He told me to go to JFK where his private plane is waiting for me. I think he's flying me to Russia," Austin replied, the panic apparent in his voice.

"Okay, calm down. This is exactly what we wanted."

"I know, I just didn't think it would happen so fast. We just spoke last night," Austin continued.

"Damien trusts you. He has no reason to introduce you to his operation slowly. Now that you gained his trust for Project: Hercules, he's probably going to reveal a lot to you and that's exactly what we want. The more information you get, the quicker we can put this nightmare behind us," Mike explained.

"Yeah, I guess you're right."

Mike smiled on his end. "Good, now go pack. You have a plane to catch."

Austin quickly stuffed a duffle bag and texted Nick. As Austin left his apartment, Nick opened the opposite door.

"What's going on?" Nick whispered, not wanting to alert Josh.

"Damien called me. I'm heading for JFK now," Austin informed.

Nick's eyes widened. "You're going to his compound already?"

"Looks like it. Here." Austin handed Nick his personal phone. "I don't want to risk my family finding out about all this. While I'm there, if anything happens, just cover for me."

"Wait, what do you think will happen?" Nick asked, already worried of the answer.

"I think we both know the possibilities."

"No, that won't happen. Damien would never, not to you," Nick continued.

"Listen to me, we don't know what Damien would do, not any more. Just cover for me and hopefully, he doesn't keep me there forever."

Nick stayed silent for a moment as he stared at Austin's phone in his hand.

"All right, don't worry. I'm on it," he said confidently.

"Thanks."

Austin gave Nick a quick pat on the shoulder and darted down the hallway. Nick watched as his friend turned the corner towards the elevators.

"Good luck, Austin."

The drive to the airport was quiet, Austin spending the entire time thinking of what lay ahead of him on this unknown journey. What exactly was he walking into and could he handle the situations that were inevitably going to arise?

Austin parked his car in the parking garage and headed through the front entrance of the airport. Just like Damien had said, a man was holding a sign that simply said "Michaels" on it. Austin walked up to the man but, before he could introduce himself, the man was already walking towards the gates. Austin was confused but quickly followed behind.

Without a single question, Austin was escorted through the entirety of the airport, bypassing security and all their checkpoints all while following the stoically silent man. Upon arriving on the large airfield, the man climbed into a small shuttle. Austin didn't question it and hopped in as well. The shuttle drove across the field and into a large hanger on the far end where a luxury plane was stationed.

"This is Damien's?" The question came out almost involuntarily.

As usual, the man said nothing and simply gestured for

Austin to board. Austin walked up the steps of the hatch and onto the plane, now seeing just how luxurious it truly was. Soft, beige, leather seats, each with their own personal granite topped tables. Thick, plush, carpet lined the floor with lacquered dark oak wood finishing surrounding the interior of the cabin.

A glass of bubbling champagne was already waiting for Austin on one of the tables. As he dropped his bag and plopped into the comfortable seat, the hatch closed and the intercom turned on.

"Welcome, passenger, this is your pilot speaking. We are preparing to taxi onto the runway and will depart shortly. Please fasten your seatbelt and enjoy your complimentary glass of champagne. Normally, this flight would take around seven hours but, in this state of the art aviation vehicle, it will only take us five. We're scheduled to touch down in Moscow at approximately nine p.m.. Russian time."

The intercom turned off and, just like that, Austin was alone, left in his own solitude of silence. He quickly gulped down the glass of champagne as the jet began to move out of the hanger.

Just as the pilot said, the jet softly landed on the foreign runway five hours later. It quickly taxied into a hangar and stopped.

"It is currently 8.47 local time. I hope you enjoyed your flight and appreciate the speed at which we arrived. You can exit whenever you are ready, just please don't forget your belongings," the pilot spoke through the intercom once more.

Austin grabbed his bag and stood up from his chair. Suddenly, his heart pounded in his chest as the realization hit him: he was in the beast's den. Although the mission always came with its dangers, there was a certain level of safety Austin felt being in familiar surroundings. That safety was gone and, with it, the added confidence. Austin gripped his duffle bag strap tightly and took a deep breath.

"Just step off the plane. Whatever happens after that, deal with it." Austin psyched himself up while staring intently at the hatch door.

He grabbed the handle and paused for a moment.

"Come on, I can do this. There's no danger, not yet. Damien trusts me. If I believe that I'm here to help, he'll believe it too."

Austin took one last deep breath and opened the hatch, the staircase flipping down and landing softly on the hangar floor. Already, the biting cold air shot through Austin's body. Austin looked out and saw three men standing at attention. The man in the center, with his hands folded behind his back, smiled and nodded.

"Hello, Mr. Michaels. We've been expecting your arrival. Welcome to Russia."

Austin took his time walking down the stairs.

"Moscow right?" he asked.

"That is correct. Mr. Church is able to operate in a more secluded environment here," the man continued.

"Makes sense." Austin nodded. "And your name is?"

"Of course, how disrespectful of me. My name is Boris. Boris Morozov."

Boris was a slender individual, his slim fitted suit still somehow falling loosely on his body. He stood up straight, still, and proper, his body at attention. Boris's accent was bold and heavy, native to the region, yet accurate and cultured.

"There will be plenty of time for pleasantries later. For now, let's get you home and unpacked." Boris smiled as one of the other men grabbed Austin's bag for him.

He tossed it into the trunk of a stretch limousine that was

stationed at the front doors of the hangar, the engine already running. The two escorts sat in the front cabin while Austin and Boris climbed into the back. Before the limo even made it off the airfield, the heavy snow began to fall. As Austin and Boris sat in silence, the latter clicked a button on the door, raising the partition between them and the men in the front.

"There are a couple of things to know before arrival. One, when dinner is announced, it is imperative to arrive at the table promptly. Mr. Church hates tardiness for meals. Second, you go where Mr. Church goes, you stick to him like glue. If you are caught walking the grounds unsupervised, there will be problems for you. And third, and perhaps the most obvious, nothing you see here must ever be spoken of to anyone outside this organization. Am I clear on those three things?" Boris explained sternly.

Austin took a moment, as if processing all of Boris's orders.

"Yeah, sounds easy enough," he answered.

"Mr. Church has told me much about you. I hope you do not disappoint."

"I don't plan to. Damien is like family; I wouldn't hurt family," Austin continued, his lies already building up.

The limo eventually turned off the expressway and into a dense forest, only the slim dirt road untouched by the large trees. Eventually, the fierce snowstorm slowed down and revealed a large, fortified, snow-covered compound in the distance. Austin had seen glimpses of the compound through Agent Lancer's video but none of that did its sheer size justice.

The surrounding walls were thick and reinforced with multiple layers of brick. Guard posts were stationed at each corner with the back right corner post sharing its space with the familiar shed from the footage. In the center of the compound stood an overwhelmingly large mansion, thick columns lining the front entrance. Austin looked out the window in astonishment. Boris caught Austin's reaction and chuckled.

"I'm sure you didn't expect Mr. Church to have this sight waiting for you when you arrived."

"I had no idea he had anything close to this," Austin replied honestly.

"Yes, that happens a lot. Mr. Church is a man of many secrets, some of which I'm sure you are still unaware of," Boris continued.

Austin leaned back in his seat. "Oh, I bet."

The limo stopped in front of the mansion and the passenger quickly ran to the back and opened the door. Boris and Austin stepped out and Boris led him to the front doors.

"Mr. Church is waiting inside." Boris pushed the two large double doors open, revealing the beautiful interior for the first time.

Behind the front doors was a large, elegant lobby. Marble tile lined the large floor leading towards the back of the mansion where Austin couldn't even see any more. To the left was a seating arrangement, two brown leather couches surrounding a mahogany coffee table. To the right was a thick, wood table covered in ornate statues and vases.

The walls were covered in a dark red paint but were made into something much more elegant thanks to the sophisticated designs painted on them in thin gold. A large, crystal chandelier hung above the lobby with two crescent staircases wrapped around the sides, joining at the second floor landing where Damien was already standing with a smile.

"Welcome to my home, Austin. You have no idea how much joy it brings me to see you here. Knowing you're now a member of my cabinet does nothing but make me smile. For now, let's not waste any more time. Boris will show you to your room so you can unpack and, afterwards, we will meet in the dining hall for dinner," Damien announced, his smile stretching from ear to ear.

As instructed, Boris escorted Austin to his room. Boris opened the door and revealed a room on par with a five-star suite. Austin walked in slowly, admiring the various amenities he would have. A massive T.V. imbedded in the wall across from a king-sized bed. A plump, leather couch sitting under the bay window. A marble-tiled bathroom with a shower and jacuzzi.

"Guess Damien does consider me family," Austin murmured in astonishment.

"Don't flatter yourself, every bedroom in the mansion looks like this," Boris rebutted and closed the door, leaving Austin alone.

Austin tossed his duffle bag onto the bed and sat beside it. He pulled his secure phone from his pocket and stared at it for a moment.

"I can do this. Just take it one step at a time. First things first, don't be late to a meal."

Austin stood up, put the phone in his back pocket, and walked to the door. Upon opening it, he jerked in shock to see Boris still standing there.

"Are you ready to walk with me?" he asked.

Boris directed Austin to the dining hall. As they walked through the archway of the room, Austin sat in the first empty seat he saw.

"Austin," Damien spoke as he walked through the opposing archway. "Your seat is right here next to me."

Damien sat at the head of the table and gestured to the seat to his right. Austin stood up and made his way over, sitting down right across from Boris who sat to Damien's left. Austin shared a massive feast with Damien, Boris, and a number of his staff members. Austin took the opportunity to eavesdrop on any conversations around him. He didn't have to focus much on keeping up his act when his mouth was full of food.

To Austin's surprise, the conversations were tediously normal. The man to Austin's right was discussing a basketball game from the night before with the man across from him. Towards the other side of the long table, four people were discussing their daughters' joint dance recital the following week. At the other head of the table, three men were laughing about a show they had watched the previous night. All the while, Damien and Boris ate in silence and Austin ate in disbelief.

These weren't stone-cold drones who would kill you as easily as they breathed. They weren't mindless soldiers just existing to serve Damien. Austin finally realized something that had escaped him up till this point, this wasn't like the movies. These were regular men and women just doing their job, their job just so happened to be working for one of the most dangerous men on the planet. As the empty dinner plates were removed from the table, Damien rested his hand on Austin's shoulder.

"Come on, I'll give you the proper tour."

Damien showed Austin around the mansion, showing him the rest of the residential wing, the enormous living room, the kitchen, and the basement. He gave him a quick peek at the backyard though it was covered in a blanket of snow making very little of it visible.

Along the tour, Austin found many opportunities where he could have grabbed Damien but Grant's words echoed in his head; don't just kill the man, kill the legacy. Damien continued to show Austin exquisitely decorated rooms and introduced him to many of his staff members.

"You've been awfully quiet throughout this whole thing," Damien spoke as he and Austin walked down a hallway.

"Just trying to soak it all in, I guess," Austin responded honestly.

"I'm sure you have many questions and I'm ready to answer them."

"What made you make all this out here?" Austin asked, waving his arm around dramatically.

"The forest provides cover; the empty area provides seclusion and safety. I'm able to do pretty much whatever I want out here," Damien answered.

"And why Moscow?"

"Russia is just a tad bit less restrictive than America when it comes to…" Damien paused, thinking of the right phrase. "Extra-curricular activities."

"I know, you said why you kept your secret from me but why did you keep the money a secret? You never carried yourself like you had all this waiting for you at home," Austin inquired.

"I like to keep my life compartmentalized; it makes everything easier in the long run. Keeping Reign separate from my organization makes it simpler to run both," Damien responded.

"But are they really separate?" Austin pushed.

Damien giggled deeply. "I see you're more observant than I gave you credit for. Reign does overflow a bit into this part of my life but only when it's beneficial to me. Otherwise, everything is separate and isolated, just the way I like it."

Damien and Austin made it to the second floor landing that overlooked the entrance lobby. When they did, Austin caught sight of Boris speaking with a man near the front doors.

"Okay, another question. How is he your number two?" Austin pointed over the railing to Boris.

Damien laughed heartily and said, "Boris doesn't need to look intimidating; his mind is more than adequate. When I first started this venture, I wouldn't have even made it past the starting line if it weren't for his initial connections. And as we went on, he established new connections for me that made things even easier. He may look meek but his mind is extremely dangerous."

Damien pointed down to the man talking to Boris.

"Now *that* man, he *is* extremely dangerous."

"Who is he?" Austin asked, leaning his hands on the guard rail.

"Alexei Petrov, a Russian native. You ever want to meet a stone-cold killer, there he is. I hired him on as my head of security," Damien informed.

"Is he really that bad?" Austin asked, slightly worried.

"Oh yeah, that bad and worse. Even after I hired him, he made it very clear to me that if I got on his bad side, no amount of money would save my life. He doesn't care about loyalties; he only goes where the money takes him. And if you're unfortunate enough to piss him off, all the money you have to your name will be useless, it'll only act as casket stuffing for your funeral."

Austin's mouth went dry. He stared at Alexei with fear, knowing that there was a high chance that they would cross paths by the end of the mission.

"Listen." Damien snapped Austin out of his fear-induced trance. "There is something very special I want to show you but I'll save it till tomorrow. It's already late and I want us to get an early start in the morning."

"All right, should I wait here for Boris?" Austin asked.

"What for?" Damien replied, confused.

"He gave me a bunch of house rules to follow and one of them was to never walk around unsupervised," Austin explained.

"Oh nonsense! You aren't any old staff member, you're different from everyone else. Don't listen to Boris, those rules don't apply to you. I'll make sure to update him on the situation the next time I see him." Damien grabbed Austin's shoulder playfully with a smile stretched across his face.

Again, Austin couldn't believe what he was seeing. Damien truly saw Austin like a son and treated him as such. Austin was already given liberties that many others simply did not have.

"Now go on, head back to your room *unsupervised* and get some sleep. I'll see you in the morning," Damien said with dramatic flair and began to walk away.

Austin did as Damien instructed and headed back to his room. For a brief moment, he contemplated sneaking around the mansion with his new found freedom but decided against it as it was only his first night there. Austin got back to his room and plopped into bed. He removed his phone from his back pocket and shoved it under his pillow as he put his head down, falling fast asleep almost before his head even landed.

The next morning, Austin was jolted awake by a vigorous knock at his door. He jumped off the bed and quickly answered it, seeing Damien standing before him with a smile.

"Morning, Damien."

"Good morning, Austin. I didn't mean to wake you but I just couldn't wait any longer. Get changed and meet me in the lobby, it's time to show you my destiny."

Damien walked away before Austin was even able to respond.

"His destiny?" Austin thought. "Could he already be

showing me the lab?"

Austin changed quickly, making sure to stow his phone away in his back pocket once more. He jogged down the crescent staircase and reunited with Damien by the front doors. Damien wasted little time walking with Austin through the compound to the back. There it was, the same shed from Agent Lancer's video and Austin was about to get a firsthand view.

"Here it is." Damien gestured.

"You wanted to show me this old shed?" Austin asked, keeping up with his act.

"It's not about the shed, Austin, it's about what's hidden beneath." Damien beamed as they made it to the shed's door.

Damien lifted a small panel next to the door, revealing a handprint scanner. Damien pressed his hand against it and instantly, the door hissed open, revealing the small room Austin had seen in the video. The two stepped into the elevator and Damien pressed the only button on the interior panel.

"So the old-looking shed is just a cover?" Austin asked as the elevator hummed down the shaft.

"Exactly. In the event that my compound was ever compromised, seeing an old shed at a glance would seem insignificant. It was made to be a final deterrent against any invaders knocking at my door," Damien explained proudly.

Finally, the elevator stopped and the doors opened, revealing the underground lab seen on Agent Lancer's footage. Damien and Austin stepped out onto the overlooking catwalk, Austin portraying all his shock and awe. Damien wrapped his arm around Austin's shoulder.

"Austin, welcome to my true calling."

"All this, all this is under the compound?" Austin asked, still keeping up his charade.

"Good morning, Mr. Church," Boris greeted, waiting patiently by the elevator.

"Good morning, Boris. Is everything in order for today's test?" Damien asked.

"Yes, Sir. We're just waiting for your appearance," Boris answered.

Austin leaned over the catwalk's railing and admired the massive lab down below. Countless men and women were working diligently on sophisticated lab equipment and monitors. Just as in Lancer's video, Austin saw the rows of pods towards the far end of the lab and already knew what was inside them.

"Come on, I'll give you a closer look before the test," Damien exclaimed.

Damien, Austin, and Boris walked down the staircase and onto the lab floor. Immediately, Damien took Austin to the pods. Austin stared through the front glass dome in disbelief. Although Austin had already seen this exact sight in the footage, seeing it in person evoked an entirely different response. Austin was astonished and appalled by the sight of countless unconscious human beings laid up in pods like lab rats. Without realizing it, Austin wasn't able to keep his emotions from rising to the surface.

"I don't blame you," Damien said, snapping Austin back to reality.

"What?" Austin asked.

"I saw your face, your reaction," Damien continued.

Immediately, Austin stammered trying to quickly come up with a reason behind it but Damien stopped him.

"Relax, I think it would frighten me more if you *didn't* have that kind of reaction. This is not a sight you would see every day. But I hope you can also appreciate exactly what it is I'm doing here. All this, everything you see, is necessary," Damien exclaimed.

"All these people, they volunteered to be subjected to something like this?" Austin inquired.

"Some, yes. Others I took from Reign," Damien answered.

"From Reign?" Austin winced with confusion.

"Like I told you last night, I allow overlap of my various interests as long as it benefits me. Reign gave me an opportunity for infinite candidates."

Austin pondered for a moment, pretending to put the pieces together for the first time. "The losers from the matches."

"Exactly!" Damien cheered. "Most of the people who walk into Reign, whether to fight or to watch, are nobodies. They have no friends, no families, barely have a home. They're tethered to society by a tiny insignificant thread and try to use Reign as a last-ditch effort to make something of their lives. Once they lose, they have no reason to continue so I use them instead. At least here, I give them purpose. You've delivered me quite a few yourself actually."

Damien stopped in front of a pod and gestured towards it. Austin stepped closer and wiped the condensation off the glass, revealing a familiar face inside.

"That — that's Rick. I fought him a few weeks ago," Austin replied with genuine shock.

"The explosive power he displayed in your fight was impressive. And when a fighter impresses me, I see potential in them. That's how I decide who to use and who to let be," Damien added.

At that moment, the group walked up to an older man, his pure white lab coat draped over his body.

"Good morning, Mr. Church," the man said.

"Morning, Doc. I want to introduce you to my new cabinet member," Damien replied, gesturing to Austin.

"Ah, yes, you must be Austin. It's a pleasure to meet you, Mr. Church has told me so much about you." The man shook Austin's hand erratically.

"Austin, this is Dr. Arushka. He's the lead scientist on Project: Hercules," Damien informed. "Is everything ready?" he added, turning solely to Dr. Arushka.

"Absolutely, Mr. Church. The new subjects are prepped and ready for their first combat test. We believe we have finally discovered the proper ratio to the formula. We are confident this test will breed very positive results." He smiled proudly.

"Then lead the way," Damien said gleefully.

Dr. Arushka led them through a pair of automatic doors and onto another catwalk that overlooked a large room even further below. They stopped in the center of the catwalk and Damien leaned in close to Austin.

"Austin, you're about to witness the future."

Dr. Arushka pressed a button on the tablet he was holding and two doors on the far side of the room below opened, a man walking out of each. The two men looked normal, healthily fit but nothing to assume they had any extra physical abilities.

Dr. Arushka informed his viewers of the subjects. "The one on the left is subject 115 and the subject to the right is 802."

"What are they working with, Doc?" Damien asked, examining them from afar.

Dr. Arushka readjusted his large glasses. "115 is the control. He was given the same dose we used previously. 802 was given a new chemical cocktail with a much higher dose of adrenaline. We believe the increased adrenaline will balance out the sluggish symptoms that 114 was dealing with prior."

Damien folded his arms onto the railing as he leaned over. "Then let's see what they've got."

Dr. Arushka waved his hand in the air. "Nachinat'!"

Austin assumed the word meant begin because suddenly, both men erupted towards each other and collided in the center, sending tremendous punches into each other's faces. Subject 115 grabbed ahold of his opponent and hurled him across the room. Though it was done with great ease, Subject 802 flew through the air as if he were as light as a feather. He smashed into the wall and jumped to his feet quickly, only to be tackled once more into it.

As the combatants fought, Austin noticed something peculiar. Damien quickly noticed Austin's expression and inquired about it.

"What's on your mind?"

"Those two are already bleeding a lot from all the haymakers but neither seems to be bothered by it. It's like they don't even feel it," Austin explained.

"That's because they don't." Damien smirked. "One of the chemicals in the formula we're creating causes total nerve severance. Every pain receptor throughout the body is destroyed, leaving the host complete freedom to fight continuously despite whatever pain they are meant to feel."

"They don't feel pain?" Austin asked, still looking down at the hellacious fight.

Subject 802 grabbed an incoming punch from 115 and instantly snapped his arm in half. Still, Subject 115 had zero reaction to it and simply continued to fight. Unfortunately, with only one working arm, it wasn't hard for 802 to gain the advantage, grabbing 115's head with both hands, twisting it violently, and severing the spinal cord at the neck. As the loser's body slumped to the floor, the room went silent.

"802 is the winner!" Dr. Arushka announced. "Pozdravlyayu!"

"Yes, congratulations indeed, 802," Damien added.

"Damien, this — this is intense," Austin admitted.

"Progress is intense, Austin. Evolution is intense. We are working towards an entirely new level of existence. Imagine people walking the streets with enhanced strength, durability, speed, and who are impervious to pain. The normal citizen in this world would never be able to compete with that. That is the revelation I am trying to bring to light. The present human race is superior only until the next evolutionary stage overthrows it. This is that evolution," Damien exclaimed robustly.

Damien began to discuss with Dr. Arushka while Austin stared frightfully at the subject below. He turned his head slowly, locking eyes with Austin, his deathly stare piercing through Austin like an arrow.

"This is too dangerous," Austin murmured to himself.

"So do we think this is it? Are we ready to progress to further trials?" Damien asked excitedly.

"I'm sorry to say but that remains to be seen. Even before this combat trial, anomalies were still showing up on the routine CT scans we were doing. Until we figure out what is happening to the brain, I can't, in good conscience, move on to the next step," Dr. Arushka replied.

Still, Austin stared at Subject 802 but, suddenly, he gave Austin a devilish smirk.

"Guys, something's wrong," Austin warned but nobody was listening.

"Isn't there another chemical we can add to the formula to reduce the effects on the brain? I'm not trying to make drooling zombies; I want functional humans," Damien continued.

"Guys! Something's not right!" Austin shouted.

Everyone looked down at the subject just in time to watch him leap through the air and onto the catwalk in a single bound.

"Otstupit'! Otstupit'!" Dr. Arushka shouted. "Stand down 802!"

Subject 802 ignored the doctor's commands and swung his arm into his head, knocking him straight to the floor. Two guards immediately ran over while Damien and Austin backed away slowly. They tried to restrain him but he easily tossed them both over the railing with ease.

"To hell with restraining him! Put him down!" Damien ordered.

Two more guards held their assault rifles up and fired relentlessly into the assailant. Austin was stunned to see the bullets bounce off his body with no lasting effect. With no reaction, he simply walked through the hail of bullets and disposed of the two guards. He turned his head, locking eyes with Damien and began to slowly walk towards them like a lion stalking its prey.

"Austin, let's go," Damien said, pulling Austin away nervously.

Before Austin could even respond, Subject 802 was standing right in front of him. In an instant, he slammed his fist into the side of Austin's head. Austin's body dropped to the floor instantly, his head already pounding from the impact. Damien backed away slowly, the experiment still stepping closer. Damien took another step back and stepped on a dropped rifle from one of the guards, tripping over it and landing on the floor.

"Stand down 802! Final warning!" Damien shouted sheepishly.

Subject 802 lifted his hand above his head, ready to strike, when suddenly, his eyes widened. His breath became shallow as his entire body tensed up. He dropped to his knees and slumped over onto the catwalk, dead. The room went silent as several guards nervously stepped closer. Upon confirming the subject's death, the tension in the room quickly dissipated.

"Sir, are you all right?" Dr. Arushka asked, rushing to Damien's side.

"I'm fine, check Austin," Damien replied quickly.

Within seconds, a medical team was examining Austin.

"Can you follow the light for me?" one man asked, waving a pen light in Austin's eyes.

"I told you I'm okay. You don't need to run a concussion test on me," Austin replied.

Just then, Damien walked over.

"Austin, I know you hate this part but sometimes, it's necessary. Just let them check on you."

Again, Austin could hear the worry in Damien's voice, his concern was genuine.

"Fine," Austin replied reluctantly.

After being cleared by the medical team, Austin walked over to Damien and Dr. Arushka who were standing over the corpse.

"What could have caused such a drastic reaction? Aside from the outburst, he seemed perfect," Damien questioned.

"I believe the increase in adrenaline, while balancing the effects of the other chemicals, was too much for his heart to take. I will know more once I open him up and run his blood but my educated guess is sudden cardiac arrest," Dr. Arushka explained.

"Damn it, I really thought this was it," Damien groaned.

"We will continue to tweak the formula. It's only a matter of time before we find the perfect ratio and, when we do, subjects like this will be mass produced."

"So bullets can't stop them either?" Austin asked as he joined the group.

"No, their skin is impenetrable. The only thing that could break their skin would be another just like them. Bullets might as well be pebbles to them," Damien answered.

"So if this guy didn't just suffer a massive heart attack, how were you going to stop him?" Austin asked, slightly angered by the ordeal.

Damien didn't respond.

"Is this the first time this has happened?" Austin inquired.

"Yes, no other subject has ever had an outburst quite like this. We've dealt with restlessness and agitation but nothing to this degree," Dr. Arushka interjected.

"I know I can't be the only one here who realizes how dangerous this is. He could have killed every single person in this room without breaking a sweat," Austin continued.

"Of course I know it's dangerous!" Damien barked. "But this is what it will take to change the world. Whatever it takes, my vision will be realized."

Austin stared at Damien intently who had a worried expression of his own. If this event showed Austin anything, it was that Damien feared his own creation.

The rest of the day was spent talking to the lab technicians and waiting for bloodwork results. Damien, Austin, and Boris observed Subject 802's autopsy from a viewing window. Damien waited patiently until Dr. Arushka lifted his head from the body and gave a confirming nod.

"Damn it, it was his fucking heart," Damien murmured.

"Don't worry, Mr. Church, we will solve this issue like we have solved all the rest," Boris comforted.

"I know, I just wish we had all the answers already," Damien said, swinging the door to the viewing room wide open.

"Remember what you always say, Sir, you can't rush perfection." Boris chased after Damien.

Austin stayed behind for a moment, staring through the window at the body on the autopsy table. Countless thoughts raced through his head: the potential of such a dangerous weapon, the state of the future if Damien succeeded. Yet all Austin was able to do at that moment was stare idly by while Damien pushed closer and closer to making such a nightmare a reality.

The next morning started with breakfast in the dining hall and an invitation to Damien's personal study. Austin knocked on the door.

"Come in!"

"Boris said you wanted to see me," Austin said as he closed the door behind him.

"Yes, I wanted to know how you were holding up after yesterday's incident," Damien answered from behind his large, oak desk.

"Yeah, nothing a little aspirin couldn't fix." Austin chuckled.

"That's good to hear." Damien exhaled. "Even with the life I live, that's the closest I've come to my own mortality in a very long time."

"I won't lie, what you're doing here is ridiculously dangerous," Austin replied as he sat in the chair across the desk from Damien.

"Do you remember the trainyard?" Damien asked abruptly.

Austin's heart skipped a beat. "The trainyard? Yeah, of course I do. Why?"

Austin's first thought was that Damien was going to tell him about the storage unit and his real reason for being there that night.

"It seems like just yesterday that I found you and Nicholas at the mercy of those thugs. If I didn't show up when I did, you might not even be here today."

"Might? I definitely wouldn't be here. You saved my life that night," Austin replied, his tone now somber and subdued.

"Both our lives changed forever that night. I would have never thought the kid lying in the trainyard gravel that night would grow up to become such an important part of my life. And yesterday only strengthened that feeling. I know I say it a lot but I'm truly proud of you, Austin, and I'm happy you're here." Damien explained.

"I'm..." Austin paused for a moment, his brain sifting through the lies and truths swirling around in his head. "I'm happy I'm here too. I owe you a lot, Damien. After that night, you took a stupid, lost kid under your wing. You taught me how to control my emotions and channel my anger. From the very beginning, you cared about me, more than my own father ever did, and you helped me turn my life around."

At that moment, Austin wasn't speaking to Mr. Church, he was speaking to Damien, the man he knew as a father figure for many years.

"You weren't stupid, Austin. You were just confused and angry. And as much as you think I saved you, you saved yourself. If you weren't willing to learn and change, none of my words or lessons would have done anything for you." Damien pushed himself out of his chair. "There is something I would like you to have."

Damien leaned over to the end of his desk and pulled a box

close, setting it down in the center. He unclipped the latch and opened the lid, revealing the interior to Austin. Inside the box was a pistol mold with the gun sitting inside it, a single magazine lying next to it.

"Damien, what is this?" Austin asked in astonishment.

"It's a gun, Austin." Damien giggled.

"You know what I mean," Austin groaned. "Why are you giving this to me?"

"If yesterday's incident taught me anything, it's that I need more precautionary measures in place. We got lucky yesterday but if another subject were to attack, we can't rely on a sudden heart attack again," Damien stated.

"But bullets just bounce right off of them," Austin rebutted.

Damien smirked. "Not these."

He took the gun and magazine from the box, loading it quickly.

"The bullets in this gun were specially made as a contingency plan. I never needed to carry it on me but, after yesterday, I think it's time to bring it out and I want you to be the one to hold it. If you need help on your shooting, I'll set up training."

"What's so special about these bullets?" Austin asked as he took the pistol from Damien's hands.

"Those bullets are encased with a special Tungsten-Titanium penetrator. That unique blend will rip through any Kevlar armor like paper and will even pierce through any rebellious subject's skin. I want you to be my hammer of judgement on anyone else who steps out of line." Damien smiled excitedly.

"But what about that guy, Alexei? Isn't that what he's for?" Austin questioned.

"Alexei has his own role here and plays it wonderfully. This is a job I want you to have. It's as simple as that." Damien continued to smile.

"All right," Austin said reluctantly. "Thank you."

Damien placed his hand on Austin's shoulder. "No, Austin, thank you."

Austin gave Damien a quick smile but then looked back down at the gun in his hand. He stared at it for a long while, amazed at the fact that Damien just willingly handed him the one thing that could stop his project. Damien had full trust in Austin and expected nothing, all Austin had to do was play his part and Damien would ruin himself.

The rest of the week was mundane in comparison to Austin's first few days. Dr. Arushka spent his time analyzing more blood samples and creating more variations of the formula. In the meantime, Austin stood by Damien as they made routine visits to the lab and around the grounds.

As the sun peaked through the clouds on Saturday morning, Austin awoke to a knock at his door. Austin opened the door and saw Boris standing in the hallway.

"Good morning, Mr. Michaels. Mr. Church had business to attend to but instructed me to give you this letter."

Boris handed Austin an envelope and proceeded down the hallway.

"A letter? He couldn't just send a text?" Austin thought as he sat on the side of the bed to open the envelope.

Austin,

I didn't intend to be rude but something came up and I won't be able to join you this morning. That said, I didn't get the chance to tell you about your plans for the weekend. After breakfast, a car will be waiting for you out front to take you back to the airfield. Enjoy your time with your friends and family and make sure all your affairs are in order for next week. On Tuesday morning, I will have a car waiting for you outside your apartment to bring you back. But as usual, I'll see you before that on Monday night. Safe travels.

Love, Damien.

Love. There it was again. Damien's genuine emotions breaking through the harsh exterior of a wanted criminal. The last two words written on the page consumed more of Austin's attention than the rest of the letter and it took a moment for him to realize what the letter was actually telling him.

"I'm going home!" Austin exclaimed aloud.

The events of the morning rushed passed Austin as his mind was obsessed with the idea of getting to go home. For the next few days, he would be home, safe and secure, living his life somewhat normally.

Austin dropped his duffle bag on the plane's cabin floor and leaned back slowly into his seat. He rested his head back and closed his eyes, the calming feeling of relief washing over him like a tidal wave of reprieve.

Chapter 12

A Little Time Off

Austin made it back to the parking garage but upon seeing his car, he practically sprinted to it. As he jumped into the driver's seat, he realized just how much he missed the usual things he took for granted. Although it was only a few days, pretending to be someone he wasn't made that time feel like an eternity.

He drove home and dashed to his apartment, anticipating the unmatchable feeling of security he would get from closing his door behind him. As he fidgeted with his key ring, trying to find the correct key, his door swung open and Josh lunged into his arms with excitement.

"So did you fight Superman or what?" he exclaimed, a smile stretching from ear to ear.

Austin was stunned silent. His brain couldn't even calculate what he had just heard and his mouth was suddenly incapable of forming any coherent words.

Nick ran to the door.

"I'm sorry, he figured it out on his own," Nick groaned.

"He figured out Damien's entire plan on his own?" Austin reiterated, the disbelief present in his voice.

"Not that!" Nick exclaimed. "He figured out we were hiding something. After that, he poked holes in every lie I came up with. He's actually really good at investigating."

"And here I was thinking I was just nosey." Josh chuckled

163

and pulled Austin inside, closing the door behind him.

The three sat in the living room and Josh wasted no time prying.

"So, tell us everything!"

"There's not much to tell that you don't already know. It wasn't easy getting through the week. Pretending to be okay with everything I heard and saw was the worst part," Austin explained.

"Yeah, yeah, I'm sure you struggled with your morals, but what happened with the supermen?" Josh pressured.

"You gotta stop calling them that," Nick chimed in.

"Nothing happened. I saw a few in action and it's just as terrifying as you would think," Austin responded.

"Man, I am so glad you guys moved across the hall from me five years ago cause this shit is cool." Josh giggled excitedly.

"It's cool in comic books and movies but when your staring into the eyes of someone who feels no pain and could break you in half with less strength than it takes to open a can, you feel fear right down to your core," Austin explained solemnly as if channeling his own experience.

The room went quiet.

"Okay, getting the terrifying part a little more," Josh admitted as he slouched back into the couch.

"Do Mike and Grant know all of this?" Nick asked.

"No, I came straight home from the airport and I couldn't call them either." Austin tossed the pile of scrap that used to be his D.A.R.C. phone onto the coffee table.

"Aren't they going to be wondering what's going on?" Josh questioned.

Just then, there was a knock at the door.

"Speak of the devil," Josh mocked dramatically.

Austin walked to the door and turned the knob but before he

164

could even open it himself, Grant stormed in like a freight train.

"Are you fucking kidding me?" he shouted.

"Hey, Austin," Mike said calmly as he walked in behind Grant.

"Look, before you start flipping out, let me explain," Austin stated as he closed his apartment door.

"Explain! Explain which part exactly? How you failed to mention you were returning stateside? Or maybe explain why we lost track of you less than twenty-four hours into your field trip! Or maybe explain why yet another civilian now knows of your mission!" Grant exploded.

"Okay, that last one's on Nick," Austin cut in.

"I swear to God, I will end this entire operation right now! What the hell happened!"

Since the day he met him, Austin only knew Grant to have one emotion and it was anger but even he had never seen him this enraged. For once, Austin didn't match Grant's level.

Austin made sure to speak calmly. "Grant, you're right to be angry. I'm sure it all looked horrible from your end but just give me a chance to explain."

Grant's eyes shot over to Mike who gave a concurring nod.

"Sit and speak," he ordered through his clenched teeth.

Austin sat and began, "You lost track of me because the phone you gave me broke."

Austin gestured to the scrap on the table.

"I saw them, the subjects for Project: Hercules. They're terrifying but unstable. One tried to attack Damien."

"You fought one?" Mike asked with astonishment.

"I wouldn't call it a fight, he put me down with one swing. But that's how the phone broke. And I had no idea I was coming home until I woke up this morning. Damien said he'll have a car here Tuesday morning so I can go back. That's pretty much my schedule for him."

"And Josh knowing is on me. I had no intentions on telling anyone but he sorta figured it out on his own," Nick interjected.

Grant pinched the bridge of his nose in frustration.

"Grant, this was his first time in the field and he already outlived O'Neal. He hasn't done anything wrong, let's give him the benefit of the doubt." Mike tried to defuse Grant before he erupted again.

Grant looked at Mike for a moment but immediately swung back to Austin.

"Tomorrow morning, I want your ass in the C.O.R. for a full debriefing. I want to know every damn detail. If you had steak, I want to know what sides were served, do you understand?"

"Completely," Austin answered.

"You're lucky Hardwick had a meeting today or else I'd be dragging your ass back right now. He wants in on all debriefs for this mission," Grant continued.

"Sorry to have stormed in like this," Mike apologized.

"For God's sake, Mike. Grow a pair! You don't have to apologize for doing your job," Grant fired back.

"Grant's right, Mike. You don't have to apologize for coming here. However, I would like an apology for the bug that's planted somewhere in my apartment," Austin exclaimed.

Immediately, Grant's head whipped around.

"Come on, I may be new to this whole thing but I'm not stupid. If you couldn't track me, then you could have only known I was back once I got home. Let me guess, you heard my voice and flew over here, am I right?" Austin smirked.

Grant looked at Austin and gave a disheartening grunt before storming out of the apartment. Mike smiled widely.

"Oh boy, you really got his number. The bug was totally his idea. I'm gonna hear about this the whole way back to HQ." Mike chuckled.

"Do you think you could get rid of it? I don't think I really need to be bugged, do I?" Austin inquired.

Mike grinned playfully as he walked over to the other side of the apartment, reaching underneath the countertop of the half wall separating the foyer from the kitchen. He quickly removed a small device from the underside and raised it up for everyone to see.

"Consider it done." He smiled and headed towards the door. "Enjoy the rest of your day, fellas."

As the door closed, Josh jumped up from the couch.

"So what do you guys wanna do?" He smiled.

"Actually, I was going to see if Alyssa was free tonight," Austin stated.

"Aw, did you miss her all week?" Josh mocked.

Austin grabbed his jacket.

"I would say you guys can stay but you live across the hall. Get the hell out." He laughed.

"Austin, before you go see Alyssa, I would suggest paying your mom a visit," Nick advised as he handed Austin back his personal phone.

Austin's eyes widened. "You're right, I almost forgot all about this."

"Well I didn't. You know how hard it was to find excuses why you couldn't talk on the phone? Why can't your mom be obsessed with texting like everyone else?" Nick complained, following Josh out the door and closing it behind him.

Austin decided to save Alyssa for later and rushed over to pay his family a visit. Before long, he pulled into the driveway of his childhood home.

"Hey, Austin, it's been a while!" the neighbor, Mr. Francis yelled from his porch next door.

"Hey, Jerry! How's Darlene?" Austin responded, closing his car door.

"She's good, her and your mom went out just last weekend for lunch."

"Let me guess, my mom didn't let her pay." Austin smiled.

"Of course not! I never heard the end of it when Darlene got home. She swears she's gonna repay your mom for all their lunches one day." Jerry laughed.

"Not if my mother has anything to do with it."

Austin jogged up the front steps and unlocked the door with his key.

"There's a bell, you know," Christian stated from the living room, sprawled out across the couch with the T.V. remote in his hand.

"Careful what you say, as soon as you graduate high school in June, you're gonna be just like me," Austin joked as he leaned over the back of the couch.

He ripped the remote right out of Christian's hand, Christian jerking up immediately.

"Come on, every James Bond movie just got added on Netflix. I have to watch them all before they move again." Christian complained.

"Where's Mom?" Austin asked, holding the remote high above his head.

"She's in my room, now give me the remote."

Austin tossed the remote back to Christian and headed up the stairs. Austin knocked on Christian's bedroom door and opened it.

"Hey, Mom."

"Well, look who it is! And here I thought I imagined having two sons." Debbie smiled, giving Austin a cheek-to-cheek kiss.

Debbie turned back and continued sorting on Christian's bed, putting certain items in a large box in front of her.

"Yeah, sorry about that, Reign has kept me busy and I—"

Debbie groaned disgustedly. "You know how much I hate that horrible place and you know how much more I hate that you're a part of it. I don't wanna hear that name in this house."

"Okay, well, *that thing* has kept me pretty busy. But since I was free today, I thought I'd stop by and say hi," Austin explained. He looked closer at what his mother was doing. "Are you packing for Christian? He's got a few more months till he graduates, you know."

"God, no! Are you crazy? Christian would never let me touch his things. This is all the stuff he's not taking with him. It's all going in the attic," Debbie replied.

"Yeah, that makes more sense." Austin chuckled.

Debbie placed an old baseball trophy into the box.

"So, are you going to tell me where you really were this week?"

Austin's eyes expanded with surprise. "What do you mean?"

"Come on, Austin. You don't think I can tell when my own son is texting me and when he isn't? I'm guessing I had a nice, long chat with Nick, am I right?" Debbie asked, turning around to Austin.

Austin was speechless, trying desperately to come up with an excuse but his mother's stern stare made it impossible to formulate a thought.

"Well, where were you?" Debbie asked again.

"I — I can't tell you," Austin admitted.

"Austin, what did you get yourself involved in? Does this have anything to do with that bastard, Damien?" Debbie snarled, already angry at the possibility.

"Technically yes, but I swear, it's not like that."

"Oh, Austin, come on!" she shouted. "What are you doing? Don't you know what Damien is? How bad of an influence he is? You weren't raised to make such stupid decisions."

"Mom, I promise you, it's not what you think. It's actually a good thing, a very good thing."

"Then why can't you tell me?" Debbie continued.

"Because I just can't but, I swear, you have nothing to worry about. I'm not making bad decisions, I know I'm not, not this time," Austin consoled.

Debbie stared at Austin for a moment and then let out a heavy sigh, turning back to the storage box.

"I really hope you're not lying to me, Austin. You're not a kid any more, you're twenty-three. There's no more room for stupid decisions," Debbie explained, still packing up the box.

Austin sat back in the computer chair next to him.

"Do you ever think about Dad?" Austin asked.

Immediately, Debbie's head whipped around.

"What?" she questioned.

"Do you?" Austin repeated.

Debbie exhaled and sat down on the side of the bed. "To be honest, I find myself thinking about him a lot."

"Do you miss him?"

Debbie thought for a moment. "Well, when I think about him, I get angry. Angry that he left, angry at *the way* he left, angry that I never got the chance to speak my mind about it. But then I think about all the memories we made together, all the fun we shared, and the two beautiful children we made. And then I just find myself sad and confused."

"You think he deserves your sadness?" Austin questioned.

"I know it doesn't entirely make sense but I can't lie to myself about how I feel. Yes, sometimes, I still miss him. Whether he deserves it or not, I can't speak to. All I can do is be honest with myself," Debbie continued.

Austin stayed silent for a moment but Debbie pulled him out of his silence.

"Where did that loaded question come from?"

"I've been thinking a lot about him lately. Just wanted your input," Austin answered.

"Austin, are you sure everything's all right?" Debbie asked sincerely.

"Yeah, Mom." Austin smiled. "Everything's fine."

"Good, then can I ask a question of my own?" Debbie proceeded. "Why do you still involve yourself with Damien and that place?"

"I know you never approved of it but, to me, it was a good choice. It gave me purpose; it gave me a way to channel my anger. And the money's not bad either," Austin explained.

"Maybe I would have bought that when you were eighteen but you're not eighteen any more. Are those reasons really still good enough for you?" Debbie pushed.

Austin stared into his mother's eyes for a moment.

"Honestly, no, they're not. At first, I thought it was the best thing for me. I was making money to fight and I was *really* good at fighting. But now, I just go through the motions. It's not the same anymore."

"I hate that you ever did it in the first place but it makes me feel good to know you're starting to realize how useless it is. If it's not fulfilling any more, than why don't you just stop?"

Debbie inquired.

"Well, I have a feeling I'm gonna be done with that place pretty soon anyway. And when that time comes, I think I'll be satisfied," Austin continued.

"That's good to hear." Debbie smiled.

Austin stood up from the chair.

"I didn't think this visit would be so full of self-revelations," he joked.

"That just goes to show, you never know what you're gonna get when you come to visit your mom. Make sure Christian knows that when he moves in with you." Debbie laughed and the two shared a tight hug.

"Are you staying for dinner? I was gonna order something soon," Debbie asked.

"No, I actually have one more stop to make but rain check?"

"I'll hold you to it." Debbie winked.

Austin took his leave and headed to his last stop, Shaw's. He opened the door and, immediately, his eyes locked on to Alyssa handing a receipt to a full table. Alyssa turned to walk away and caught his gaze, a smile instantly spreading across her face.

Alyssa walked up to Austin. "Hey, stranger. It's been a while."

"I know, trust me, if I had a choice, I wouldn't be away for so long. But I actually came here to ask you something."

"I'll ask to leave early, pick me up at seven." Alyssa smiled.

Austin stammered through his words but finally, he managed to get out, "Okay, perfect."

That night, Austin pulled up in front of Shaw's with a few minutes to spare. With a quick check in the visor mirror, Austin was ready for his date. Alyssa walked out of the diner and over to Austin's car, jumping in with a smile.

"So, where are we going?" she asked.

"Well, I know this great little diner on the corner. It's new but good," Austin joked.

"You're lucky I know you're joking." Alyssa laughed. "I'd leave right now."

"Don't worry, I have something nice planned." Austin smiled and drove off.

Austin pulled up in front of a restaurant, the valet already waiting to take the keys.

"Austin, this place looks really expensive. I'm not even dressed for this place; they won't let us in." Alyssa panicked.

"Would you relax? Don't you think I thought ahead about all of that?" Austin chuckled.

"There he is!" a man yelled from the Maitre d' stand.

"What's going on, Jesse, everything set?" Austin asked as he gave him a fist bump.

"All set, bro, you two enjoy the night." Jesse smiled.

Austin smiled and escorted Alyssa towards the back of the restaurant.

"So that's why we came here? Because you have a connection?" Alyssa asked.

"There's nothing wrong with knowing a few people. He owed me a favor so I called it in." Austin chuckled.

Austin opened the French doors that led to the outdoor patio, revealing a single table with two chairs that overlooked the Hudson River.

"Oh my God, Austin," Alyssa gasped.

"He owed me a pretty big favor," Austin jested.

Austin pulled out a chair, allowing Alyssa to sit down before pushing it in slightly.

"I would have never guessed the guy I jogged past all the

time would have such manners. And know how to 'woo' his date so well." Alyssa giggled.

"I'll be honest, I'm pretty new to this kind of thing but I figured I'd give it a shot." Austin sat in the chair across from Alyssa.

"Just for me?" she asked.

Austin stared into her eyes. "Just for you."

"Is that why my outfit didn't matter? Because we're outside?" Alyssa asked, still smiling over the entire situation.

"*That* and the view," Austin answered.

"It really is amazing," Alyssa said as she turned to look out at the water.

Austin's eyes never left Alyssa. "Yes it is."

Austin and Alyssa finally had a chance to talk and get to know each other in a way they couldn't previously. They shared stories about their childhood, they laughed about ridiculous things, and they revealed more about their different relationships with their fathers.

"A bodyguard?" Austin exclaimed.

"Yes! I'm not even kidding! My father wanted to hire a bodyguard to escort me around wherever I needed to go. I don't know who lied to him and told him he was a Kennedy." Alyssa laughed.

"I'm sorry, I know I should be trying to impress you tonight but that sounds completely ridiculous, no offense to your father." Austin laughed back.

"No, total offense! I'll offend him too, it's stupid! That was the last major fight I had with him. I think, after that, he kinda got the hint that I wanted a lot less to do with his weird paranoia."

"But what does he do that makes him so worried? Is he in politics? A lawyer maybe?" Austin asked.

"Nope, just stocks. Since he was younger, he's always made a killing in the stock market and has been able to coast ever since. A few 'buy and sells' a year and he keeps everything afloat. I've never seen luck like his."

"Smart businessman doesn't sound like the 'life in danger' career I thought you were going to say." Austin chuckled as he took another sip of his wine.

"Exactly! I have no idea where this obsession started but he takes it very seriously. He's overly cautious to a fault, a big fault."

"It causes problems?" Austin asked and Alyssa went silent, the air quickly changing around her. "I'm sorry, I didn't mean to pry. It was stupid, I shouldn't have asked that."

Alyssa giggled. "Would you stop? You didn't do anything wrong. Yes, it causes problems. Before he buys a new stock, he goes to discuss it with the business first. He always wants to know what they're about before he buys in. So more often than not, he's away. My mother isn't the biggest fan of that but she understands it, tolerates it. My brother is a different story."

"Oh, your brother. Sean right?"

"Yeah, Sean. He's a couple of years older than me. Family is really important to him so whenever my father is gone, he gets really upset with him. They constantly get into arguments over family obligations and responsibilities. One thinks gatherings and moments are more important and the other thinks stability and security are more important. It's a constant battle in my house whenever there's luggage at the door," Alyssa explained.

"That sounds intense," Austin confessed.

"It is but hopefully soon, it won't matter," Alyssa stated.

"Why is that?"

"My dad keeps talking about this big stock that he's been

sitting on. It started out tiny, each stock was worth less than a penny but it just keeps growing and growing. Think Bitcoin but like five times bigger. He keeps saying just a little bit longer and he'll never have to buy another stock again. When that happens, I plan on moving out and getting my own place. With his big career ventures behind him, the paranoia should die down and I'll finally be able to get away," Alyssa explained with optimism.

"Sounds like you got it all figured out."

Alyssa stabbed the last bit of steak on her plate and popped it into her mouth.

"I would hope so. I've been planning this out for a long time. I saw a couple of nice apartments by you actually."

"Really?" Austin's smile appeared involuntarily.

"Yeah, but who knows, I hear California is really great too." Alyssa smirked as she finished her glass of wine.

"You're lucky I know you're joking." Austin smiled. "I'd leave right now."

"Ouch, using my words against me, nice touch."

Alyssa's hand reached over and grabbed Austin's.

"This has been really great." She smiled.

"I think so too."

The two stared at each other for a moment but for the first time, they each leaned forward over the table. Their lips locked in a passionate kiss, one the two had been unknowingly urging for.

As the night wound down, Austin drove Alyssa home, pulling up in front of a large estate.

"This is me." She pointed.

"*This is you?*" Austin exclaimed, staring out the window in utter shock.

"Like I said, my dad's good in stocks, really good," Alyssa

said awkwardly.

"Alyssa, this house is beautiful, if you could even call it a house."

Alyssa clicked a button on the fob on her keyring causing the large front gates to open automatically. "You can just pull up through there." Alyssa pointed at the crescent pathway that rounded to the front steps.

Austin slowly pulled the car up to the front.

"Do you want to come in? My dad should be home tonight," Alyssa asked.

"I would love to but now I think *I'm* underdressed. Another time, okay?"

Alyssa laughed. "You're ridiculous but okay, another time. I'll hold you to it."

Alyssa leaned over and gave Austin another kiss.

"I had a great time tonight." She smiled happily.

"Me too."

Alyssa stepped out of the car and closed the door behind her before turning around and leaning back into the open window.

"Goodnight, Austin."

"Goodnight, Alyssa." Austin smiled.

Austin watched Alyssa run up her massive front steps and through the large heavy oak double doors.

Austin put the car in drive and had one final thought on the night. "Stocks."

Chapter 13

No Rest for the Wicked

Austin opened his eyes the next morning to his personal phone vibrating. Without lifting his head from the pillow, he reached over and grabbed it, unlocking the screen to see a text message.

"Here's HQ's location. It's time you take yourself here." The message read.

After all this time, there it was, right there in front of him: an address he could easily input into his GPS as if he were going to the supermarket. Austin prepared himself for the day and jumped into his car ready for his first debriefing with D.A.R.C.

When Austin made it to the address, he looked up at the building and knew he was in the right place. A quick look around revealed where the parking garage was. Austin turned the car into the garage and parked in the first spot he saw. As he continued through the motions, he found an elevator to take him up to the main floor.

When the doors opened, he stepped out into the lobby right in front of the card scanner. He turned to the agent standing guard nearby.

"Could you give me a swipe?" Austin asked.

"State your business," Agent Luder demanded.

"My business? I'm here to see Agents Hall and Walker."

"I'll have to verify that information. Wait here, please," Luder continued.

"Verify? You've seen me here before," Austin replied in confusion.

"I got it, Agent Luder, thank you!" Mike yelled as he ran over.

Mike swiped his own card and allowed Austin to step through.

"What the hell was that about? He acted like he didn't even know me," Austin whispered to Mike as they walked towards the stairs.

"Don't mind him. Some agents are a little resentful of you for getting in our good graces so quickly," Mike answered as he looked around diligently.

"What the hell are you talking about?" Austin questioned.

"Most of our agents come with years of experience in the military or some other branch of the law. The ones who don't come from there come from the Initiate Recruit Program. But even then, not everyone has the opportunity to work so closely with Grant and myself. You came in through an even quicker channel than the I.R.P. and jumped right into the C.O.R. with D.A.R.C.'s two Elite Special Agents," Mike explained.

Austin looked around the lobby and caught several pairs of eyes staring through him.

"I see jealousy isn't above D.A.R.C.'s finest," he scoffed.

"Here, this should make things easier from now on." Mike handed Austin a card.

Austin looked at it and saw that it was his very own D.A.R.C. I.D. card.

"Thanks but don't I need all those other cards too?" Austin asked.

"They're being printed as we speak." Mike smiled.

"You're late," Grant growled as Mike and Austin stepped

into the C.O.R.

"How can I be late? There was no time discussed," Austin rebutted.

"Doesn't matter. If I think you're late, then you should have been here sooner."

Austin rolled his eyes.

"Can we start this thing before I say something I'm going to regret?" he asked as he turned to Mike.

"We're just waiting on Director Hardwick," Mike stated.

As if summoned by those words, Hardwick charged into the C.O.R. with haste.

"I'm ready to hear every word," he said as he sat in his seat with great anticipation.

"All right, Austin, tell us everything," Mike added, setting himself up by his computer.

"From what you saw, how far along is Damien on completing his formula?" Grant asked.

"He has the main ingredients figured out already. All he's working on now is finding out the perfect ratio. Apparently, he's dealing with a lot of negative side effects from different dosages."

"Do you know what the formula is comprised of? I know we were still missing an ingredient on that list you found in the trainyard," Hardwick inquired.

"No, I never got a chance to find that out. I guess Damien didn't think it was necessary to share. The secret ingredient is still a secret."

"And what about the test subjects? I was told you confronted one," Hardwick asked.

"There was some type of show they put on between two of the subjects, different dosage and ratios of the formula. They were seeing which one was better. After the fight was over, the guy fought back and nobody in the room was able to put him down. Bullets didn't even break his skin."

"They're bulletproof?" Grant exclaimed.

"Yeah, seems like it. He walked straight through a hail of gunfire like they were shooting spitballs at him. If the heart attack didn't put him down, he would have killed every one of us," Austin continued.

"Great, if Church's sick dream isn't bad enough, he's creating his own Frankenstein's monster," Hardwick stated.

"Yeah, complete with the fact that he can't control his own creation," Mike added.

"Seeing those things in person is a completely different experience, it's terrifying," Austin admitted as he leaned onto the table. "Super strength, zero pain receptors, and bulletproof skin."

"Damn it, are we going to be forced to drop a nuke on these bastards to put them down?" Grant asked rhetorically.

"Actually no." Austin smirked.

"You have more?" Mike asked.

Austin reached behind his back and placed his pistol onto the table.

"Damien gave me this gun as a contingency. He created custom bullets that can break through the skin, they have a unique Tungsten-Titanium penetrator. Use these bullets and you can shoot these things like they're normal people."

"He gave you this?" Grant asked as he picked the pistol up to examine it.

"Damien's afraid of what he created, there's no doubt about it. But right now, the formula still isn't perfect. As long as the ratio isn't figured out, we still have our window," Austin stated.

"And what about when it *is* figured out? We have to get more information on his operation as a whole," Mike interjected.

"I'm going back Tuesday morning so I'll see what else I can find out," Austin replied.

"Speaking of which, you'll need another one of these." Grant tossed a new phone to Austin. "Try not to break this one."

Suddenly, Austin felt a sudden, immense pain in the side of his neck as Mike walked behind him.

"What the hell was that?" he exclaimed, grabbing his neck in panic.

"Nano-tracker. It's an undetectable device that sits just underneath the surface of the skin. With this, we'll be able to track you anywhere in the world, even when your phone breaks. This is usually reserved for full-time agents but after this past week, I'm not taking any more chances of losing you." Mike smiled, sitting back down with the injector in his hand.

"You could have warned me first." Austin continued to rub the injection site.

"Is there anything else?" Hardwick asked.

"Actually, yeah, there is. I found out a lot about Damien's mindset about this whole thing. He knows what he's doing seems crazy but, in his mind, he's doing something necessary for the world and the human race. And in his own twisted way, he really does care about me. He sees me as a son, it isn't an act."

"Is that supposed to mean something to me? Are you feeling sorry for this prick?" Grant barked.

"Grant, calm it down," Hardwick ordered.

"No, I'm not feeling sorry for him," Austin answered sternly. "I just wanted you guys to know that he isn't being manipulative, he really sees us as family. We may be able to use that to our advantage going forward."

"You're really getting the hang of this agent thing." Mike

chuckled.

"Oh, one more thing, his cabinet members," Austin stated.

"His what?" Grant asked.

"Cabinet members. It's what he calls the people he relies on the most. His right-hand man, Boris Morozov, and his head of security, Alexei Petrov. He sees me at that level too."

"Wait a minute, did you say Alexei Petrov?" Mike asked, already typing away on his keyboard.

"I figured you guys would know his name. He seems like a world class piece of shit," Austin replied.

Within seconds, Mike opened up a full dossier on Alexei.

"Alexei Petrov, the most infamous hitman in Russia and one of the most ruthless in the entire world. All his kills are cold and calculated yet merciless and sadistic. One of the highest body counts of any killer. His alias is The Carpenter," Mike explained.

"Do I want to know why that's his alias?" Austin questioned.

"All his kills are done with his bare hands, zero weaponry," Grant cut in.

"Well, Damien has him on his payroll too." Austin leaned back.

"The more we discover, the more dangers are present besides the Hercules subjects," Mike said, running his hands through his hair in frustration.

"We'll continue to take it one step at a time. No matter what Damien has in his arsenal, we'll take our time and dismantle his operation," Hardwick announced. Hardwick turned to Austin with a smile. "That's good work, son, very good work. Keep it up."

"Thank you, Sir."

Grant handed the pistol back to Austin. "Next week when you get back, this is your first stop. You don't go home, you don't

183

go shopping, you come here, is that understood?"

"Understood," Austin said simply.

Grant held up a single bullet that he took from the magazine in Austin's pistol.

"In the meantime, we'll get this to R&D and see if they can replicate it. If we can mass produce these bullets, we'll put both sides on an even playing field."

Austin stood up, putting the pistol back in his waist. "And we'll be one step closer to ending this whole thing."

The next night, Austin packed his duffle bag for his weekly visit to Reign. When he met Nick and Josh in the hallway, Nick was wearing a worrying expression.

"What's wrong?" Austin asked.

"Knowing the truth about everything, it makes this feel weird now. Like we're going to get figured out," Nick admitted.

"We're not. Damien has no idea of what's really going on. As long as we act like nothing has changed, he won't think anything has. The only way he'll find out is if we let him."

"Don't worry, I'm really good at acting oblivious." Josh chuckled and jogged his way down the hall. "Come on! We have a fight to get to!"

As the three made it to the club and squeezed their way through the dense crowd, Austin glanced up to the viewing box and saw Damien smiling down onto the crowd.

"I still can't believe the losers become his lab rats," Josh whispered to Austin as they headed towards the center ring.

"I know, I hate that I have to keep this up but I have no choice. If I refuse to fight, Damien will become suspicious. All I can do is hope that I stop him before anyone else becomes a victim."

"Hey! You ready for your match?" Demi asked, her usual

bubbly personality fully on display.

"Aren't I always?" Austin replied, dropping his bag on the nearby bench.

"And how about you?" she asked as she turned to Nick.

"Of course. When am I not ready? It should be just as obvious as Austin," Nick replied, slightly annoyed.

"Relax, killer, I'm just playing around. Let's get you over to your ring." Demi wrapped her arm around Nick playfully.

"And there they go again," Josh chimed in.

"Mr. Michaels, we're ready," the official informed as he approached.

Austin made his final preparations and stepped into the ring, his opponent already staring him down.

"Austin, ready?"

Austin gave his usual nod.

"Kevin, ready?"

Kevin did the same and the moment the official called for the start, he exploded off his side with tremendous speed. Austin was caught completely off guard and felt a hail of swift jabs across his face and sternum. Kevin sent a stiff kick into Austin's chest sending him bouncing against the cage wall and delivered a strong roundhouse kick into his face as he bounced back.

While on the mat, Austin tried his best to regroup, quickly analyzing the fight so far. Kevin pulled Austin to his feet but Austin grabbed him and threw him aside with all his might. Kevin rolled along the mat but sprung back to his feet in an instant and, in that same instant, lunged back in to continue his assault.

Austin attempted to block Kevin's violent knee strikes but even they were too fast for Austin to fully register. He managed to get a small window to attack but his punch struck empty air as

Kevin swiftly dodged it and responded with a strong jab in Austin's ribcage. Austin winced at the sudden pain but pushed through, grabbing Kevin again and hurling him even further.

To everyone's surprise, including Austin's, Kevin sprang from the mat and latched on to the cage wall to avoid colliding with it. Without warning, Kevin propelled off the cage wall towards Austin, hoping to end the fight with a devastating strike. As he approached, Austin thrust his fist upwards as hard as he could, striking Kevin under the jaw with frightful force. Kevin dropped to the mat in a heap, instantly unconscious.

Austin's hand was raised and, upon exiting the ring, Josh handed him a towel.

"That looked close for a second."

"Yeah, little bastard was quick." Austin panted, wiping away the excess blood from his face.

"Nice win!" Nick praised as he walked over, Demi already running and hugging Austin from behind.

"I just wish you and Nick could both always have easy matches. I hate seeing you guys get hurt," she admitted.

"I'm fine, nothing I can't handle," Austin replied with a confident smile. "What do you guys say to the diner?"

"You already know what I say." Josh smiled widely as he wrapped his arm around Austin's neck.

"Yeah, at this point, I was just asking Demi and Nick."

"I'm good with that."

"Yeah, me too."

"Great, let me just say bye to Damien and I'll meet you guys out front."

Austin jogged up the stairs and into Damien's office.

"Impressive as always, Austin." Damien turned to him. "Although I will say, Kevin provided quite a challenge for you.

He will make a very capable subject for Project: Hercules."

Austin paused for a moment, the idea of him practically sending Kevin to his death sinking deep into his soul.

"Can't wait to see what he can do," Austin forced the words through his lips. "Well, I'll see you tomorrow."

"One moment, Austin." Damien stopped Austin as he headed for the door.

Austin's heart began to rattle. Instantly, Austin's mind raced trying to think of what Damien wanted to say and what he could reply with to defend himself.

"Before you head home for the night, I want to show you something. Let's take a drive."

Damien walked past Austin and down the stairs. Again, Austin's mind began to wander, deep in thought. Where could they possibly be going? Was it a trap? Did Damien somehow find out the truth? Austin followed behind Damien, making sure to stay focused.

Damien said goodbye to several people in the crowd as he walked past them, cutting through like a piercing arrow. As they made it outside, Nick and Josh caught Austin's gaze.

"Hey, Damien, are you coming to the diner with us?" Demi asked innocently.

"No, not tonight. In fact, I'm stealing Austin away tonight to show him something very important. I hope none of you mind," Damien replied.

"Aw, man, okay but you owe us. Next diner trip, you're coming, and it's on you," Demi joked.

Damien chuckled. "That sounds fair."

Nick and Josh stood silent, practically holding their breath.

"Do you want us to wait for you guys?" Nick asked, trying his absolute best to act naturally.

"We might be a while so I think it's best if you guys just go on without us," Damien answered quickly.

Nick glanced at Austin who gave him a slight nod.

"Okay, well, if you guys change your minds, let us know."

Damien and Austin wrapped around the building into the alley where Damien's car was parked as Nick, Josh, and Demi headed down the block towards the diner.

"Do you really think we should let him go?" Josh whispered to Nick as Demi was engrossed in her phone.

"We have no choice. We're not supposed to know anything and we're not even part of D.A.R.C. Grant will kill both of us if we screw up Austin's mission. Damien doesn't know anything; Austin will be fine," Nick whispered back.

Austin climbed into the passenger side of the car as Damien turned it on.

"So where are we going?" Austin asked.

"Somewhere very special to both of us." Damien smiled as he pulled out of the alley.

Damien stayed vague and otherwise silent as he drove, Austin cycling through possible locations. Despite Austin's mental preparedness, he was still surprised when Damien pulled into the trainyard.

"The trainyard? Why are we here?" Austin asked.

"Because meeting here all those years ago wasn't just a coincidence, it was fate and I'm going to show you why."

Damien drove to the far end of the trainyard near the storage units and stopped.

"I had no idea these were over here." Austin continued to act unaware.

Damien slammed the car door. "Inside one of these units is the reason I was here when you were."

"You said you heard us as you walked by."

"That was a lie. I *did* hear you but it wasn't from outside, it was from over here."

Austin followed Damien down the rows of units until they stopped at a familiar one.

Damien looked at the gate and scoffed, "Seems like someone broke the lock off, this place really has gone to hell."

"You don't seem to care that much," Austin admitted.

"I have other security in place. The lock was just a surface defense," Damien answered.

Damien rolled the gate upwards and opened the door, Austin stepping inside with him. Again, the stale dust invaded his sense of smell but the surroundings were of no surprise. Similarly to when Austin broke in, the red light aimed at Damien's chest as the gun rolled out of the shadows.

"State authorization password," the voice spoke.

"Project Hercules," Damien said calmly.

"Password accepted, welcome back, Mr. Church."

The gun powered down and rolled back to its original position. Austin knew how he had to act.

"Damien, what the hell was that about?" Austin exclaimed with widened eyes.

"Like I said, I had other security in place." Damien grinned.

The lights turned on in the unit, revealing all the nightmares Austin remembered seeing.

"Austin, this is what I wanted to show you. This is why I was there that night we met," Damien announced pridefully as he walked through the room.

"Damien, this…" Austin paused. "What is all this?"

"I know it might seem like a lot but it means a lot to show you this. Just try to absorb it slowly, don't overlook anything."

"Why don't you walk me through it, maybe that'll help more," Austin stated, still selling how overwhelmed he was.

Damien smiled. "I'd be happy to."

Damien escorted Austin to the back wall, the numerous drawings covering it. "These were early concepts of my idea. I took a deep dive into the human body. I wanted to analyze how muscles worked, I mean *really* worked. When they flex, when they tense, when they tear. I wanted to know everything I could about how the body worked physically. It wasn't until later on I had to worry about chemical reactions."

"Isn't this like what Leonardo Da Vinci did?" Austin asked as he looked closely at the drawings.

"I'm glad you could appreciate how important and influential these drawings are. Yes, I was heavily inspired by Da Vinci's drawings. Even all those years ago, he was able to learn invaluable information simply by studying and examining."

Damien turned to the racks of blood bags.

"This concept was a little less theoretical." Damien began to comb his fingers through the countless bags. "When I first started thinking of such a formula as Project: Hercules, I knew there would be some reactions but I didn't know what they would be, how to identify them, or even how to track them. So I knew the only way to get those answers was to do it hands on."

"So you tested the first trials on blood samples instead of people?" Austin asked as he joined Damien.

"Precisely. Of course, even that couldn't tell me all the adverse reactions the subjects would get but it supplied me with a good foundation to my research. That along with the physical studies I did," Damien continued as he pointed to the blood-stained floor. "Everything you see around you was the building blocks to what I have now. If it weren't for everything in this storage unit, my dream wouldn't be so close to becoming reality."

"Is that why you brought me here?" Austin questioned.

Damien nodded proudly. "You saw the successful side of my operation last week. The compound, the enormous staff, the subjects, but I wanted you to see where it all started. I wanted you to see my humble beginnings. It really puts everything into a different perspective."

Again, Austin couldn't believe how delusional Damien was about the entire matter. He spoke as if he were discussing his career as an athlete or actor.

"This was not something I decided on yesterday. This dream, this passion, has been in my mind and heart for many, many years. All the planning, testing, studying, money, resources, it'll all be worth it very soon."

"I appreciate you bringing me here, Damien. I had no idea something like this even existed," Austin pretended.

"I knew you'd appreciate it." Damien smiled widely. "Come on, let's get you home, you have a plane to catch in the morning."

"You're still going tonight?" Austin asked.

"Yes, there's some business I have to handle before your arrival tomorrow. I usually leave straight from Reign but tonight, I made the exception. Unfortunately, business doesn't stop and it sure as hell doesn't wait for one man." Damien chuckled.

Damien pulled up in front of Austin's apartment.

"I'll see you tomorrow, son."

Austin paused. With only slight hesitation, Austin responded, "Night, Damien. Have a safe trip."

Austin stepped out of the car and Damien quickly drove away.

"Son. Could his mind really be *that* twisted? None of this

seems wrong to him," Austin thought as he shuffled around for his keys.

Austin made it into his apartment and quickly prepared himself for the following day, when his second week would officially begin.

Chapter 14

Back to Business

The next night, Austin was already back in Russia, prepared to play his role as usual. He knocked on Damien's office door and stepped inside.

"Boris said you wanted to see me?"

"Yes, there is a matter that I want you to handle for me. I didn't want to mention it until you were already settled in and had eaten." Damien stood up from his desk chair and stared out the window.

"What is it?" Austin questioned curiously.

"I have scheduled an exchange for tonight, a couple of hours from now in the town nearby. I want you to handle it."

"Me? Why don't you just send your security or Alexei?" Austin asked.

"As you may have noticed, Alexei isn't around much. I usually have him handling exterior situations. I need you to handle this for me. What good is my new cabinet member if I can't ask for such a simple request?" Damien chuckled. "And as for my security, I am sending three guards to the exchange but I want you to oversee it."

"Okay, what's the play?" Austin asked, sitting down in the chair across from Damien.

"You are going to meet with a man named Anatoly who is going to provide you with a resource that is precious to my operation."

"What kind of resource?"

"It's a very unique chemical known as Trimoxil Dimene. Without it, the Hercules formula would be nonexistent. For a long time, I wasn't able to even synthesize an actual formula until Boris told me about this chemical. That was the first example of Boris's worth," Damien answered.

"Maybe that's the chemical Damien was missing on his list in the trainyard, the spot with all the question marks. He knew he needed something; he just didn't know what," Austin thought to himself, still acting engaged in the conversation.

"Testing so many different variations of the formula has depleted my supply and I need to restock if I want the testing to continue. You'll trade a vial of the chemical for this." Damien tossed a duffle bag at Austin.

When he caught it, he unzipped it and saw that it was filled with cash.

"Damien, how much is in here?" Austin asked stunned.

"Five hundred thousand."

"That much for a single vial?" Austin exclaimed.

"Yes, it's very expensive but Boris is able to use his connections to supply me with it whenever I need more. Although I will admit, I hate relying on others for my work. That's why I have a small team working on creating an artificial version of Trimoxil Dimene but until they succeed, I need to continue paying for it."

"And how long does a single vial last?" Austin questioned.

"It depends on how many variations we have to make. Sometimes, it can last one month, sometimes one week. My hope is that we can create the artificial before I have to replace the one you're buying tonight."

"All right, sounds good to me," Austin said as he stood up, hanging the duffle bag over his shoulder.

"Excellent, the guards will meet you at the entrance whenever you're ready."

Austin exited Damien's office, making a mental note of everything they had just discussed. It still surprised Austin how much Damien trusted him. Information D.A.R.C. would have never discovered on their own was being thrown at Austin on a daily basis.

Austin met the guards at the entrance, the group getting into a car and driving into town. As the car drove down the scarcely lit road, Austin stared out the window, up at the starry night sky. With nothing to distract him during the quiet drive, Austin began to ponder the exchange.

"Damien trusted me with this, why not just send Boris if they are his connections? What if the vial breaks before we get it back? What if the money isn't accurate and they think we're tricking them?"

Austin ruffled his hair with both hands trying to wipe out the paranoid thoughts that quickly enveloped his mind.

"We are here," the driver informed as he pulled into an alleyway.

He parked at the very end of the alleyway where it opened up into a large dead end. The three guards stood in a row, Austin standing in front of them holding tightly onto the duffle bag.

"Austin, can you hear me?" Damien's voice rang out in Austin's ear.

"Yep, communicator's working fine," Austin whispered.

"Excellent, Anatoly should be there any minute."

Suddenly, the glow of headlights washed across the alley.

"They're here," Austin said simply.

The car pulled up across from Austin's group and turned off. Two armed men exited the vehicle, a third exiting from the back with a metal case. He slowly walked up to Austin, now standing mere feet from him.

"Ty govorish' po-russki?" he spoke.

Austin stared at him for a moment in complete confusion.

"He asked if you speak Russian?" one of Damien's guards stated.

"Oh."

Austin looked back at the man and shook his head.

"Ah, English then," he said. "You are Austin?"

"Yes, are you Anatoly?" Austin replied.

"Da. I assume that is money," Anatoly said, glancing down at the duffle bag.

"And I assume that's the vial," Austin responded in a firm tone.

"Da."

Austin slowly placed the bag on the floor and unzipped it, stepping back slightly to give Anatoly space. Anatoly knelt down and looked into the bag.

"Am I to take your word that this is all of it?" Anatoly asked.

"Depends how much you trust Boris's word," Austin fired back.

Anatoly stared at Austin for a moment but then broke out into laughter.

"Good answer, good answer. I like you." He chuckled.

Anatoly put the metal case on the ground and slid it to Austin's feet. Austin lifted it from the ground and opened it, revealing a single vial of purple liquid sitting comfortably inside a foam casting.

"So, this is Trimoxil Dimene," he thought to himself.

Austin handed the case over to one of the guards near him.

"Package secured," the guard spoke into his communicator.

"Excellent." Austin heard Damien's voice through his own earpiece as well. "Kill them."

Austin's eyes shot open in shock as he heard the words but, before he could even react, the guards pulled out their pistols fitted with silencers and opened fire on the opposing group.

The two men standing guard near Anatoly were quickly gunned down as Anatoly quickly dashed by.

"Go after him! Get the money back!" one guard shouted.

Austin hesitated for a moment but began to run after Anatoly, still in shock at the situation. Anatoly cut down an alleyway to the right and Austin quickly gave chase. Anatoly ran into a dead-end opening and quickly turned around to see Austin approaching. Anxious and cornered, Anatoly dropped the bag of money and pulled a switchblade from his pocket.

"Anatoly, listen to me, I don't want to fight you. Just hide and I'll tell my guys that you escaped," Austin informed.

Thunder began to boom overhead as dark storm clouds rolled across the sky.

"Do you think I am idiot? I put knife down, you kill me," Anatoly replied in his simplistic phrasing, now slowly stepping around Austin, making sure to watch his every move.

"You're wrong. I don't want anyone else to die tonight. I didn't know this was going to happen. Please, Anatoly."

Austin stared at Anatoly with sorrowful eyes but Anatoly didn't respond, instead gripping his knife tightly and darting at Austin. Austin dodged frantically as Anatoly swung at him violently.

"Anatoly, please! Stop!" Austin yelled as the thunder roared even louder.

Anatoly continued to ignore Austin's words as he chased him down with his knife. No matter how much Austin begged and pleaded, Anatoly hunted him, disregarding any words that came from Austin's mouth. To him, they were mere distractions and lies in order to manipulate the situation.

Austin backed up and bumped into the brick wall behind him. Anatoly quickly lunged forward with his knife but Austin dodged and swiftly disarmed him. As the knife clattered against the cobblestone, Anatoly leapt at Austin with even more desperation. Austin slammed against the ground with Anatoly on top of him, his hands now wrapped tightly around his neck.

"Anatoly... please... don't," Austin begged through short breaths as his airflow stopped.

He frantically grasped at Anatoly, wanting to grab anything that would loosen his grip but nothing worked. Austin could feel his lungs struggling and a single thought crossed his mind; he was about to die. Anatoly was gripping as hard as he could and he wasn't going to stop until he was holding a corpse within his hands.

Suddenly, Austin's peripheral vision caught the switchblade lying on the ground just a few feet away from him. As the dark clouds released an abundance of rain down onto the streets of the town, Austin stretched his right arm out as far as he could. He extended and stretched, his fingers spreading out to their limits just to reach the very tip of the handle. Austin began to feel dizzy, his vision becoming blurry. If he passed out, he was as good as dead.

With only seconds left, Austin's index finger reached the handle, pulling it just close enough to fully grab with his hand. Without warning, Austin plunged the blade into Anatoly's side, Anatoly's expression immediately shifting from anger to pained shock. His suffering stare caught Austin's eyes and Austin quickly looked away.

With one more thrust, Austin plunged the knife in even deeper. Immediately, the grip around Austin's neck loosened and the moment it did, Austin managed to murmur two simple words.

"I'm sorry."

Without a final word, Anatoly tumbled over onto his side. Austin turned over, his body alternating between exaggerative gasps and coughing violently as the air rushed back into his lungs. Anatoly's blood was already flowing through the joints of the cobblestone, quickly reaching Austin thanks to the rain. Austin crawled away from the incoming blood as the rain camouflaged the tears streaming down his face.

One of his escorts arrived on the scene and, without a word, grabbed the bag of money and dragged a silent Austin away. With both the chemical and the money in hand, the group made their way through the storm and back to the safety of Damien's compound.

The moment the car pulled up in front of the mansion, Austin exploded out of the backseat and through the front doors. Without breaking his stride, Austin made his way to Damien's office, swinging the door open unannounced.

"What the fuck was that?" he shouted as he stormed across the office floor.

"Excuse me?" Damien questioned calmly.

"Why did you give the kill order? We had the chemical and they had the money, the deal was done!"

"Exactly, they had the money and I wanted it back. We had the chemical already, there was no reason to continue playing pretend," Damien answered, his tone calm as if there was nothing wrong with the events that unfolded.

"So what? You do this every time you need another vial of Trimoxil Dimene? How do you keep getting a supply?"

"Boris has many connections, all of which are unrelated to each other. We put the cash on the lure until someone bites with the chemical. When they do, we set up the exchange and leave with the money and the chemical. Gets me what I need while leaving my pockets nice and full." Damien chuckled heartily.

Austin slammed his hands down onto Damien's desk.

"Damn it, Damien, I killed someone tonight!"

Damien's stare became stern.

"I know it must be hard to come to grips with what transpired tonight but that does not give you free range to come into my house and shout in my face!"

Instantly, Austin saw a different side of Damien, a side he had never witnessed before. The aggression, the anger, the coldness, Damien snapped straight into this different persona without a moment's hesitation.

"You killed someone to get back half a million dollars, big deal! Do you have any idea how many people I've killed for less? Get over it!"

Damien walked around his desk, now standing face to face with Austin.

"After all these years, I expected you to be more calculated than this, colder."

"What happens in the ring is one thing, I've made peace with *that* possibility during a fight. But this was in a back alley in the middle of the night. Anatoly's body is lying in the rain like trash," Austin exclaimed, his stare stern and serious.

"No, it's not. I already sent out a cleanup crew. The three bodies will be removed within the hour. Can't have special individuals like Anatoly showing up on the news, now can we?"

Austin stayed silent as he stared at Damien, his disdain anything but concealed.

"Is there a problem, Austin?" Damien asked as he leaned in close, his stare still coldly locked onto Austin.

Austin wanted nothing more than to unleash all his emotions onto Damien but, somehow, a small seed in the back of Austin's head expanded and Austin remembered his mission. If he made himself feel better now, the mission would be over and Damien would win. Austin inhaled deeply.

"No, no problem, Damien. I'm sorry."

"That's better," Damien said sinisterly. "Let me make one thing very clear to you now that you've calmed down. Just because I brought you into this like family does not mean I won't cast you out like an enemy. Nothing and no one, not even someone I love like a son, will stop me from achieving my destiny. Is that clear?"

Austin couldn't shake Damien's stare. He could see the unhinged anger and bloodlust sitting just beyond his gaze.

"Yes, Damien. I understand."

"Perfect." Damien smiled. "Now go wash up and get some rest. We'll continue our work in the morning."

Damien walked back to his chair as Austin turned to exit feeling defeated and ashamed.

That night, Austin tossed and turned in his bed, sleep being the furthest thing from his mind. Every time he closed his eyes, all he envisioned was Anatoly's pain-stricken face. Before long, the sun's rays beamed through Austin's window and onto his face. He continued as normal and met the staff in the dining hall.

"Good morning, Austin. You're just on time," Damien greeted as he walked over.

Austin was stunned by Damien's tone and expression. It was

as if their argument never even happened.

"I believe you remember when I told you about Alexei but you never had a chance to meet him face to face."

Alexei walked over and extended his hand.

"Pleasure," he said simply in his low, gravelly voice.

"Nice to finally meet you," Austin replied as they shook hands.

Austin could feel the thick, rough skin of Alexei's hands, his callus-covered palm rubbing aggressively against Austin's as they shook.

"Come, let's go to the basement," Damien stated.

As the three walked, Austin contemplated the intention. He was about to enter the basement with one of the world's most dangerous killers. Was Damien getting rid of Austin quietly after their altercation the night before? Did Austin already fail?

Austin stepped down the stairs hesitantly as Damien and Alexei waited.

"Last night opened my eyes to something I should have noticed sooner," Damien said.

Austin's heart sank as his anxiety-driven blood rushed through his body.

"I've seen you do incredible things inside the cage but that's all inside a very little bubble. You may be a deadly weapon inside the octagon but in a situation like last night, you are just as vulnerable as anyone. That's why I pulled Alexei from his exterior duties. While you're here, Alexei's sole job will be to train you."

"Train me?" Austin questioned.

"You're playing on an entirely different level now, Austin. You need to be calculated and unstoppable when put in a situation like last night. As good as you are, you can be better."

Damien smiled with a playful punch into Austin's arm.

"If that's really what you want," Austin replied.

"Do not worry, you are in good hands." Alexei grinned evilly as he cracked his knuckles.

"Now, you two play nice. I'll be back later on to check how things are coming."

Damien walked up the stairs and closed the door, leaving Austin alone with Alexei. As he stood across from the intimidating figure, Austin remembered everything he had heard from Mike and Grant about Alexei. Cold, unmerciful, killed with his bare hands, all traits that alerted Austin's self-preservation response but he knew he had to fight through it. At this moment, Alexei was not an enemy, but an ally, and Austin was going to take advantage of the situation any way he could.

Immediately, Austin understood what Damien meant. Even while innocently sparring, Austin could feel the unwavering force behind Alexei's strikes. His strength was almost intimidating as he taught Austin what he knew. Disarming tactics, solid defensive strategies, and even several ways to silently kill someone, which left Austin with an uneasy feeling in his stomach as he flashed back to his fight with Anatoly.

As morning turned to afternoon and eventually evening, Austin contemplated if this could be considered torture. Bruising across Austin's arms from blocking and deflecting Alexei's strikes, blood streaming down his head from Alexei's fist that made it past Austin's blockade, and the overwhelming taste of iron in his mouth as Austin spit out yet another glob of blood onto the floor. As difficult as the training was, Austin made sure to absorb every bit of information, seeing it as a perfect opportunity to further prepare for the inevitable takedown of Damien's operation.

Finally, the basement door opened again and Damien casually walked down.

"Well, well, color me impressed." He smiled as he caught sight of Austin across the basement.

Austin was sitting on the floor with his back against the wall, practically hunched over in a heap of bruises and blood trying desperately to catch his breath.

"Impressed... from what?" Austin asked, breathing deeply in between words.

"I didn't expect you to still be conscious," Damien admitted.

"What?"

"I didn't want to say anything as we trained but no one has ever withstood a whole day with me," Alexei confessed with a smirk.

"You exceeded my expectations as usual, Austin. Go get cleaned up and get some rest, you deserve it."

Damien helped Austin to his feet who stayed silent. Whether from shock or exhaustion, Austin had no words to express. He silently walked up the stairs and out of the basement.

"How'd he do?" Damien asked as he turned to Alexei.

"I must admit, I am very impressed. He has an iron will, toughest son of a bitch I've met in a very long time."

"So he didn't waver?" Damien questioned, his tone becoming serious.

"Anyone who would put themselves through the abuse he went through today would not do it unless they believed in why they were here. Austin did not waver; he did not hesitate."

Damien smiled. "Excellent."

Chapter 15

Flip of a Coin

The week continued as normal, or as normal as it could have. Austin stuck to his role and did it well. Damien was pleased and Alexei was impressed. Though nothing of further interest happened throughout the remainder of Austin's stay, his mind was still flooded with the nightmare he experienced earlier in the week.

Instantly upon thinking of it, Austin was taken back to that very moment. He could feel the warm, thick blood oozing down his hand as it gripped the knife's handle. He could hear the harsh rain smash against the cobblestones around him. But most importantly, it was the stare. Anatoly's stunned and empty stare, his gaze piercing deep into Austin's soul.

Austin sunk deep into his chair on the private jet as it headed towards home, something Austin hoped would help relieve him of his waking nightmare. The plane landed several hours later and, as instructed by Grant the previous week, Austin made his way straight to headquarters.

Austin walked through the front doors and stood at the card terminal.

"State your business," Agent Dawson stated sternly.

"Come on! We're not seriously still doing this, are we? I don't have my card on me, just let me through," Austin quickly argued.

"State your business," Dawson repeated, pausing briefly between each word as if emphasizing his statement.

Austin exhaled with annoyance. "I'm here to meet with Agents Hall and Walker for a debriefing. Do you want to be the one to tell Grant you're the reason I'm late?"

Dawson stared at Austin with an unamused expression, almost as if still deciding whether or not to let him through. Finally, Dawson swiped his own card and allowed Austin safe passage.

"Thank you," Austin exclaimed, still very much annoyed.

Austin made his way through the lobby and up the stairs, all the while still feeling the numerous stares following him. As Austin reached the second floor landing, the door to the C.O.R. opened, Mike standing in the doorway with a smile.

"Safe trip?" He beamed.

"Is there any way you can have an I.D. card waiting for me here too? I obviously can't bring it with me when I work with Damien but then I get stopped coming back here," Austin complained as he walked past Mike.

"Just give it some time, Austin, the hazing will stop. Sooner or later, the other agents are going to have to recognize your contribution. Once Damien is taken down, I bet those same people will want to shake your hand," Mike continued as they walked down the center aisle.

"Welcome back," Grant greeted.

"Good to see you again, son," Hardwick added.

Grant gestured towards a nearby chair. "Take a seat, let's hear what you have to report."

"Please tell me he hasn't made more progress with his subjects," Hardwick chimed in.

"No, the status of the formula is still the same. They didn't run any new tests this week, at least none that I was aware of. But I did find out a crucial ingredient to the formula, one that was most likely the question marks back in the storage unit."

"Austin strikes again." Mike smiled.

"He called it Trimoxil Dimene. I've never heard of it before but based on how he has to acquire it, I don't think you'll see it at your local pharmacy any time soon. He was trading half a million dollars for a single vial of the stuff. According to Damien, his formula is useless without it," Austin continued.

"Do you know who his supplier is?" Grant asked.

Mike spun his chair towards Grant. "You're thinking to burn the supplier?"

"Maybe and, if we're lucky, maybe plant a supplier of our own. Then we'd have two agents on this."

"That won't work," Austin cut in. "Damien changes his supplier for every batch he needs. Besides, he has a team working on creating an artificial version of the chemical. Once they do, he won't need to buy it anymore."

"He changes suppliers? Why? Seems like a useless hurdle to put in front of yourself. Are you sure that info is correct?" Grant asked skeptically.

"Yeah, I'm sure. He has to change because he always has the current supplier killed."

"Killed? He drops bodies every time he needs more of this stuff?" Mike asked, surprised.

"I don't mean to question your intel but this all seems a little counter-productive," Hardwick admitted.

"I know what it seems like but that's the way it is. I know because…"

Austin stopped as if frozen in his seat. He didn't speak another word and barely took another breath.

"Austin?" Mike questioned.

Austin inhaled deeply as he leaned onto the table.

"I know because he made me do it."

"What do you mean?" Grant asked sternly as he slowly sat down across from Austin.

Mike pulled his chair in towards the table as Hardwick further sat up at attention. Immediately, Austin could tell he had the full attention of the room, more so than he did a moment ago.

"He had to get another vial this week so he had me do the exchange. I had no idea what his plan was until I was already there with three of his guards. The second we got the vial he ordered his men to kill the supplier. The guy who I made the trade with, Anatoly, ran off and they ordered me to chase after him. I didn't want to say no and blow any leads we had so I did. When I got Anatoly alone, I tried to explain the situation to him. I didn't want anyone else to die but he wouldn't listen to me." Austin positioned his arms vertically, his hands balled together as they propped up his head. "He came at me. I kept trying to convince him that I wasn't his enemy but he just wouldn't listen. He was scared, desperate, I don't blame him, I just wish he took a second to hear me."

"Austin, what happened?" Grant asked again.

"He was going to kill me, right there in the alleyway. I was a second or two away from death so I did exactly what I tried to prevent: exactly what Damien wanted."

Mike's eyes were widened with shock. "You killed him."

Austin didn't respond verbally, instead just looking away and nodding.

"How are you handling it?" Hardwick asked solemnly.

"I can't stop thinking about it. I can't stop seeing his face, his eyes just staring at me as I stabbed him. He knew he was dying and spent his last seconds alive burning his stare into my brain."

"I have to be honest, even from your reaction right now, you seem to be handling it pretty well. I've seen people lose their minds in hysterics from killing someone," Mike stated.

Austin pondered for a moment before responding, "Look, I don't pretend to be a saint. Hell, most days I wouldn't even say I'm a good person. I beat people half to death at least once a week just for other's amusement."

"Did you ever kill anyone in Reign?" Grant asked.

"No, but I never ruled out the chance. Every time I step into that ring, I know there's a possibility that I kill someone or I get killed myself. But for some reason, as long as it was within those caged walls, it was different, almost excused. Every fighter who steps into those rings knows what they're there to do and knows how it could all end. That danger is there every single fight."

"So what made this so different?" Mike asked.

"Because this wasn't in those caged walls. This was in a dingy alley and the guy I killed wasn't my opponent. He was there to make an exchange. He had no idea Damien was such a bastard and neither did I."

"But you tried to save him, you tried to reason with him. He's the one who didn't listen. You did everything you could, Austin," Mike continued.

"We should have never been put in that situation to begin with. From that point on, I just kept reliving the moment in my head and I haven't been able to forget it."

"And you won't, probably for a long time. What you did isn't easy, Austin," Grant stated, the rare tone of sincerity in his voice.

"How did you guys do it?" Austin asked.

"Do you want to answer this, Sir?" Grant asked as he turned to Hardwick.

"No, no, you have the floor. It's been quite some time since I was in those shoes anyway," Hardwick replied.

Grant turned back to Austin who was still waiting patiently for a response. "You go to visit your mother and brother after this meeting but, when you get there, the front door is broken in and a stranger has them both at gun point. You know he doesn't see you and you only have one chance to do something. If you don't do something drastic, your mother, your brother, or both are going to die. Now, Austin, would you kill that stranger?"

"I mean, I guess I would if they were going to be killed," Austin replied honestly.

"What you did in that alleyway was no different. And what we've done in our pasts was no different except we didn't do it to protect one or two people, we did it to protect hundreds of millions or more."

"How many have you killed?" Austin asked directly to Grant.

Grant looked at Austin for a moment as if deciding to give him that answer.

"Fifty-six and another thirty-one undiscernible."

"Undiscernible?" Austin questioned.

"When an entire squad is shooting at the enemy, it's hard to tell who caused which bodies to drop."

"Do you all remember your numbers?" Austin asked as he quickly glanced at the other two agents.

Both nodded.

"You have to remember," Grant interjected once more. "If you're going to live with the choices you've made and the things you've done, then you better know every fact. I would feel worse if I didn't know how many lives I was responsible for."

"Why?" Austin asked slightly confused.

"Because the moment I lose track of my kills is the moment I realize I've killed irresponsibly and if I've killed irresponsibly, then I'm no better than the scum D.A.R.C. goes after. That's what separates us from them, Austin. We kill with purpose, with responsibility. We don't hang the innocent from the city square or mow down a village of strangers for kicks. Whenever we take even a single life, it's to protect hundreds of thousands more."

For the first time, Austin heard Grant speak with genuine sincerity. It was as if this topic struck a certain chord with Grant that was previously untouched. Even Mike stared at Grant with approval for the speech he was giving.

"It may not be ideal and others will still look at us as monsters but, at the end of the day, we do what we do so that the masses can continue living their blissfully unaware lives. We protect the innocent by any means necessary. We stand confidently on one side of the line and do what we must so that the other side never touches the ground on ours. We are the last line of defense against people like Damien Church who think the world is their playground and every person in it is just a disposable toy. Without us, people like Church would go unchecked and, at that point, the world gets put on a timer, it won't last forever."

Austin stared at Grant intently, his words resonating deeply in Austin's mind and heart.

"What you did wasn't animalistic or heartless, it was necessary. Necessary so that you could survive to continue your mission and save countless lives by the end. If you want to feel sorrow for Anatoly, be my guest but never question why you did it. Mike and I have been in this line of work for more years than we can damn well remember and Hardwick for even longer and I speak for all three of us when I say you did nothing wrong."

"You always look at it that way?" Austin asked.

"It is the only way *to* look at it. In this life, the life of someone who deals with people like Church, we live on two sides of the same coin." Grant reached into his pocket and pulled out a quarter. He began to twiddle the coin between his fingers, showing off both sides. "To the casual outsider, both sides do questionable things or things that are deemed 'wrong'. But what separates us from the other side of the coin is what we do those things for." Grant held the coin up to Austin, facing the head's side towards him. "On one side, we are the courageous, the virtuous, the selfless." Grant flipped the coin to the tail's side. "On the other side, they are tyrants, victimizers, over-powered and unchecked psychopaths who want to see the world burn or rule it themselves. Just like Church: he kills, he tortures, he steals, he betrays, all for himself, his own goals and aspirations." Grant flipped the coin back to heads once more. "On our side, we do similar actions but in order to protect the innocent, to stop monsters like Church, and to try and prevent another from becoming just as dangerous or worse. That is the nature of our lives but, believe me, in no world is our side the monster in your closet."

While still staring at Austin, Grant flipped the coin into the air and allowed it to clang against the table several times before slamming his hand down on it to stop it. Never breaking his stare with Austin, he lifted his hand and revealed the coin, lying heads up on the table.

"We are always on the righteous side and you'll be wise to remember that."

Austin smiled slightly, the tension immediately deflating

from the room. Grant smiled back at Austin.

"Without people like you, like everyone in this building, the world would be a much darker place. Death and destruction would be commonplace and every single person living on this planet would fear for their lives every day. Next time you want to question what you did or why you did it, just remember that."

Grant handed the quarter to Austin.

"Keep this as a constant reminder of that fact."

Austin took the quarter and stared at it for a moment.

He looked back at Grant. "Thank you, Grant."

"Is there anything else we should know about your time there?" Hardwick asked.

"Oh, yes, one more thing. After what happened with Anatoly, Damien put Alexei's external duties on hold to train me."

"Wait, Petrov is training you personally?" Mike exclaimed.

"Yeah and I have to admit, he's a tough son of a bitch but I'm learning a lot."

"It was bad enough when Alexei was just on Damien's payroll but now he's training our own inside man?" Hardwick groaned.

"What do we do, Sir?" Mike asked.

"Wait, why is this such a bad thing? Alexei is just making me more prepared to stop Damien and he doesn't even know it," Austin debated.

"If Alexei continues to train you and sees the same promise in you that we did, he may want to use you for his own jobs. Next thing you know, Damien is sending the two of you off to God knows where to do God knows what. Anatoly's death will just be the tip of the iceberg if we leave Alexei unchecked," Grant explained.

"If Alexei is training Austin while he's in Russia, I want Geer training him when he's homebound. Mike, get Geer up to speed," Hardwick ordered.

"Consider it done, Sir."

"Who's Geer?" Austin asked.

"Lincoln Geer, he's one of our top agents and leads our most elite squadron in D.A.R.C., Gladiator Squad. If anyone can compare to Alexei's physical skill, it's Agent Geer," Mike answered.

"How long did he train you during your stay?" Hardwick asked.

"The first day was practically morning to night but after that, it was about three hours a day."

"All right, then we'll do the same. Tomorrow morning, I want you here bright and early and you'll spend the entire day with Geer. After that, starting next week, you'll spend three hours with him on Sunday," Hardwick explained.

"Understood, Sir. I'm ready."

"Good, you'll need to be. Don't think that just because Geer is on our side means he's any less ruthless than Alexei. He's going to push you," Grant chimed in.

"Push you!" Mike exaggerated.

Austin chuckled. "Understood."

"All right, son, dismissed." Hardwick smiled.

Austin stepped out of the C.O.R. leaving the three agents alone. As he stepped out of the building, his phone rang. He looked at the screen and immediately answered.

"Hey, Alyssa."

"Hey yourself. Listen, I'm sure you were super busy all week since that's the only reason I could come up with as to why you didn't call or text."

Austin chuckled. "Yeah, definitely busy. Sorry, I didn't mean to ghost you."

"Don't worry, it's okay. I wasn't waiting by the phone for you. No offense."

"None taken but I'll be honest, it's really good to hear your voice," Austin admitted.

"You too."

Austin could practically hear the smile on Alyssa's face.

"Listen, I was hoping your busy schedule breaks up once the weekend hits because I wanted to know if you were free for dinner."

"Dinner? Yeah, I can definitely do dinner."

"Don't be so quick to say yes because I was wondering if you would come over for dinner."

"Come over as in come over to the small village you call a house?" Austin joked.

Alyssa laughed. "Yes, that kind of come over."

"I would love to."

"Great, be here by eight. And my dad should be home tonight which is a bonus. I think you two will really hit it off."

"That's great. I can't wait to meet your whole family."

"Great, see you then."

Alyssa hung up and, as Austin removed the phone from his ear, he couldn't help but smile. For some reason, Alyssa just had that effect on him. Whenever she was involved, he had to smile.

Chapter 16

Connections

Austin made his way home and prepared for his dinner that night. Before long, it was time to leave. Making sure to pick up a nice bottle of wine beforehand, Austin drove to Alyssa's house. As he pulled up to the front gate, he clicked the button on the nearby intercom.

"Who is it?" a voice asked.

"Hi, it's Austin. I was invited by Alyssa," he replied, slightly unsure of his response.

Suddenly, a buzzer rang out and the front gates opened. Austin drove up around the crescent pathway and parked in front. As he stepped out of his car, Alyssa ran down the front steps and jumped into his arms.

"It's good to see you," she said after giving him a kiss.

"You too."

"Come on, I'll give you a tour."

Alyssa grabbed Austin's hand but he stopped her.

"What about the car? Should I move it?"

"Don't worry about it, just leave your keys in the dish by the door, one of the staff will move it."

"One of the staff?" Austin exclaimed.

"Yeah, we have a few live-in staff, did I forget to mention that?" Alyssa asked.

"Uh… yeah!" Austin replied still stunned.

"Well, doesn't matter, come on!"

Alyssa dragged Austin inside, Austin quickly dropping his keys in the dish as instructed. Austin could hardly believe his eyes as they gazed upon the beautiful interior of the mansion. Sleek hardwood floors stretched down the length of the house until a break in the floor continued on with large, square tiles. Two crescent staircases wrapped around the center room leading to a second floor landing, a round, wooden table sitting between them. The light champagne-colored walls were covered with beautiful art pieces and a large, crystal chandelier hung gracefully above.

Austin stood, mouth agape, now only imagining what the rest of the house could look like. Austin wondered if it was his feelings for Alyssa that caused him to feel that Damien's compound paled in comparison to what was before him.

"Please don't think of me differently now," Alyssa said worriedly.

"Different? No, why would I think of you different?" Austin replied sarcastically. "If anything, I feel sorry for you."

"Sorry? Why?" Alyssa questioned with confusion.

"It must take you forever just to grab a snack."

Alyssa playfully punched Austin in the arm as she let out a giggle.

"Come on, let me introduce you to my family."

Alyssa pulled Austin across the large floor towards the back of the house where the kitchen was located. The moment Austin stepped onto the tiled portion of the floor and into the kitchen, his amazement resurfaced once again.

Maybe it was the espresso-colored cabinets that wrapped around half of the room or maybe it was the high end appliances sprinkled throughout. Maybe it was the thick, beautiful, white and gray granite countertop or its matching piece which topped a large island in the center of the room.

Maybe it was the long, dark dining table which sat across from the kitchen or its matching chairs covered in elegant upholstery. Austin's trance was interrupted by Alyssa's words.

"Mom, this is Austin."

A woman had just finished washing her hands by the sink when she turned around and smiled.

"It's a pleasure to meet you, Austin," she spoke as she shook Austin's hand.

"Likewise, Mrs. Moore," he replied.

"Please, call me Susan. There's no need for formalities here." She chuckled.

"Understood." Austin smiled back. "You have a beautiful home."

"Thank you very much. The credit for the size has to go to my husband but the credit for quality goes to me. I can't imagine what this place would look like if I let him interior decorate."

Austin laughed. "Speaking of your husband, I'd like to meet him too."

"You will, he should be home by the time we sit down for dinner." Susan turned to Alyssa. "In the meantime, go show Austin the rest of the house."

Austin followed Alyssa through the large corridors, his eyes persistently scanning his surroundings. They reached the top of a staircase that headed down into the basement.

"Sean! Come up here!" Alyssa shouted.

A young man ran up the stairs, a smile already on his face.

"You must be Austin. I've heard a lot about you," he said as he and Austin shook hands.

"I hope all good things," Austin joked.

"Hey, I could tell you everything she said. I'm sure you'll love to hear—"

Suddenly, Alyssa elbowed him in the side, stopping his thought.

"Very funny, go back downstairs where you can't annoy anyone," Alyssa growled.

"Hey, you called me up here." Sean chuckled. "I'll catch you at dinner, Austin."

"Sounds good."

As Sean raced back down the stairs, Alyssa pulled Austin in yet another direction. They stepped slightly down into a large, cozy living room, the fireplace already roaring on the other side.

"Alyssa, your house is unreal," Austin admitted as they both sat down on one of the espresso-colored leather couches.

"Like I said, I really don't want you to think of me differently."

"I won't though I have to admit, I would have never guessed you had all this," Austin admitted.

"Why not?"

Austin pondered briefly before responding, "For one thing, you aren't—"

"Stuck up?" Alyssa finished Austin's thought.

Austin smirked. "Yeah."

"Yeah, that's the usual thought process when people see this place for the first time. But like I told you last weekend, the money that bought this place didn't come without its own price. There's only so many family get-togethers you can miss out on before you start to think that all of this isn't really worth it," Alyssa explained.

"But your dad doesn't think that, does he?"

"No way. If it were up to him, he'd buy a place twice as large but, fortunately for us, he isn't the only one living here. It was a group agreement to buy this house but, even then, it was a struggle to get him to settle."

"Settle? *This* is settling?" Austin asked in shock.

"Exactly!" Alyssa exclaimed and started to laugh. "But my plan still stands. Once this last big stock venture ends, I'm going off on my own. I don't want to be tied down by this place. I want to live on my own, experience life like… like—"

"Like us normal folk?" Austin joked, now finishing Alyssa's thought.

She looked at him for a moment, her face slightly flush from embarrassment.

"I totally didn't mean it to sound like that."

"Relax, I'm joking. I know what you mean." Austin giggled. "You just want to be able to live your life how you want, not how you're told to."

Alyssa went silent as she just stared at Austin before letting out a light scoff.

"What?" he questioned.

"I just find it so amazing. You barely know me and yet you can put my feelings into words better than I ever could."

"What can I say, I'm a good listener," Austin jested.

"You're more than that," Alyssa replied, leaning in and planting a loving kiss on Austin's lips.

"Dinner's ready!" Susan shouted from the kitchen, interrupting their moment.

"Kitchen or dining hall?" Alyssa yelled back.

"Dining hall!" Susan replied.

"Wait, that wasn't your dining room table?" Austin asked, surprised.

Alyssa just looked at him and smiled. Upon entering the

dining hall, once again, Austin was floored.

"I don't know why I'm still surprised," Austin stated as he looked around the beautiful room.

A staff member walked in with the last tray of food for the table followed shortly after by Susan and Sean.

"Don't wait for an invitation, help yourself," Susan stated.

"What about your husband?" Austin asked.

"He's running a little bit late. What else is new?" Susan scoffed. "But he should be here soon."

The four sat down to eat, Austin immediately impressed with the cooking.

"Wow, this is delicious." Austin quickly cut another piece of the chicken he was eating.

"Don't get too attached to it, not like Alyssa can cook it for you." Sean laughed.

"Shutup, Sean! I know how to cook," Alyssa argued back.

"Really? What was the last meal you cooked yourself?"

"Last week I made myself smoked salmon. You would know but you went on a weekend club binge and didn't come home."

Sean thought for a moment.

"Okay, I'll give you that one but only because I can't remember that weekend."

"Are they always like this?" Austin whispered to Susan.

"Every day," she replied simply causing Austin to chuckle. "So, Alyssa tells me you have some mysterious job that keeps you busy, care to elaborate?"

Austin slowly finished chewing the food that was in his mouth, hoping to buy himself time.

Finally, he answered, "It's not so much a mystery as it is something I just don't like to discuss. I help run a small, independent fighting gym."

"Woah, like UFC?" Sean cut in as he heard the conversation.

"Yeah, something like that. We're still small, up and coming but we have some good talent." Austin continued to morph the truth.

"So do you just help run it or are you one of the fighters?" Sean continued, the sparkle of intrigue in his eye.

"I'm a fighter too."

"That's so sick! Can you teach me some moves?" Sean exclaimed.

"Austin has better things to do than waste his time teaching you things you'd never use," Alyssa quickly retorted.

Sean stayed silent, shoving another forkful of food into his mouth, his angry glare locked on to Alyssa.

"Isn't that dangerous?" Susan asked, returning to the topic of conversation.

"There's always a danger to it but fortunately, I haven't lost," Austin replied.

"In how long?" Sean asked.

Austin turned to him, a prideful smile forcing its way onto his face. "Ever."

"You're undefeated? How come you guys haven't expanded yet? I'm sure an undefeated record would grab some attention," Sean asked, helping himself to another serving of string beans.

"It's not easy pushing through to mainstream especially when we're not the first ones to do it."

Austin almost frightened himself with how good he was at lying to Alyssa's family. For every question, he had an answer, and for every answer, he had an explanation. As Sean continued to gush over Austin's news, Austin turned slightly and stared at Alyssa who was already looking at him. The moment their eyes locked, a smile stretched across her face. Austin smiled back as the same thought from earlier popped back into his head; whenever Alyssa was involved, he had to smile.

"Sorry I'm late!" a voice spoke from the corridor.

Austin's eyes widened, his heartbeat stopping as his fork clanged against his plate. That voice, he knew that voice, knew it all too well. Could this really be happening? Could the world be so inconceivably small, that something like this could be possible?

"My last meeting ran a bit late."

The man walked in and stood by his seat at the head of the table.

"It's fine, dear. Alyssa brought a guest for dinner," Susan stated.

Austin could already feel the man's gaze upon him but some imaginary force was holding his head down, keeping his eyes locked on his half-empty plate. As the mere seconds felt like never ending hours, Austin realized there was no force holding his head down, it was something much more relatable, fear.

Austin knew he had to act, slowly and reluctantly lifting his head toward the man. Their eyes locked for the first time, both men trying to hide their overwhelming shock. Austin stared into his eyes, the disbelief still flooding his mind.

"I wasn't aware we were having company but the more the merrier. And your name?" the man asked, an insincere smile on his face.

"Austin," he managed to say simply.

"It's nice to meet you, Austin, I'm Damien."

"Austin was just telling us of his job at a fighting gym," Susan stated.

"Oh, is that so?" Damien asked, his eyes locked on Austin with intrigue.

"Yeah, says he's undefeated," Sean added.

"To be honest, I'm more interested in how you two met," Damien said, sharing his glance between Austin and Alyssa.

"Actually, we always pass each other on our jogging routes." Alyssa smiled as she grabbed Austin's hand.

"Yeah, and the diner she works at isn't that far from my apartment," Austin added.

"And so the world works its magic." Damien smiled faintly.

Austin continued to play along, all the while trying to figure out what Damien was truly thinking. Was this going to jeopardize the entire mission? Had Austin already sealed his fate through this chance encounter?

Suddenly, the ocean of paranoid thoughts flooding Austin's mind was parted with a single idea. If Damien was going to put up an act, then Austin could do the same.

"So, Damien, Alyssa tells me you're quite successful in the stock market," Austin said, right before taking another sip of his wine.

Damien paused for a moment but only a brief one.

"Yes, I've been quite fortunate to have made so many good decisions in what I buy and sell. But I always make sure to do my research first," he replied confidently.

"Yeah and all it takes is another week long trip to Japan," Sean interjected with an attitude.

"Not tonight," Damien barked, Austin once again seeing Damien's dark side peek out through his tone.

It was the same tone he gave to Austin when they discussed Anatoly's death. With that single statement, Sean went silent. Despite Damien's almost silent threat to Sean, Austin knew he had to continue.

"Well, whatever the case may be, you've clearly done well

for yourself. I mean this house is tremendous from the outside and beautiful from the inside." Austin chuckled.

"Like I said, Austin, I get credit for the interior decorating." Susan laughed.

"Either way, I know I don't have a staff of workers living in my guest wing," Austin joked.

"They really are like family." Alyssa smiled. "Still makes me sad to think about Evan."

"Who's Evan?" Austin questioned.

Damien took a deep breath. "Evan used to work here. He grew very close with the family but then, one day, he decided to move back to Ireland to stay with his family. He was already on a red-eye by the time we read the goodbye letter he left."

"I didn't even know the guy *had* family in Ireland," Sean chimed in.

"Sorry to hear that," Austin played along.

"But enough about sad news. Let's celebrate some good news." Damien raised his glass. "To Austin, the new guest in our home. May he one day soon, have the title of *guest* stripped from his identity."

"Cheers to that!" Sean exclaimed.

Everyone raised their glasses and gently clanged them together. Through the fanfare of the glasses banging together, Austin caught Damien's stare.

Later that night, as the house was winding down, Alyssa walked up to Susan.

"Hey, Mom, have you seen Austin?"

"He's on the upstairs balcony with your father," Susan answered.

"What? Dad already pulled Austin away? I have to go get him."

"Leave them, Alyssa. Your father only wanted to talk to him. It's normal for a father to want to get to know the man his daughter is seeing. For once, let your father be a father."

Alyssa paused for a moment, giving Susan a worried look.

Susan smirked. "Relax, it'll be fine. Austin seems like an amazing young man. I'm sure the conversation is going great."

"Damien, what the fuck is all this?" Austin exclaimed as he leaned backwards against the balcony railing.

"Keep your voice down," Damien replied.

"Damien, this is insane. You have a family? Is your real name Damien Moore?"

"Of course not. I didn't let my wife and kids take my last name. Moore is Susan's last name." Damien joined Austin on the railing, him facing outward. "Of all the woman in New York City, you had to meet my daughter."

"Would have helped if I knew you even *had* a daughter. Just another life secret, I guess," Austin groaned.

"I told you, I like to compartmentalize my life. I like to keep every aspect separate from the others."

"So they have no idea about Reign or Project: Hercules?" Austin asked in awe.

"Susan knows that I'm not completely honest about my career or daily activities but nobody knows the truth." Damien turned to Austin. "I made sure to keep it that way, at least until you came along. You somehow found your way into all three alleys of my life."

"Is there a fourth I should know about?" Austin continued.

"Nope, you've hit them all." Damien chuckled. "You're lucky it's you."

"Why is that?"

"Because the last person to blend the lines didn't really like my reaction."

Austin thought for a moment.

"I'm guessing Evan never made it to Ireland."

Damien took out a pair of cigars and handed one to Austin. As he began to prep and light them, he explained.

"Evan was a good man, hard worker. But Alyssa was right, the staff is like family and, sometimes, they don't know where the line is drawn. Evan ended up getting too close to me and found out about Reign. Instead of talking to me about it, he showed up one Monday night looking to fight."

"Why don't I remember this?" Austin asked.

"You have no reason to remember it. It's not like I announced him as my employee. He participated just like any other fighter. Based on his one-sided loss, he clearly didn't know what he was dealing with."

"He lost? So does that mean he became one of your subjects for Hercules?" Austin wondered.

Damien took a big puff of his cigar. "No, I didn't want him jumping into that third area of my life. He had already made a mess of things so I knew he had to be disposed of."

Austin stared at Damien intensely as Damien stared out into the open sky.

"It really was a shame; Evan was a damn good worker." He turned to Austin with a gentle smile. "Like I said, you're lucky it's you."

Austin remained quiet, his insides screaming with the idea of the new web he found himself in. Without waiting too long, Austin took a puff of his cigar and responded.

"So stocks, huh?"

Damien laughed heartily.

"That's actually true, at least it used to be. That's how I

originally funded Reign and by the time I started Project: Hercules, I had made enough money to become self-sustainable. I kept my money flowing, making just enough investments to turn a profit all while using the bulk of my money to create what I have in Russia. Haven't had to look back ever since."

Once again, Austin's true feelings found their way out of his mouth.

"Damien, this whole time, I really thought I knew you, knew who you were. After finding out about Project: Hercules, I had to rethink that idea. Eventually, I was able to piece it back together including what I had found out but now this? Damien, you have a wife and two kids and you never told me about them."

"I told you, Austin, I like to keep my life—"

"Yeah, I know, you like to keep everything separated!" Austin cut Damien off, his voice rising in frustration. "But Damien, this is me you're talking to. You always told me you saw me as a son but you *have* a son, a real son, twenty feet from you right now. Was anything you ever said true?"

"No! Don't do that!" Damien snapped. "I meant every word of it. I do see you as a son and Sean has nothing to do with this. Yes, Sean is my son, my biological son. He was born from my wife and I and I watched him grow up; but us, Austin, you and I, our bond was forged in fire. It withstood the harsh realities of the world, realities that Sean could only imagine. We know what life is really like, how unforgiving it can be. My family inside have no idea about any of that. All they know is the lavishness within those four walls. Austin, what I see in you, I see in no other person, not even Sean. So when I tell you I see you as a son, I damn well mean it."

Again, Austin could hear the passion and truth in Damien's voice and he could see it in his eyes as he stared at him. There wasn't an angle Damien was playing and this wasn't just another lie to avoid a problem; Damien was being sincere. Before Austin completely lost himself inside the rabbit hole that was Damien Church, he cycled back to the discussion.

"You know not everyone in there is about the lavish life you provided them," Austin stated.

Damien nodded begrudgingly as he looked back through the glass-paned doors. "Alyssa, the constant reminder that I can never become complacent."

"What do you mean?" Austin asked.

"Doing what I do, living my separate lives, I have to stay on my toes but Alyssa makes sure I never stop. She isn't happy with the mansion, and the six cars, and the Olympic-sized pool. She wants to move out, live on her own in an apartment she paid for with her own money that she earned."

"Yeah, how dare she want to be independent," Austin said sarcastically.

"In my life, that kind of idea could cost you everything." Damien's tone became stern. "As long as everyone is here, they are safe under my watch. I don't have to worry about where they are or what they're doing. It gives me time to focus on what really matters. If I don't give a hundred percent of myself to things like Reign or Project: Hercules, then they fall apart, crumble right from within my hands."

"Damien, Sean and Alyssa aren't going to stay home forever. Eventually, even all this is going to not be worth it. They'll want to live their own lives; Alyssa already wants to."

"I know but I just need it to stay this way a little longer. After that, it won't matter where they go or what they do, I know they'll be safe and I won't have to worry about them."

"You mean after the formula is completed," Austin stated.

"Yes, once the formula is perfected, my new world can begin and, once that happens, there isn't a place on this planet where my children will have to worry."

"Alyssa said you were working on one last big trade in the stocks. Could she be thinking that Hercules is that stock?" Austin questioned.

"Yes, I always use stocks as my cover but even she knew that this one was different. But I meant what I said, this is the last one."

"Because once Hercules is perfected—"

With a sinister grin spread across his face, Damien finished Austin's statement, "The world will never be the same."

As the night finally ended, Alyssa and Austin walked down the front pathway towards the street where Austin's car was already waiting for him.

"I'm so sorry again for leaving you with my father. Are you sure he didn't say anything stupid to you?" she asked.

"I promise you; it was fine," he lied. "We just talked; it was nice."

"Austin, there's something I want to tell you but I'm not sure if this is the right time," Alyssa admitted.

"Well, my car is another six miles away, we have plenty of time," Austin joked.

"Stop, I'm serious!" Alyssa laughed. "I feel..." She paused. "I feel like I'm falling for you so fast, is that bad?"

Austin stopped and turned to Alyssa.

"Is it bad that I feel like I've already fallen?" he asked.

Alyssa stared into his eyes.

"Do you really mean that?"

"I do."

Without another word, the two shared another kiss under the

light of the full moon. As they pulled away, Alyssa smiled widely.

"I'm really glad you came tonight."

Austin smiled back. "Me too."

Chapter 17

Making the Most of Little Time

Austin jumped out of bed, fueled with a new purpose and fresh information to relay. Without a moment of hesitation, Austin walked through the card terminal, swiping his card with confidence.

"Now that's the walk of an agent." Mike smiled. "Are you ready to meet Geer?"

Austin walked straight up to Mike. "Not yet, we need to talk."

Within minutes, Austin's emergency debriefing was underway.

"His daughter?" Grant exclaimed as he shot up from his chair inside the C.O.R.

"Yeah, I didn't believe it either. Damien was hiding another layer of his life from me. First Project: Hercules and now this," Austin replied.

"Austin, does Alyssa know the truth about her father?" Mike asked.

"No, not that I can tell. She always just talks about his dealings in the stock market."

"She could be playing you just like you're playing her," Grant stated.

"I don't think so and I'm not playing her. I really care about her. I'm not letting Damien ruin what I have with Alyssa," Austin exclaimed.

"It's gonna be hard to have a nice candle-lit dinner sitting across from the person who turned your life upside down," Grant continued.

Austin slammed his hands on the table in frustration.

"I won't let it happen. I won't let him take this away from us. He's had his way with everybody and everything for this long, he doesn't get this too."

"All right, all right, calm down. First, let's focus on what we can do today." Mike neutralized the situation. "Are you ready for your training?"

Austin exhaled in annoyance.

"Yeah, I'm ready."

Mike jumped up from his chair. "Good, then let's go."

"While you guys go meet with Geer, I'll fill Hardwick in on the new intel and see what else I can find out about Church's clan," Grant announced as Mike and Austin left the room.

Mike escorted Austin into one of the sub-levels of the facility, into a large training room.

"Your student is here!" he shouted into the large, empty room.

A man slowly turned out from one of the columns in the room, already taping up his hands, his solid frame standing firmly in the center. With one glance, Austin could tell his everyday outfit wasn't a suit like the agents he was used to working with.

The man lifted his eyes slightly from his hands and locked eyes with Austin, his piercing blue stare freezing Austin in place. Fades of black streaking through his fully white hair, as if his hair was trying to hold on to the youth that now escaped him, his gray facial scruff the only thing void of actual color.

Mike patted Austin on the shoulder. "Good luck."

As Mike walked away, Austin stepped into the room.

"Hi, I'm—"

"I know exactly who you are. Mike filled me in on everything I need to know about you. I have to admit, going in to take down Church on your first go around takes balls. Name's Geer," he explained.

"So they told you about Alexei?" Austin questioned.

"Yeah, I never crossed paths with the guy myself but I've heard of his work. We have a lot to do if we're gonna keep up with his training," Geer replied.

"So what's so different about this training? Aren't you both just doing the same thing?"

Geer scoffed lowly. "Do you think you could win any fight you're in?"

Austin looked on perplexed.

"Yeah, I think I could."

"Really? So you think you could beat me right now?"

"Listen, I'm not looking to start a proving ground here," Austin stated.

"And I don't expect you to, just answer the question," Geer pressed on. "Do you think you could beat me?"

Austin thought briefly.

"Every fight I go into is with someone I don't know. I don't know their strength, their speed, their style, but every time that decision is made, my hand is raised. To me, this isn't any different. I don't know you yet but I will and when I do, I'll win."

Geer chuckled and tossed the roll of hand tape to Austin.

"That's some answer, kid. Anyone ever tell you you're arrogant?"

"I'm sure that word's been thrown around before," Austin sneered.

"And how about if I brought the rest of Gladiator Squad in here. Do you think you could win then?"

"Against all of you? No, that's crazy," Austin replied, stunned by the question.

Again, Geer scoffed.

"I know about your fights in that club of yours and your combat training during your inauguration. From what I hear, you're damn good but you're not the best, not yet. Against one opponent, you could definitely hold your own but what about two or four or six? What then?" Geer walked right up to Austin and stared into his eyes. "I'm not here to teach you how to fight, I'm here to teach you how to win."

Austin couldn't help but smile at the claim, already excited at what he could learn from such a confident fighter. Geer readied himself.

"Are you ready to begin?"

For the entire day, Geer pushed Austin rigorously, somehow outmatching Alexei's performance. After training with Alexei, Austin didn't think anyone else could be so ruthless and aggressive but Geer proved him wrong. His punches were swift and powerful, deliberate with every strike. He wasn't just training Austin, he was pushing him to his absolute limit, hoping to pull out all the potential Austin hadn't realized he had.

As their sparring continued and the floor became covered in blood and sweat, Austin began to feel a fire ignite within him. Suddenly, he didn't feel as though he was training any more. He began to look at Geer like an opponent he couldn't defeat.

"I see that look. That's good." Geer smiled.

"So you know what I'm thinking?" Austin asked back, matching with his own intrigued smile.

"You finally realize that you can't beat me and it's eating

235

you up inside. You want to beat me; you want to be better than me."

"And if that's true?" Austin quickly wiped the blood from his nose.

The two men began circling each other, waiting for the next round to begin.

"Then I'm doing my job. When you trained with Alexei, there was only so much you could do. If my theory is correct, you didn't want to push the issue too hard because you didn't know how Alexei would respond. You were on their grounds playing by their terms, I don't blame you for playing it safe. I'm sure you just kept your mouth shut and listened to what Alexei was teaching you; you were his student. But I don't want you to be my student, I want you to become my equal."

"So you don't want me to just learn new moves or techniques from you?" Austin asked.

"No! That shit is boring! I want you to fight me! If you fight me with everything you've got and I fight you with everything I've got, you'll realize what you don't know. It's faster for you to learn through the actual experience than for me to break down a new disarming tactic step by step."

Austin smiled with excitement.

"You know, I think I'm really going to like this."

Geer raised his hands up and gestured them towards himself. "Good, then come at me!"

As the day wound down, Mike casually walked back into the training room.

"Hey, Austin, we're working on dossiers for all of Damien's family, figured it could help to have," Mike informed without actually lifting his eyes from the floor.

When he did, they widened with awe. The room was uplifted

in chaos. Furniture was overturned and broken, several wall paddings were ripped down, and the long mirror at the end of the room was shattered.

"What the hell happened? This was supposed to be a training session!" Mike exclaimed.

Austin and Geer sat in the center of the room, both panting heavily with wide smiles on their faces.

Geer turned to Mike, still catching his breath. "It *was* a training session. Austin is doing just fine." He turned back to Austin. "Same time next week?" he asked, extending his hand.

"Count on it." Austin smiled as they shook hands.

That night, Austin crawled his way into bed, his entire body screaming in aches and pains. As his head finally hit the pillow, he hoped his body would have enough left to get him through his Monday fight.

As if traveling through time itself, Austin found himself already standing in the ring inside Reign, his hand being confidently raised by the official. As Austin exited the ring, he was greeted with his usual congratulations.

"Another one in the books." Demi beamed.

"Yeah, as usual." Austin smiled faintly.

"Go say your little goodbyes, we'll meet you outside," Nick joked as he gently directed Demi towards the exit.

He and Josh gave their nods to Austin and, as they headed towards the door, he headed towards the stairs. Austin opened the door to Damien's office but was slightly taken aback by what he saw. Damien stood by the window with a stranger standing by his side.

"Good, I'm glad you're here," Damien said as he turned around.

"Who's this?" Austin asked quickly.

"This is Matthew. He is one of my subjects for Project: Hercules," Damien replied.

Austin found himself lost in his own head trying to piece the puzzle together as quickly as he could.

"He's one of your subjects but he isn't trying to kill you. Does that mean the formula was perfected?" Austin questioned, hoping with his entire being that it wasn't.

"It appears so." Damien smiled proudly. "Dr. Arushka has confirmed zero adverse reactions in the last five subjects including no cardiac arrest upon increased stress."

"And what about the aggression?" Austin asked.

Damien put his arm around Matthew.

"Like you said, he isn't trying to kill me. I think we've finally done it."

Austin wanted to jump out of his very skin but had to mask his utter fear with overwhelming joy. "That's fantastic! It's finally ready!" he exclaimed with as much happiness as he could muster. "So what now?"

"That's actually why I brought him along tonight. We aren't meeting up tomorrow, we're leaving straight from here," Damien stated.

"We're going back to Russia together?" Austin asked.

"No, we're going to Japan, Osaka to be precise."

"Japan? What for?"

"I already have a buyer interested in the formula but he wants a demonstration before we talk numbers. The meeting is set for tomorrow at midnight so we have to be fast if we want to make it on time. My plane's already waiting for us, it should get us there fast enough," Damien explained.

"A buyer? Already?" Austin's heart raced at the thought.

His worst nightmare was beginning to take shape and he

could do nothing but walk alongside Damien and watch it happen. Again, Austin snapped back to reality, ready to keep up his role.

"So what are we doing standing around here for, let's go." He smiled.

The three men rushed from the club and into a limo out front, Nick, Josh, and Demi watching Austin get into the back.

"Aw, come on! Another night Damien steals from us?" Demi whined.

Nick didn't reply, instead turning to share a worrying look with Josh.

"Another Monday, another mystery."

Chapter 18

The Sit Down

"So have you spoken with the buyer already or has it been anonymous?" Austin asked as the rented limo drove through the streets of Osaka.

"No, we've spoken, several times in fact. His name is Haruto Nakamura," Damien responded.

"Isn't Nakamura Enterprises his company?" Austin questioned.

"One and the same."

"Nakamura Enterprises is one of the largest and richest companies in the world. I never thought he would be interested in something like this. He's so—"

"Public?" Damien asked, cutting Austin off. "One thing you have to realize is that for as large as someone's public face is, their shadowed face is larger. Haruto didn't get to where he is today because of his nice smile. His backdoor deals are what gave him the necessary resources to build his company up and when you make deals like that, you make enemies. Haruto knows what this formula could mean for him and his company."

"But he still wants that demonstration first," Austin said and turned to Matthew. "Are you ready?"

"All I have to do is go in there and do what I was made to do, simple as that," Matthew answered confidently, a coldness in his voice.

"Before we get there, take this." Damien handed a briefcase to Austin. "I brought one dose of the Hercules Formula with us in case he wants to make a purchase today. Sell him the one, reel him in for an entire pallet's worth."

Austin opened the case and saw the small vial, the light green liquid swishing about inside the glass. He stared at it for longer than he planned, thinking of how much destruction a single vial could cause and how he was moments away from allowing it to happen. Someone was going to get their hands on the formula and would be free to create their own walking weapons. The moment everyone feared was upon them and Austin had a front row seat to the beginning of the end.

"Austin," Damien said, snapping Austin back.

Austin closed the case.

"You okay?" Damien asked.

"Yeah, I'm fine, just can't believe it's actually perfected," Austin lied.

Immediately, Damien smiled. "I know, it's hard for me to believe as well. But the fact remains that the hard work paid off. Now it's time to reap the rewards."

The limo finally pulled up in front of a large office building. As they stepped out, a guard bowed to them.

"Before we enter the building, I must pat you down," the guard stated.

"Of course." Damien opened his arms up and Austin and Matthew did the same.

The guard patted Damien and Matthew but when he got to Austin, he discovered the pistol in the holster on his hip. Before the guard could say a word, Damien interjected.

"The gun stays with him. He's my muscle just like I assume Mr. Nakamura has plenty of his own muscle with him tonight."

"Very well," the guard replied after pondering for a moment. "Please, follow me."

As they walked into the large building, Austin noticed how empty it was.

"This meeting really is after hours, huh?" Austin asked.

"Something like this could never be done during company time. At this point, Nakamura is just as liable as we are. I wouldn't be surprised if all the cameras were down too," Damien stated, looking around at the different cameras throughout the interior. "Listen, when we get into the meeting, let me do all the talking. We want this to go as smoothly as possible. Get in, show off, get paid," Damien whispered as they walked with a quickened pace down a long hallway.

The guard guided them to an elevator at the end of the hall. The group stood in silence as they waited for the elevator, the steady chimes of passing floors the only sound to entertain them. As the doors opened and everyone stepped inside, the guard waved his keycard across a flat scanner, a small panel under the scanner opening to reveal a small keypad.

As the guard entered the correct code, the elevator doors shut and traveled down into the depths of the building, lower than the lit screen could even display. The doors finally opened, revealing a dimly lit concrete hallway in front of them, two additional armed guards standing across from each other.

The group walked past the guards and down the hall, finally entering a large, concrete room, two tables stationed across from each other on either side. The guard waved his hand towards one of the tables, gesturing for their group to sit. Austin placed the briefcase on the table and took a seat next to Damien as Matthew stood at the side of the table.

A door at the other end slowly opened and four armed men

stepped out followed by an older man. As the man sat down, Damien made his greeting.

"Good evening, Mr. Nakamura."

"More like good morning, and please, call me Haruto," he spoke, his voice low and strained.

"I'm glad we were able to make this meeting happen in such a timely manner," Damien stated.

"I am as well. I am impatient when face to face with such a fruitful proposal."

Damien chuckled. "Understood." He stood up and began to walk around the table. "As I told you over the phone, the Hercules Formula is a game changer and could turn the tide of any war but it is also extremely dangerous. Even if you're buying the completed formula, it must be treated with respect."

"In my entire life, I have never come across anything that struck fear into my heart. I built this company from the ground up and have conquered every enemy that stood in my path. I have surrounded myself with the strongest men these streets could breed. Your formula is nothing more than an extra layer to my empire," Haruto exclaimed, the tough confidence oozing from his aging stature.

Damien smirked. "Care to put those words to the test?"

"If you are asking if I want the demonstration to begin, I would love nothing more." Haruto smiled back.

Damien turned and nodded silently at Matthew who walked past and stood in the center of the room, several guards now surrounding him.

"Whenever you're ready," Damien stated as he sat back down next to Austin.

Austin's hands laid tensely on top of the briefcase as he anticipated seeing the controlled power of one of Damien's completed experiments up close. Haruto stared intensely at the situation in front of him and simply raised a single finger at his men. Suddenly, they lunged towards Matthew with reckless abandon, preparing to strike him down any way they could.

Instantly, Austin noticed something frighteningly obvious about the fight. While Haruto's men were exerting all their energy fighting Matthew, he looked as if he were barely even paying attention to them, let alone strategizing how to fight them. Even if one of the unfortunate attackers managed to land a solid hit on Matthew, he continued to act as if he didn't even register the contact. Before the onlookers were able to comprehend the fight in their heads, it was over. Matthew stood in the center of the room, unscathed, surrounded by five unconscious men.

"Very impressive, Damien." Haruto smiled widely.

"I assume you're now ready to discuss a price," Damien replied confidently as he placed his hand on the briefcase. "I took it upon myself to bring a sample size for you to buy today though I assume, after that demonstration, you're ready to order a whole lot more."

"A confident man, I like that." Haruto grinned, flicking his finger toward himself, gesturing for the briefcase to come to him.

"Go ahead," Damien ordered.

Austin stood up from his seat, holding the case by the handle. As he slowly walked across the room, he wished time would just stand still, slow down just enough for him to think of a plan. He was mere steps away from handing the formula over to its first buyer and sending it off into the world, making it absolutely unstoppable.

He stood in front of Haruto and placed the case on the table, unlocking both latches. As he spun the case around, Haruto was able to see the single vial inside.

"That vial can create exactly five soldiers providing the correct dosage is distributed," Damien informed.

"So much power in such a small package." Haruto's eyes sparkled at the sight. "I'll give you fifty million U.S. dollars."

"Fifty million? Haruto, you insult me. A single component of that formula costs me half a million alone not including the laundry list of other chemicals, equipment, staffing, labor, research, incubation, and diagnosing. All that combined produces ten completed vials so, at the very least, we're looking at a hundred million and that's *if* I don't want to turn a profit," Damien exclaimed with a snarky chuckle.

Haruto stayed silent as he exchanged glances between Damien and the vial. His eyes moved one last time to Matthew and that is when he made his decision.

"I'd be willing to double your bottom line but he stays with me." Haruto pointed sternly at Matthew.

"Matthew isn't part of this exchange, Haruto. You get the formula, not a finished specimen," Damien debated.

"Take it or leave it, Damien. If you want to walk out of here with two hundred million dollars, he becomes my property."

"Your what?" Matthew snarled, the anger already consuming him.

"They will leave and you will become my property, my weapon, my pet, doing whatever I deem fit for you to do."

"Haruto, I beg you to change your tone right now," Damien warned, his voice already shaky with panic.

Matthew stepped up next to Austin, staring intensely into Haruto's eyes. "I am nobody's pet and I do what I want."

"Is that so?" Haruto asked and then turned back to Damien. "Your specimen is quite disobedient, Damien. Perhaps you should alter the formula to make them more compliant."

"Haruto, please! I implore you to watch your words!"

"I would listen to the man if I were you," Matthew warned.

"Is that so? You must truly not know your current situation." Haruto snapped his fingers and, immediately, the room filled with countless guards, all wielding assault rifles. "You will obey your new owner, dog."

Matthew snapped and grabbed Haruto by the throat. Before he was able to make another move, the guards opened fire. Austin instinctively grabbed the case and dropped to the floor, crawling hastily towards the door. Damien rushed out into the hallway and dropped down.

"Austin, come on!"

Matthew dropped Haruto and immediately waged war against the small army in the room. As Austin met up with Damien, he helped him to his feet and the two ran down the long stretch of hallway towards the safety of the elevator. Without any effort at all, Matthew violently disposed of every man in the room except for one.

Haruto crawled backwards into the corner of the blood-soaked room, convulsing with fear. Matthew slowly walked up to him and picked up where he left off, with his hand around Haruto's neck. He lifted him off his feet and into the air.

"Please," Haruto pleaded with tears streaming down his face.

"It's always a shame when pets turn on their owners, don't you think?" Matthew grinned sinisterly.

Haruto screamed agonizingly as Matthew forcibly ripped his head from his spine.

"They're all dead, Damien, he killed them all," Austin exclaimed as Damien pressed the elevator's call button.

"I know, I know. We need to get out of here," Damien

replied frantically as he repeatedly slammed his finger into the call button. "Come on, come on, please."

Austin was overwhelmed by the situation, his body flooded with anxiety and fear but a single thought was able to pierce through those feelings: the fact that Damien was terrified.

"Damien!" Matthew shouted from the end of the hall; his body covered head to toe in thick, dark blood.

Damien pressed the button harder and faster and, finally, the doors opened.

"You weren't planning to leave me behind, were you!" Matthew shouted maniacally as he began to run towards them.

Damien jumped into the elevator and began to press the button to close the doors.

"Austin, get in! For Christ's sake, he's going to kill us!" Damien shouted.

Austin stood his ground and reached for the pistol on his hip. As he took aim, Matthew was sprinting towards him and closing in fast. Austin pulled the trigger once, twice, three times, sending all three specialized bullets into Matthew's chest. Matthew's momentum stopped as he dropped to his knees and fell backwards onto the floor, a pool of blood quickly surrounding him as he died before Austin's feet.

"Get in, we have to get out of here," Damien continued as he stared at Matthew's fresh corpse.

Upon exiting the elevator, Damien and Austin sprinted through the corporate building and out to the limo that was still waiting. They lunged inside the back as Damien shouted to the driver.

"Get us back to the airport now!" he ordered.

As the limo drove through the dense city streets, the two men began to catch their breath and reflect on the events that had just transpired.

"I'm glad you grabbed the vial. Wouldn't want someone to get that for free." Damien chuckled playfully.

"Enough, Damien!" Austin snapped. "Don't you get it? This isn't working! You're creating something that can't be controlled!"

"Don't say that, Austin. We're so close, I know we are. We just need to do some more research, find a way to inhibit aggression. I'll ask Dr. Arushka if he can look further into the hypothalamus," Damien replied, his speech quickened with anxiety.

"Is this before or after one of them kills you!" Austin shouted.

"It's going to work!" Damien barked back. "I know it is, it has to. We're so close, *I'm* so close. I can't give up now, it'll work. It'll work, I know it'll work."

The car went silent as Damien began to murmur the same mantra repeatedly to himself and Austin stared defeatedly out the window. He placed his hand under his chin for support but found that it was still trembling from the incident. He quickly pulled his hand away, grabbing it with the other for stability. In his head, Austin began to recite his own mantra.

"This'll all be over soon, it's almost over."

Chapter 19

Half Truths

Austin sat in silence as he swiveled about in his chair, the C.O.R. seeming quieter than usual. The dense silence was finally broken by Austin's superiors stepping into the room.

"Welcome back, Austin. You know the drill, run down your week," Grant ordered as the three men sat down.

Austin took a deep, frustrated breath. "I didn't meet Damien in Russia this week. We left Monday night and traveled to Japan. Damien had a meeting with a potential buyer for the completed Hercules Formula."

"He's already selling it?" Hardwick exclaimed.

"God damn it!" Grant growled.

"He tried to but it was a complete failure. He brought one of his subjects to demonstrate but the whole meeting went to shit, we were the only two to get out alive."

"What happened?" Mike asked curiously.

"Physically, his subjects are complete but he still can't get their emotional state under control. They're impulsive and quick to aggression. He was the reason the meeting failed. By the end, he was coming after us, I had to put him down," Austin continued.

"Are you okay with that? I know how you felt about Anatoly," Mike inquired.

Austin paused briefly in thought. "You know, somehow, this

didn't bother me as much. Damien's subjects just don't seem all that human any more once they come out of those pods."

"What happened next?" Grant asked.

"Nothing, we made it back to his compound and the week continued as usual. I did some training with Alexei and Damien had a conference with his scientists."

"Started eventful, ended with a dud," Hardwick scoffed.

"I can tell you one thing; Damien is starting to lose it. Deep down, he knows this isn't going to work but he's in denial about the whole thing. He won't stop until his vision becomes a reality but the truth is, it never will."

"Unfortunately, we can't close this case on Damien's perpetual failures. He might become even more dangerous unhinged. You did great, Austin, keep up the good work," Grant stated.

"Now it's our turn to debrief." Mike chuckled, spinning around towards his computer.

Several files appeared on the large screen.

"As I mentioned last week, we began building dossiers on Damien's family members. We now know everything about Susan, Sean, and Alyssa."

"Was all this necessary?" Austin asked.

"We can't take any chances with Church. For all we know, he could be using his family to hold more secrets," Grant added.

"From what Alyssa has told me, it seems like everyone is pretty fed up with him and after finding out it was Damien, it makes even more sense. He keeps his family, Reign, and Project: Hercules completely separated from each other."

"And you're sure Alyssa has no idea about her father's true motives?" Hardwick questioned.

"Alyssa has no reason to lie to me, we met on neutral ground and Damien pretended not to know me at dinner. He's one big, walking secret."

"So Alyssa doesn't know who you are just as much as her father," Grant stated.

Austin froze, his eyes glossed over in realization.

"She doesn't know who I am," he muttered.

"Austin?" Mike questioned.

"When I met Alyssa, I thought she was a stranger. All that time we spent together was genuine but now, after finding out Damien is her father, it seems like she was all a part of the mission," Austin explained. "I'm actively trying to take down the father of the girl I'm falling for."

"Austin, the mission comes first. I'm sorry that your girlfriend got wrapped up in this whole thing but that's just the way it is," Grant said sternly.

Austin didn't respond right away but finally, he answered Grant with a half-hearted response.

"Yeah, I know. The mission comes first."

Austin said one thing but his face expressed another and Mike saw that; he knew what Austin was truly thinking. Austin wanted to tell Alyssa everything, scream it out from the closest rooftop in pain-stacking detail.

"I think we've gotten all we can out of this meeting. Same time next week," Hardwick announced.

As the room dispersed, Mike chased Austin out the main door.

"Austin, hold on a sec."

"Need something else?" he asked.

"Come with me."

Mike took Austin into a small room that resembled a living room, dining room, and kitchen all wrapped into one. A minifridge sat underneath a small counterspace, a coffee machine sitting on top. A round table, big enough to fit three people uncomfortably, was stationed in the middle with a small love seat against the back wall.

"Isn't there a huge lounge downstairs?" Austin asked as he looked around the room.

"There is but this one is more private." Mike sat in one of the chairs at the table. "Please, sit."

"Mike, this is getting weirder by the second, please tell me why we're here," Austin pleaded as he reluctantly sat across from Mike.

"I know what you just said in the C.O.R. was bull."

"What do you mean?" Austin asked.

"You want to tell Alyssa, don't you? You want to tell her everything," Mike pushed.

"Mike, I meant what I said in there, I know the mission comes first, I can't jeopardize that for Alyssa," Austin explained.

"Austin, Grant isn't here to piss off and Hardwick isn't here to disappoint, it's just me. You can talk to me," Mike said sincerely.

Austin refrained from answering for as long as he could but finally, he let it all out.

"Of course I want to tell her! I want to tell her everything! I want to tell her everything about her father, I want her to know who really walks through her front door. I want to tell her everything about me, everything that I'm doing." Austin shot up from his seat and leaned on the countertop. "And I want to beg her to understand it all. I want to beg her not to hate me for everything that I'm doing. I want to beg her to believe me when I say that none of this was planned and these two worlds just collided by chance."

"I understand your frustration but, before you go off spouting government secrets, I just want to ask you one question," Mike spoke calmly.

Austin turned to him awaiting his inquiry.

"Deep in your gut, do you honestly believe she'll accept everything you have to say? You said you want her to believe you and understand you but even if she did everything you wanted, do you think she'll accept it? She could believe you wholeheartedly but that doesn't guarantee she'll be okay with it all. Maybe she'll believe everything you say about her father but what if she chooses to side with her family regardless?"

Austin shook his head. "No, she wouldn't. She's a good person, she wouldn't want to become part of that and neither would Sean or Susan."

"You never know, Austin. People change when faced with overwhelming decisions. I've seen people go against the very person they were, turn their backs on everything they believed in when faced with a life changing situation. In the end, she might decide to stick with her family in such a difficult time and then what? What did you accomplish by telling her everything? You blew the mission, broke her heart, and lost her forever even though you were doing what you thought was right."

Austin slowly sat back down, lost in thought over what Mike was explaining to him. He looked at Mike, the tears at the brink of releasing from his eyes.

"What the fuck do I do, Mike?"

"In my opinion, there's only one thing you can do. You won't like it and it'll hurt but I think the best thing you could do for Alyssa and her family is end it."

"You want me to break up with her?" Austin asked, the tears now rolling down his face.

"I think it's for the best. If Damien catches wind that you two broke up, he might ask you about it but, in the end, it'll still be between two adults. He won't tear everything down because someone broke his daughter's heart and your cover will still be intact within Project: Hercules." Mike stood up. "And who knows? Maybe after everything is said and done, you can try again."

"No." Austin shook his head. "I'll never be able to go back from this but after Damien walked into that dining room, what else should I have expected?"

"For what it's worth, I'm really sorry." Mike patted Austin on the shoulder before heading for the door. "Take as much time as you need. Think of what you're going to say."

Austin sat alone in the small room with nothing but his drowning thoughts. Just then, as if the nightmare was meant to manifest, Austin received a text and, when he looked at his phone, he saw that it was from Alyssa, inviting him to come over at once. He exhaled heavily and responded with a simple "okay".

Austin went home simply to grab his car and headed straight for Alyssa's house, the entire time thinking of what to tell her. He parked the car by the front steps and walked up to the door. Before he could even ring the bell, the door swung open, Alyssa standing in the doorway with a smile spread across her face.

"I missed you." She gleamed.

"I missed you too." Austin's reply was genuine but somehow, that made what he had to do hurt even worse. "Where is everyone? I thought you guys have valet service here," Austin joked, more for himself than Alyssa, anything to distract him from the inevitable.

"Actually, I sent the whole staff on break."

"The whole staff? Why?" Austin questioned in confusion.

"Well, Dad's not around, no surprise there. Sean went to Atlantic City for the weekend with his friends, and my mom went to the mall, she won't be back for hours."

"What's that have to do with the staff?"

"Well…" Alyssa glanced at Austin playfully. "I figured there would be no better time to have the house all to ourselves, *completely* to ourselves."

Alyssa leaned in close to Austin.

"Come upstairs."

Austin immediately read the situation and knew he had to do something now. Alyssa grabbed Austin's hand and pulled him towards the staircase but he pulled her back.

"Alyssa, wait."

Alyssa smirked flirtatiously, grabbing Austin and kissing him passionately, a burning desire to go further. Austin wanted nothing more than to melt into her kiss and let the moment take them but he knew he couldn't prolong this any further. He quickly pulled away from Alyssa and stepped back.

"What's wrong?" she asked.

"Nothing, I just — I'm sorry, I can't do this."

"Is everything okay, Austin?" Alyssa rubbed his arm in support.

"Yeah." Austin paused. "No." He pulled away once more.

"Austin, what's going on?"

Austin began the conversation he never wanted to have.

"Alyssa, I care about you, more than you could imagine, but this isn't going to work anymore."

"What are you talking about? Where did this come from?" Alyssa asked, confused and frustrated.

"I just don't want to hurt you and if I continue pretending like everything is okay, then that's exactly what I'll end up doing.

I'm not the man you think I am."

"You're exactly the man I think you are. You're caring and passionate and determined. You have a good heart and a strong will. You're everything I've ever wanted and—"

"No, I'm not!" Austin shouted cutting Alyssa off. "You just think I'm those things but the truth is, I'm not. I'm the opposite and I want you to know the truth."

Tears began to form in Alyssa's eyes.

"So tell me this truth then."

Austin paused. He wanted so badly to take back every word he had already said but the words that still needed to be said were deep in his throat.

"The truth is I'm not a good person and definitely not the kind of person you deserve. I've done horrible things at best and unforgivable things at worst. The things I'm involved in now have changed me, made me someone dangerous to be around."

"Austin, none of this makes any sense. Why are you doing this?" Alyssa questioned.

"Tell her about her father! Tell her every little dark, dirty secret he has! Tell her who Damien truly is!" the thoughts screamed in Austin's head, begging to release from his lips.

Ignoring every urge his mind and body had, he didn't mention Damien at all. He knew what the ramifications could be. What it could mean for the mission, for his life.

Austin inhaled deeply, preparing to deal the final blow to Alyssa's heart. "If I selfishly stayed with you, you would get hurt or worse. I'm doing this to keep you safe. I can't be with you."

Alyssa looked up and away, her eyes trying diligently to hold back the tears. Eventually, they gave way and the tears freely streamed down her face.

"You know what, Austin? I don't need you to keep me safe

or worry about me. I don't need you to *sacrifice* for my wellbeing. I don't need you to treat me like an incapable child. The only thing I need from you is to get the hell out of my house!"

"Alyssa, I—"

"No! You're done talking. Get out," Alyssa snapped back in a stern tone.

Austin couldn't blame her for her reaction, she was hurt and he knew that.

"I just want you to know that I—"

"I said get out!" she shouted cutting him off once more.

Austin kept his mouth shut and simply turned around, opening the front door and exiting without another word. He turned back to Alyssa as she stared at him in the open doorway.

"I'm sorry," he managed to say.

"You should be."

Alyssa slammed the door in Austin's face and, somehow, he already knew in his heart that he would never see her again. Austin walked slowly back to his car knowing that even though it hurt, even though this was a day he wished he could wipe from his memory, he did it because he cared about Alyssa and if the only way to keep her safe was to suffer without her, then that was what he was going to do.

Chapter 20

Revelations

The sky roared with rolling thunder as the clouds glowed with harsh lightning. Austin's alarm blared through his bedroom as he turned over in the opposite direction.

"It is ten thirty a.m. on Monday, June 21st, 2021. It is currently seventy-three degrees with thunderstorms in your area in New York City. This is your fourth wakeup call," the computerized voice announced.

Austin exhaled strongly and crawled himself out of bed. He shuffled to the bathroom and got ready for the day though his usual enthusiasm was nonexistent. When he returned to his nightstand and lifted his phone, he saw that he had five missed calls from Nick and three missed calls from Josh.

"But no missed calls from her," he groaned.

After dragging himself into the kitchen, he heard a knock at his door. The door was knocked upon three more times before Austin casually walked over to answer it. When he opened it, Mike gave a big greeting.

"Good morning, sunshine! I brought you some energy food, protein omelet." Mike smiled, raising a plastic bag. "But don't worry, you won't eat alone. There's a bacon, egg, and cheese in here for me."

"Actually, I ate already so I'm full," Austin replied without expression.

"No you didn't, it's not even eleven yet and you haven't woken up before ten-thirty in over two weeks. Just eat, it'll make you feel better." Mike placed the bag on the counter and began to empty its contents.

"Is that why you came here? To cheer me up with breakfast?" Austin asked as he plopped himself into one of his dinette chairs. "Or should I take Grant's absence as a hint that you're gonna tell me something I won't like?"

Mike chuckled heavily. "You're good, Austin." Mike placed the tin bowl in front of Austin as he sat down with his own sandwich. "I'm here to relay a message. Director Hardwick is ready to put an end to this mission but he's giving you final say before he gives the green light."

"Why do I get final say?" Austin questioned, opening his tray.

"Everything we know about Damien's operation is from your intel. Hardwick feels like you know better than anyone if we're really ready to put this to bed. He doesn't want to jump the gun on the raids."

"I can't say his timing is bad. Damien's team already created their own version of Trimoxil Dimene so he's able to pump the formula out like a factory now."

"But D.A.R.C.'s R&D team has been working around the clock to supply us with those god-killing bullets so no matter how many soldiers he pumps out, we'll be able to meet them head on."

"He still hasn't been able to fix the aggression and impulsiveness but I think he's close. Before I left on Saturday, Dr. Arushka seemed happier than usual to find Damien."

"All the more reason to put a stamp on this and be done with it," Mike continued. "And you're sure he has no other safehouses, right?"

Austin shook his head as he stuffed a piece of omelet into his mouth.

"The Russian compound is the central hub but he has a small safehouse in Osaka, that's why he chose to do business with Nakamura first. The storage unit in the trainyard doesn't have any vials of the formula but it has all the foundational research to start all over again so we should hit there too."

"You know there's one more place we have to hit right?" Mike asked.

Austin tossed his fork down into the tray as he curled his hands together near his mouth.

"Please don't say it," he pleaded.

"I'm sorry, Austin but that's where the man lives, that's his home. It would be irresponsible of us not to raid his mansion." Mike saw the hurt in Austin's eyes. "I'm sorry."

"Promise me she doesn't get hurt. Promise me Sean and Susan will be safe too. This whole thing is about Damien, I don't want to affect that family any more than I already have."

"I promise. I'll make sure the team goes in with the bare minimum equipment. There won't be a single gun drawn, you have my word."

Austin looked into Mike's eyes for a moment, trying to find a glimmer of deception but there was none.

"Thank you."

Austin took his last bite and stood up to throw out his garbage.

"Have you spoken to her at all?" Mike asked.

"Not a word. Sometimes I'll just wait outside the building hoping she'll jog by but she doesn't. I assume she changed her running route to avoid this block altogether," Austin responded, his tone already heavy with sadness.

"Why don't you go by the diner?" Mike questioned.

"And say what? This whole thing turned upside down the second Damien walked into that house. Every moment we shared together immediately became a lie!" Austin shouted.

"But it wasn't a lie, that was all real."

"I know that but I can't prove it! And what does any of that matter anyway? We're preparing to raid her house. So what? I'm going to walk into Shaw's Diner and try to work things out just for a battering ram to smash in her front door? There's no way I can fix this, it's done," Austin exclaimed, the anger and regret manifesting as tears swelling in his eyes.

"Austin, you have to do something. Everyone can tell you aren't yourself. It takes forever for you to get up in the morning, you don't keep up with your daily exercise, you shunned away your friends, and—"

"Did you talk to Nick and Josh?" Austin barked.

"They're worried about you, Austin, we all are. This mission was personal to begin with because of your relationship with Damien but, after Alyssa, it became too personal. I know this must be so hard for you but if you don't take care of yourself, then this whole thing could be a waste. We need you at the top of your game when this goes down."

"I'll be fine," Austin groaned as he placed his hands on the counter, turning away from Mike.

Mike stood up and pushed his chair in.

"I'll see myself out but, for the little that it's worth, we're almost at the finish line."

Austin stared off into thought, the sound of the door closing snapping him back. He began to contemplate everything to himself, replaying the last few months in his head. The people he had met, the moments he experienced, both good and bad, and the mission that took over his entire life. Through it all, he came out with one final thought.

"Another fight."

That night, Austin walked into Reign alone, Nick and Josh already standing by his ring with Demi.

"Where were you? They had to postpone your match; it was almost going to be a forfeit," Josh stated.

"I got held up," Austin replied simply.

"You wanna tell us the real reason?" Nick asked, his skepticism already showing on his face.

Austin exhaled. "I just took my time tonight, I didn't rush. I'm starting to care less and less about this place these days."

"Well, keep up the charade a little bit longer because your fight's up. The crowd got restless waiting for you," Demi stated as she gave Austin a kiss on the cheek for good luck.

Austin wrapped his hands and stepped into the ring, his opponent already standing across from him with a smug smile.

"He's still lying about why he was late," Nick said to Josh as they stood by to watch the fight.

"Come on, we both know exactly where he was," Josh replied.

Nick turned. "We have to do something about this."

"Austin, ready?"

"Johnny, ready?"

As the match began, Johnny darted at Austin with deadly speed and grappled his legs, taking him straight to the mat. As he jumped on top of Austin and began to send devastating right hands into his face and body, the frustration began to build. With every punch came another thought about the turns his life had taken: Damien's sick plan, D.A.R.C.'s recruitment, Jeff's death and the deaths that Austin had caused, then, of course, Alyssa.

Everything that he tried not to think about came rushing to the forefront of his mind like an unstoppable freight train and no matter what he did, he couldn't think of anything else. Finally, Austin had enough.

In one swift motion, Austin flipped Johnny over and landed on top of him, immediately crashing his fist into his face. Just as every one of Johnny's punches unleashed a memory, every punch that Austin delivered saved him from one. Every ounce of frustration and anger was being released into his punches and everyone watching could tell. The large crowd went silent as the blood-curdling blows echoed through the underground, the sound of bone colliding with bone, and tearing flesh causing the onlookers to wince.

As violent and one-sided as the match had become, Austin didn't stop. Each punch was now accompanied by a rage-fueled grunt as Austin pummeled Johnny's face into the mat. The official frantically attempted to open the lock as Nick, Josh, and Demi looked on in horror. As soon as the door was opened, Nick and Josh rushed in, the two forcibly pulling Austin off of Johnny's unconscious body.

"Austin, stop!" Josh yelled.

"It's done! It's done!" Nick pushed Austin against the cage wall.

Austin looked at Nick as if he had just awoken from a trance, his gaze jolting to every aspect of his surroundings. The hushed crowd, the frightened officials, and finally, the body he had left in the middle of the ring.

"What the fuck was that?" Nick exclaimed.

Austin didn't reply and quickly rushed out of the ring, pushing his way through the thick crowd towards the bathroom. As he rigorously rubbed and scraped the blood from his hands,

Nick and Josh walked into the bathroom.

"We need to talk," Nick said.

"I'm fine." Austin's eyes never lifting from the sink.

"No you're not fine! You almost killed that guy in there! He's barely breathing!" Nick shouted, storming up to Austin.

"What do you care? That's what we do here, isn't it? Shit like this can happen, we both know that!" Austin snapped back.

"This isn't the same thing. You weren't fighting that guy; you were beating him to death. There's a difference," Josh intervened with a worried tone.

Austin exchanged glances with his two friends.

"I'm fine."

Austin attempted to leave the bathroom but the door swung open and Demi walked in.

"Stop and listen to them." Demi's eyes were already filled to the brim with tears, her voice hoarse as she tried not to cry. "Please."

"You didn't just take your time getting here, you went back there again, didn't you?" Nick questioned.

Austin looked at Nick, his eyes also swelling with tears.

"I just stand across the street like an idiot, I can't even take a single fucking step closer."

"Austin, you deserve to be happy. Fuck what Mike and Grant say and fuck Damien's bullshit. Tell Alyssa everything," Josh exclaimed.

"I can't do that to her. I can't expose her to all of that and put her at risk," Austin argued.

"But look at what you're doing to yourself!" Nick screamed frustratedly. "You aren't yourself anymore! It's been over a month and not a single thing has been better off because of it!"

Demi grabbed Austin by the arm. "I know everything now

and nothing's changed."

"Let's not spread that fact around, okay? I feel like Grant has some weird sixth sense that lets him know when government secrets are shared," Nick said as he looked around the bathroom with paranoia.

"Austin, you don't even know how she'll respond. Maybe she'll understand," Josh cut back in.

"Would you understand." Austin sounded defeated already. "Would you understand if your world was crumbling around you and Rebecca was the reason? I'm supposed to tell Alyssa the truth about everything, about all of it, and then she's supposed to go home and have her door bashed down so her house can be raided and swept through all while her father is being hunted down and killed. Does that sound like things are going to work out in the end? It's just better if she doesn't know. At this point, the less she knows, the better."

"But that's not your decision to make!" Nick continued. "And everything you just mentioned is going to happen regardless of whether you tell her or not. So why not just take the chance and tell her the truth? Why are you doing this to yourself? Are Mike and Grant really worth this? Is D.A.R.C. worth this? Is *Damien* worth this?"

Austin stared at Nick, his eyes stern yet hurting. Nick didn't wait for a reply and stepped up closer to Austin.

"Go to Shaw's, take that first step to cross the street, walk inside, and tell her everything. Spill every detail you have in your mind and every feeling in your heart. She deserves to know the whole truth and you deserve to tell her."

Austin still didn't say a word and just looked around the room at the people closest to him. Suddenly, the bathroom door swung open as a man tried to step in.

"Give us a fucking minute!" Demi shouted, enraged.

The man, frightened and confused, rushed backwards out of the bathroom in a panic. Josh couldn't help himself and broke the tense moment with his laughter. Almost immediately, Nick and Demi joined in on the laughter finally followed by Austin. The four joined in the middle, sharing a group hug.

"I love you guys," Austin admitted with relief.

"We love you too, now go tell Alyssa the same thing." Nick ruffled Austin's hair playfully.

Austin found himself standing across the street from the diner once more. The streets were silent and still as if the world itself was waiting on held breath for Austin's move. The diner was just about to close for the night and, through the large glass wall of the diner, Austin could see Alyssa wiping down a table before making her way towards the back.

"Just take the first step. Just move," Austin talked himself into making the move though his body was reluctant to obey. "Just tell her everything no matter what the consequences are for me. Just tell her."

Austin stepped down into the street, finally making his way across. He grabbed the handle of the front door and paused one last time before swinging it open and entering.

"Sorry, we're just about closed!" Alyssa announced from under the counter.

"I know," Austin replied.

Immediately, Alyssa popped up with surprise.

"What are you doing here?" she questioned.

Austin made his way closer to the counter. "I came to talk to you."

"It's been a month, Austin, there's nothing you can say now or ever that will change what happened."

"Please, just give me five minutes to explain," Austin pleaded.

"I thought you explained yourself pretty clearly the last time. You're a dangerous man who can't be trusted but somehow, you cared enough about me to leave me. It's all bullshit."

The anger was already bubbling in her voice as she dramatically mocked Austin's motives.

"I couldn't leave your house that day without breaking up with you. That was the goal," Austin said simply.

"Goal? Your *goal?* Are you fucking kidding me? Did you come here just to piss me off all over again?" Alyssa screamed.

"Please just let me start over and explain everything!" Austin shouted, staring at Alyssa with pained eyes. "Please!"

Alyssa folded her arms. "Go."

Austin took a moment, making sure he was precise with his words. "I wasn't completely honest with you when I ended things."

"So more dishonesty?"

Austin could feel Alyssa's stare invading his very soul.

"I wasn't dishonest but it was more like half-truths."

"Austin, I swear to God—"

"All right, all right!" Austin knew he couldn't waste another second. "When I told you I had done horrible things, I was telling you the truth but what I didn't tell you was that I was doing those horrible things under your father's orders."

Alyssa's eyes widened with confusion.

"What?"

"That night at dinner wasn't the first time your father and I met each other. The truth is I've been working for your father for the last few months and he isn't the man you think he is."

Alyssa was beside herself. "I can't believe this."

"Please, you have to believe me. Everything I'm about to tell you is the truth and I just want you to—"

"For fuck's sake, Austin, I knew!" Alyssa erupted, interrupting Austin's plea.

Austin was taken aback and recoiled from the surprise.

"What do you mean you knew?"

"I knew what my father was doing, what he was *really* doing. I've known for years."

"You know?" Austin exclaimed.

"I'd have to be a complete idiot or my brother to not realize the truth. I didn't buy my father's stock market stories for a second and after some snooping and eavesdropping, I got a hint of what was really going on. Evan's disappearance sealed it for me. Project: Hercules was what my father was really doing with his life," Alyssa explained.

"But — but if you knew, then why didn't you tell me?"

"Tell you what exactly?" Alyssa began to mimic a theoretical conversation with Austin. "Hey, I just thought you should know that my father is a psychopath murderer who is deranged enough to think he can literally create a new world order."

Austin shrugged in understanding.

"But it's a good thing I didn't tell you because then you would have just run to my father and told him and that was the last thing I needed." Alyssa paced behind the counter, not able to contain her irritation. "I'm really surprised, Austin. In a million years, I would have never guessed that you'd be involved with something so disgusting."

"You've got it all wrong," Austin stated.

"Wrong? I don't see how. Seems pretty cut and dry to me," Alyssa argued.

"I promise you, it's not. It's time I told you everything."

Alyssa scoffed, "I can't imagine what else you could be hiding."

Austin's heart raced knowing what he was about to do, what he was about to say. Everything he was strictly told never to reveal was about to erupt from his lips like a geyser.

"You're right to think I'd never work for your father. The truth is that I was recruited by a covert government agency designed to investigate, hunt down, and defend against the most dangerous people in the world. The reason they sought me out was because of my close connection with your father. They knew if anyone would be able to work their way into his operation, it would be me. They trained me and tasked me with dismantling Project: Hercules from the inside."

Alyssa stared at Austin for what felt like an eternity.

"Are you kidding me? So what, you're like a secret agent?" Alyssa questioned skeptically.

"Covert operative." Austin thought for a moment. "Partial."

"You expect me to believe that? It sounds like total bullshit," Alyssa barked.

"Oh, but your father creating super humans in another country is totally above board," Austin snapped back.

Alyssa glanced away from Austin. "Good point. But then what was the close connection you had with him? How do you *really* know him?"

"Your father is the person who turned my life around after my father left. And the night we met, he literally saved my life. After that, he introduced me to Reign, his fight club. That was my connection to him, the connection used to get inside of Project: Hercules," Austin explained honestly.

Alyssa grunted in disgust. "Yeah, Reign, I remember finding

out about that little gem too. I had no idea you were a part of them. I should have pieced it together when you said you worked for a fighting gym."

"Like I said, half-truths." Austin chuckled. "But in all my years of knowing Damien, I really never knew he had a family and I definitely didn't know that *you*, of all people, were his daughter."

"Let's say I believe this extravagant story, what happens then?" Alyssa inquired.

"Nothing happens." Austin shrugged. "I'm not telling you so you'll forgive me and jump into my arms. I'm not telling you so everything will just go back to normal. I just needed you to know... everything."

"So this mission of yours, does it include killing my father?" Alyssa asked sternly.

Austin didn't expect Alyssa to ask such a question nor did he want to answer it.

"Honestly, most likely. I can't imagine a scenario where he surrenders willingly."

"I see," Alyssa replied simply, but then said something Austin never thought he would hear. "If you get the chance, do it."

"What?" Austin exclaimed in awe. "You *want* me to kill your father?"

"My father hasn't been *my father* since I was three years old. He's come and gone like a guest in his own home and treated me like a prisoner. He used his *passion* as an excuse to hold his family hostage. He's a liar and a murderer who treats innocent people like tools for his sick mission. He's a living, breathing virus to the world. And the worst part about it all was living in a house with people who had no idea or chose to ignore it."

"You think your mother is okay with what he does?" Austin asked.

"She's either okay with it or chooses to be in denial over it and Sean is completely oblivious to it. I was the only one sickened to even look at him every time he walked past me," Alyssa continued.

"I had no idea."

Alyssa leaned on the counter. "Looks like we both lied to each other."

Austin joined her. "Yeah, and we still had a great time. Imagine if we were honest from the beginning."

The two stared into each other's eyes.

"I can't believe I'm actually considering putting all this behind us," Alyssa admitted.

"Then I won't say anything else that might screw that up for me." Austin smirked.

Alyssa tried her hardest but couldn't stop a small laugh from escaping her body. Suddenly, the chime of the front door went off again and a man walked in slowly.

"Damn it, I forgot to lock up," Alyssa groaned. "I'm sorry, Sir, we're closed for the night. We open again at six."

The man didn't respond immediately, at first just alternating his stare between Alyssa and Austin.

"Okay, thanks," he said as he turned and exited the diner, barely getting the two words out while he was still inside.

Austin watched the man as he continued towards the corner, quickly pulling his cellphone out.

"Something's not right," Austin said under his breath.

"You say something?" Alyssa asked.

The man put the phone back in his pocket and abruptly sprinted away from the diner. Two black SUVs suddenly stopped in front from opposite sides of the street.

"He wasn't ordering, he was confirming," Austin continued.

The moment the doors of the trucks opened, Austin reacted.

"Alyssa, down!" he shouted and jumped over the counter, grabbing Alyssa and bringing her to the floor with him.

No later did a barrage of bullets smash through the large glass windows of the diner and begin to tear apart the entire interior. The constant hail of gunfire tore through the chairs and booths, pummeled the counter bar, and shattered the wall of liquor behind the counter, the contents now raining down onto Austin and Alyssa as they laid low to the floor. It seemed as though the bullets would never stop, the assailants alternating their reloads so someone was always firing upon the establishment.

"Follow me!" Alyssa shouted over the roaring barrage of bullets.

Alyssa began to crawl towards the doorway behind the counter, Austin following close behind. As they made it to the back, Alyssa pushed a nearby metal rack over onto the floor. She frantically searched for a container in the mess she just made but when she finally found it, she lunged for it with relief.

"What are you doing?" Austin questioned.

Alyssa didn't answer and simply grabbed the box, pressing her thumbprint into a small biometric scanner on the top. The box opened slightly on its own, Alyssa opening it the rest of the way and removing a pistol from within it.

"You stashed a lockbox at your job?" Austin exclaimed.

"Knowing who my father is, I didn't want to take any chances! I'm glad I didn't!" Alyssa pushed the magazine into the bottom of the pistol. "Sorry, only have one!"

Alyssa stealthily made her way back to the counter and

prepared to open fire. Alyssa took several deep breaths, building her confidence to spring up into the action. Just as she was about to, she was grabbed by Austin who held her in place, gesturing for her to wait. Finally, the bullets stopped firing and they could hear footsteps slowly creeping into the diner, the shattered glass crunching beneath their boots. Austin listened attentively and shared his findings with Alyssa.

Without speaking a word, Austin held up six fingers and Alyssa nodded with understanding. Suddenly, Alyssa popped up from behind the counter and opened fire on the intruders, instantly dropping two of them while Austin vaulted over the counter and charged a third. Two men began to open fire on Alyssa who quickly dropped behind the counter once more.

Austin wrestled with his assailant, quickly disarming him and dropping him to the floor. He grabbed the sidearm from the man's holster and removed it, opening fire on the others. All three collapsed to the floor, a single bullet piercing each of their skulls.

Finally, the chaos died down and Austin and Alyssa were now alone in the wreckage of what was once Shaw's Diner. Alyssa lifted herself from behind the counter and examined the aftermath.

"Are you okay?" Austin asked.

"Yeah, I'm fine."

"I guess your firearms training was another secret you kept from me," Austin scoffed.

"Told you Dad was over protective and paranoid. He wanted to make sure his kids could defend themselves. But I could say the same about you, James Bond," Alyssa snapped back.

Austin let out a small laugh under his breath. "Fair enough."

"The police should be here any second. What do we tell

them?" Alyssa asked.

"Nothing, we have to get out of here before they show up," Austin responded.

"You want to run from this?" Alyssa questioned with surprise.

"Do *you* want to stay and explain all this? I don't like it either but we won't be helping anybody if we stay, especially ourselves. That hit squad was definitely sent by your father which means he knows about me, you, or both," Austin explained, now searching the bodies for any helpful information.

"Doesn't that mean your cover is blown?" Alyssa asked.

"Doesn't that mean he just tried to have his own daughter killed?" Austin asked back.

"Fair enough," Alyssa replied. "But how could he have found out about you?"

"I have no clue but I can't worry about that now. We have to move."

Austin wiped down the pistol he was using and tossed it aside.

"Come on, grab your clothes and let's go. You can change at my place."

"Then what?" Alyssa asked.

"Then I round up everyone involved with me and get them somewhere safe. If Damien knows everything, then he'll go after my family and friends and I can't let that happen."

As several police officers slowly stepped into the warzone left by Austin and Alyssa, guns drawn, the two survivors made it safely out the back, racing towards Austin's apartment. Before long, Austin was sitting on his couch calling who he needed to while Alyssa was showering in the nearby bathroom.

"Come on, pick up, pick up," Austin murmured as the phone

rang.

"Hey, you've reached Nick, leave a message," the voicemail began.

"Damn it," Austin groaned. "Nick, Damien knows everything. As soon as you get this, get somewhere safe and if you speak to Josh or Demi before I do, warn them."

Austin hung up and immediately tried Josh.

"Yo, yo! It's Joshy boy, fill me in," his voicemail instructed.

"I don't know where you and Nick are but I need you to get somewhere safe. Damien knows everything. Don't come back to the apartment, I won't be here long."

Just then, his phone received a text message. He quickly opened it hoping it was someone getting back to him but instead, it was Christian.

"Mom is coming with me to drop off some more of my stuff. Be there in a few," the text read.

"Get here quick. The second you do, we'll all leave together," Austin typed back.

"Leave to go where?" Christian responded.

Before Austin answered, the bathroom door opened and Alyssa walked out, tossing her bag onto the nearby chair.

"So what now?" Alyssa asked, zipping up her hoodie.

"My mom and brother are on their way here to drop off some more of his stuff. The second they get here, we'll leave," Austin replied.

"Sounds good. Maybe on the way, you can explain more of this *covert operative* business." Alyssa looked around the apartment. "So this is your place, huh?"

"Yep, I hate to admit it but I could only afford it because of the money your dad paid me in Reign. Guess that income's gone," Austin explained.

"It's a beautiful place, I wish I saw it under better circumstances." Alyssa chuckled.

Austin looked at her disappointingly. "Yeah, me too."

Alyssa looked back at him and the two simply stared in silence. The moment was brief but felt like an eternity as Austin struggled to control himself, wanting to lunge at Alyssa with every ounce of passion that had been building inside of him. Alyssa never moved her eyes from Austin's glare, as if silently begging him to make the first move. Suddenly, an abrupt knock at the door broke the tense moment.

Austin practically deflated. "That's my family."

Austin ran over to the door and swung it open without fear though the figure standing before him was not who he expected. He stared for a moment as his brain tried to piece together the small bits of information he could gather to try and identify the stranger staring back at him. Finally, his eyes widened as the identity became all too clear.

"Agent Lancer?"

Without uttering a word, Lancer sent his palm stiffly into Austin's chest, Austin's body flying back and crashing through the end table behind him.

"Austin!" Alyssa quickly pulled the gun from her bag and fired several bullets at Lancer though none had the desired effect. "What the fuck?"

Lancer grabbed the wooden console table next to him and, with one hand, hurled it across the apartment at Alyssa. Alyssa dropped to the floor to dodge the flying piece of furniture, causing it to explode against the wall into countless pieces. Austin jumped and latched himself to Lancer's back.

"I'll distract him, get out of here!" Austin yelled to Alyssa who was just getting to her feet.

"I'm not leaving you!"

"Damn it, Alyssa, he's a super!" Austin exclaimed.

Lancer grabbed Austin by his shirt and pulled him off his back, throwing him across the room. Austin smacked into the wall and hit the floor with a hard thud. As he stepped towards Austin, a thick book smacked him in the temple. Lancer turned slowly and locked his stern, empty gaze onto Alyssa who was now throwing whatever was closest to her at him.

As she continued her bombardment of household items, Lancer stormed over to her and swung his arm around, whacking her in the side and sending her hurtling into the back of the couch, the couch flipping over from the impact and landing on top of her.

"Lancer, you need to stop. You're a D.A.R.C. agent, remember? Agent Hall and Walker, and Director Hardwick. You're one of the good guys," Austin pleaded, hoping his words could penetrate the emptiness in Lancer's mind.

Lancer ignored Austin's plea and grabbed him by the throat, hurling him through the dining room archway. Austin flew over the table and crashed through the large mirror hanging on the wall. Austin's body hit the floor as shards of glass rained down on him. He tried desperately to get to his feet but his body was riddled with pain.

Suddenly, several armed men filled the apartment, all aiming their rifles at Alyssa.

"Your father would appreciate your company by his side but he knew you wouldn't come willingly," one man stated.

Alyssa stumbled to her feet. "He has a weird way of showing his love."

"Do we have to make this messy?" the man questioned.

Alyssa scoffed, "I love messy."

Alyssa broke out unexpectedly, immediately disarming one of the men. Although she fought like a caged beast, the men overwhelmed her and managed to render her unconscious with a blow to the head.

"Alyssa," Austin murmured as he saw the group carry her out of the apartment.

Abruptly, the dining room table was pushed easily to the side and Austin's body was lifted off the floor. Again, as if he weighed no more than a feather, Austin was thrown across the apartment, crashing through the sheetrock wall of his bedroom.

Just outside the building, Debbie's car pulled up by the front doors.

"I hope you don't think I'm carrying all of this inside by myself," Debbie warned.

"Of course not." Christian opened the passenger door. "I'll carry the pillow." He laughed.

As the two began to organize the boxes in the trunk in preparation for carrying them inside, another car screeched to a halt, recklessly jumping the curb.

"Are you crazy?" Debbie exclaimed angrily.

Nick, Josh, and Demi jumped out of the car and made a mad dash towards the apartment building.

"Demi, stay with them and call 911!" Nick shouted as he and Josh continued to the doors.

"What's going on?" Christian asked confused.

"Nothing, nothing," Demi replied in a panicked state.

"Is something wrong with Austin?" Debbie asked.

Demi just stared at her, the fear apparent on her face.

"Is he in trouble?" Debbie continued.

Again, Demi couldn't muster up the words.

"Screw this." Christian pushed past the two women and

headed towards the doors.

The dust and debris from the sheetrock had settled as Austin pulled his half-conscious body out of the hole in his wall. He limply raised his arm to Lancer, his equalizing weapon now in hand. Before he could pull the trigger, Lancer easily knocked the gun from his grip and grabbed him by the throat, lifting him high into the air.

"Lancer... please," Austin begged through the tight grip.

Like before, Lancer had no reply and simply slammed Austin straight down onto the floor, his body smacking against the hardwood with a sickening thud. Without releasing his grip, Lancer effortlessly lifted Austin's body and slammed it down violently once more. Austin screamed out in agony as Lancer picked him up and planted him down yet again. Again and again and again and again, Austin's body crashed into the floor like a mere toy.

"Oh my God!" Josh declared as he and Nick made it into the open doorway.

Without a moment's hesitation, Nick lunged for the pistol on the floor and tossed it to Austin's reaching hand. The gun slid on the floor, almost perfectly into Austin's hand and, in one swift motion, Austin swayed the pistol directly in front of him and pulled the trigger. The bullet pierced Lancer's skull right between his eyes, Lancer collapsing over on top of Austin. Austin's arm dropped to his side as the entire room went silent, the fight finally concluded.

Nick and Josh flew across the room, pushing Lancer's body off of Austin's. Christian came in next, his eyes bulging with madness over the scene in front of him.

"Austin?" he whimpered and ran to his brother's side.

Debbie and Demi soon followed, now seeing the aftermath

of the hellacious fight. Debbie screamed, her eyes catching Nick performing chest compressions on her son.

"Come on, Austin, wake up. Wake the fuck up, damn it!" Nick continued pressing down firmly onto his chest.

"This isn't supposed to be happening," Josh cried.

"Austin, you can't — you can't be dead," Christian stammered, his eyes swelling to the brim.

"Don't say that, don't fucking say that!" Nick screamed. "He's not dead! He's not!"

Debbie knelt down and hugged Christian from behind as the two cried together.

"Come on, Austin," Nick grunted, pressing down on Austin's chest relentlessly. "Come back to us, damn it, come back."

Chapter 21

Final Planning

The ceiling's bright light flushed the room in white as small murmurs could be heard. The voices, indistinguishable yet familiar. As his eyes opened slowly and his senses returned, the voices became clearer.

"Austin!" Christian yelled and lunged into his brother's arms. "I'm so glad you're okay."

Austin hugged him back simply out of reflex but he was still confused as to what had happened.

"Where am I? What happened?"

"You died is what happened," Nick answered as he leaned over the bed.

"What?" Austin questioned.

"Yep. Dead. Clinically dead for one hundred and forty-six seconds and laid up for over a day," Josh added as he walked over with a cup of ice cream in hand, a spoonful entering his mouth as he finished speaking.

"I've been out for over a day?" Austin asked in shock.

Nick nodded. "You were in bad shape, Austin."

"I thought I was pretty clear in my voicemails. I told you guys to get somewhere safe and not come back to the apartment," Austin exclaimed.

"After hearing those voicemails, the *first* place we were going to go was the apartment. Don't you know us at all?" Josh jested.

"Before the cops showed up, the Men in Black came and scooped everybody up," Christian stated.

"The Men in Black are for aliens, Christian, you're looking more for Mulder and Scully," Josh debated.

"They were for aliens too, moron," Christian snapped back.

"We're in headquarters right now?" Austin inquired.

"Yeah, their infirmary. They brought everybody in. Guess covert went out the window on this one," Nick answered.

Austin's eyes widened as the worst memory returned and shocked his system.

"Alyssa! They took her!" Austin popped up from the bed and immediately felt the immense pain radiate throughout his entire body.

"Calm down, who took her?" Nick inquired.

"While I was busy with Lancer, some of Damien's men came in and abducted her. They took her to him."

"But she's not in any immediate danger, right? I mean they brought her to her dad," Josh chimed in.

Austin looked at him sternly. "Her dad already tried to kill both of us. He doesn't care if she lives or dies."

Just then, a loud gasp was heard from the doorway and Debbie quickly charged into the room. She latched her arms tightly around Austin's neck.

"Not so tight, Mom." He smiled.

"You're lucky you've been unconscious. My mind has had a little time to process all of this." Debbie smiled with relief. "I'm so happy you're all right."

"I'm sorry I worried you," Austin replied.

"I'm guessing this is what you couldn't tell me when you came to visit that day. I have to be honest; my wildest imagination couldn't come up with all this," she admitted.

"I had a similar reaction." Demi chuckled as she walked over, wrapping herself in Nick's arm.

"There's one thing I don't understand. Why? Why do all this for them?" Debbie asked.

Austin looked at his mother with a genuine gaze. "They said they would find Dad."

Debbie's body jerked back in shock. "That's what all this was for? So they could find your father? Why would you do all this just for that?"

"After all these years, I still need the closure. I need him to answer for what he did, answer my questions, and explain himself. If D.A.R.C. can give me that, then I'll do what I have to," Austin explained.

Suddenly, there was a knock at the door. Geer stepped in with a smirk already on his face.

"Hey, kid."

"Hey, Geer."

"Can Austin and I have the room for a moment?" Geer asked.

Everybody made their way out of the room.

"Geer, they took Alyssa and brought her to Damien. I have to go."

"Slow down, kid. You're not going anywhere in this condition. If you really want to save her, then be patient," Geer responded.

"Alyssa doesn't have that kind of time."

Geer pulled up a chair. "Think about it, if he really wanted her dead, he would have just let Lancer do her in too. Why interrupt Lancer's fight just to take her away from it? I'm sure he has other plans for her. One thing is for sure, he wanted you dead.

How do you feel?"

"Not bad considering I was bounced like a basketball."
Austin chuckled but quickly curled up from the pain.

"That's a solid attitude to have."

"Thank you for training me. I feel like I would have never
made it through yesterday without it," Austin acknowledged.

"Don't forget, Alexei trained you too, plus you had your own
experience from your little fight club. I can't take all the credit,"
Geer joked.

"Just take the damn compliment," Austin barked.

Geer laughed. "Well, you're welcome."

Austin thought for a moment. "You know, I always wanted
to ask you, what made you get into all of this?"

"That's a loaded question, kid." Geer leaned back in the
chair.

"I've got time." Austin shrugged.

"I didn't start out in D.A.R.C. I worked my way up the ranks
in the military but once I got to a level that would take me out of
the field, I switched over to another division. As long as I was
out there instead of behind a desk, I was happy. I bounced around
a little bit and eventually found myself on D.A.R.C.'s shortlist.
They wanted me to become one of their Elite Special Agents but
I turned them down, opting to lead Gladiator Squad instead."

"Why so intent on staying in the field?"

"If I'm doing all this to fight for my country, then I want to
actually fight. I want to be out there; I want to be able to hit the
enemy myself. I take nothing away from the tech guys, they can
drone strike a town and wipe it out all from behind a computer
screen but, for me, I need to be down in the trenches."

"Why?" Austin asked simply.

"I don't know, I guess I just always felt like that was what gave me the most immediate satisfaction. But I guess training the next generation can give me just as much satisfaction, even if it isn't immediate." Geer smiled widely.

"I'll make you proud, Geer."

Geer laughed under his breath and stood up from his chair. "You already have, kid."

As the day dragged on, Austin pulled himself from the bed and slowly made his way to the C.O.R. He banged on the door and it soon opened.

"There he is! How do you feel?" Mike asked exuberantly.

"Put all my Reign fights into one, I still never came out this bad," Austin responded as he stepped inside.

"Regardless, it's good to see you on your feet again. That was a close call," Hardwick stated.

"Thank you for bringing everyone in. I know the last thing you wanted were a bunch of civilians in here but I appreciate it," Austin spoke with gratitude.

"We couldn't leave them out there to get picked off by Damien. At this point, no one is safe," Mike replied.

"What about Susan and Sean? Why aren't they here too?"

"We determined that they weren't at risk but we're keeping surveillance on them anyway. Keeping them in their normal routines might keep Damien from going into overdrive," Grant explained.

"The same can't be said for Alyssa. Damien's men took her from my apartment. We have to go save her." Austin gently placed himself in a chair.

"We're going to do more than that. We'll save her when we take down his whole damn compound." Grant pulled a chair over. "But what the hell happened? How did Damien find out about you in the first place?"

"I have no idea. Everything seemed perfectly normal when I last saw him, nothing to suggest he knew the truth. Next thing I know, there's a hit squad leveling Shaw's Diner."

"And then Lancer." Hardwick's tone was that of pure sorrow.

"He turned our own agent into one of his experiments. This bastard is going to pay," Grant exclaimed.

"Not only did he turn Lancer into one of his supers but he clearly felt like he was field ready," Mike started. "Lancer was able to, one way or another, make his way from Damien's compound back to the states and to Austin's front door. The mental and emotional instability must not be a problem any longer."

"If that's true, then we have even less time on the clock than we thought," Grant added.

"Okay, so what's the plan? Whatever you want to do, I'm ready," Austin stated.

Hardwick gave him a stern look. "Austin, you can barely walk. Car accident victims have better scans than you. You're in no condition to join this raid."

"With all due respect, Sir, he has Alyssa and I'm not going to sit back and do nothing while someone else is responsible for her safety," Austin declared.

"It would be irresponsible to let you out into the field. This raid must be a success on all levels. We can't risk something going wrong because you're not at one hundred percent."

"You also can't risk something going wrong because I wasn't there. I know that compound better than anyone else. Send in a task force for the raid but send me in to go after Damien and Alyssa."

"It's not a matter of *if* we think you're skilled enough, it's a

286

matter of if we think you're healthy enough. All the determination in the world won't matter if you collapse at Damien's feet," Grant argued.

"Guys, I swear to you, I can do this. When do you guys plan on departing?" Austin questioned.

"Tomorrow, 0600 hours," Mike answered.

"Okay, I'll be ready by then. I don't care about my injuries or the pain, I'm ready for this." Austin's stare was steeled and determined. "Let me do this."

"It's not like he'll be alone." Mike smiled slightly.

"What a surprise, you're defending him," Grant growled, tilting his head towards Mike.

Mike chuckled. "Look, one way or another, we're still sending in a massive ground force to raid the compound. With all that distraction, Austin could sneak right into the lab."

Mike moved his gaze over to Hardwick, Grant quickly doing the same. The entire room now stared at Hardwick waiting for his executive decision.

He exhaled; a reluctant expression dawned on his face. "Fine but Geer accompanies you every step of the way."

"I wouldn't have it any other way." Austin smiled.

"Mike, show him what we've got," Hardwick ordered.

Mike pulled up a digital, three-dimensional model of Damien's compound on the large screen.

"We depart at 0600 and, upon landing in Russia, we will rendezvous with our Russian contact, Vlad, at the Nexus Point which will also be where Grant and I will monitor the raid from."

"What's a Nexus Point?" Austin inquired.

"A Nexus Point is a codename used by D.A.R.C. to dictate a base of operations during large scale missions," Geer interrupted as he walked into the C.O.R.

He sat down next to Austin.

"Sorry I'm late."

"Right on time, Geer." Hardwick smiled.

Mike grabbed a laser pointer and aimed it at the digital model.

"We're planning a four-pronged attack on the compound, a ground force infiltrating on every side armed with our new magic bullets. You and Geer will be a part of Alpha Team and storm the front gate. Once inside, you'll make your way through the mansion and out the back, putting you closer to the lab." Mike clicked a button on his keyboard and the model changed to the lab structure. "Once inside, you are to plant C4 charges on all main faculties of the lab, the central computer terminal, the core processor, the cooling tanks, the chemical freezer, and the server room. For good measure, plant one in all four corners of the structure."

"Now, all charges will be prepped with a five minute timer so plant them and haul ass. With the lab destroyed, his formula, specimens, and research will be wiped out," Grant added.

"In addition to the Russian compound, we are deploying simultaneous raids on his trainyard storage unit, his safehouse in Osaka, and his home right here in New York," Mike continued.

"Once the lab is destroyed, you are free to hunt down Church with extreme prejudice," Grant announced.

Hardwick stood up from his seat. "I know I don't have to state how crucial this mission is. With this single, coordinated strike, we will wipe Damien Church and his legacy from existence. Stay sharp, stay focused. Dismissed."

The next morning, everyone gathered in the headquarters' hangar for departure. As the tiltrotor aircrafts prepped for liftoff, Austin looked back at everyone he was leaving behind.

"Austin, are you ready?" Mike walked up next to him.

"Yeah, let's finish this."

"All right, we'll see you onboard."

Mike continued up the ramp of the plane. Geer adjusted his duffle bag on his shoulder and patted Austin on his.

"Don't take too long." Geer gestured to Austin's support team.

Austin walked over to Christian.

"You okay?" he asked with a playful smile.

"Yeah, I think so. After seeing you come back from the dead once, I'm pretty sure you'll be fine." Christian chuckled.

Austin joined in on the laughter. "Good to know."

The two brothers embraced, neither shedding a tear but both knowing just how much the other meant to them. Austin stepped down the line to his mother.

"I know this is the last thing you ever expected but I promise it'll all work out. And when this is over, we can go see Dad together," Austin exclaimed.

Debbie brushed Austin's shirt slightly as if cleaning him up or prepping him. "You know, I thought I'd be shattered over all this but, for some reason, I feel like this is what you were always meant to do."

Austin scoffed. "Like a regular Gracey Burnes."

"Yeah, just like Gracey Burns. Be safe and come home soon." Debbie smiled and hugged Austin tight.

Nick, Josh, and Demi were patiently waiting next.

"When you get back, I want to hear every single detail." Josh beamed.

"Be safe, don't make me worry like on fight nights," Demi joked.

"Go take that son of a bitch down and bring Alyssa home,"

Nick added.

Austin simply looked at his friends, people who were there for him at his lowest points. People who supported him even when he didn't always deserve it and walked alongside him on this journey whether they knew it or not.

"Thank you," he said simply and lunged into the group, the four huddling together for a hug.

"Austin, we have to go!" Geer shouted from the plane's ramp.

Austin started walking backwards towards the plane, not wanting to take his eyes off any of the people he was leaving behind. As the planes finally took off, Austin prepared himself. He was on his way to Damien and the final moments of his long, arduous mission.

Chapter 22

No More Games

The aircrafts landed vertically in the center of a large forest clearing. As everyone exited, a small group of soldiers were standing by to greet them.

"Michael, Grant, how are you, my friends?" The man standing upfront smiled.

"Not too bad, Vladimir," Grant replied.

"And we'll be even better after this godforsaken mission is behind us," Mike added.

Vlad locked eyes with Austin as he walked down the ramp. "You must be Austin? I was briefed quite heavily about you before your arrival."

"Nice to meet you." Austin shook Vlad's hand.

"Very good, let us move this meeting into the camp. It is right beyond that tree line."

D.A.R.C.'s forces went over the plan one last time with Vlad's men and prepared their equipment for the next morning. As nightfall fell onto the forest, Austin laid in his cot inside one of the many tents set up around the camp. He stared, wide-eyed, up at the top of the tent, thinking of his lengthy journey so far.

"Just wanted to check up on you before tomorrow. Think your body can make it?" Geer stepped into the tent.

Austin sat up. "A couple of aches here and there but I'll live. Fighting for Reign all these years, I'm pretty used to pain."

"I thought you were undefeated?" Geer smirked.

"I was, doesn't mean I never got hit." Austin chuckled.

"Well, just in case." Geer tossed a bottle to Austin.

Austin caught it and began to read the label.

"I don't understand a single word on this," he admitted.

"You don't have to. Just know it's from D.A.R.C.'s R&D department and it's a pretty cutting edge pain blocker. It may not be Project: Hercules level but it'll get you through the mission," Geer explained.

"Are these safe?"

"Trust me, D.A.R.C. wouldn't spend money and resources to create something that will kill its agents." Geer thought for a moment. "As long as you don't take two at once."

Austin laughed. "Thanks for this."

"So body's fine, what about your mind. Where's your head at?"

"I'm good, I've made peace with what has to be done. I learned at the start of this whole thing that Damien is not who I thought he was. Tomorrow is long overdue. It's crazy to think about how far we've come."

"You mean how far *you've* come. Don't get me wrong, I appreciate the inclusion but this was all you. Mike, Grant, myself, even Hardwick, have been doing stuff like this for longer than we'd like to admit. You came into this as a civilian but proved yourself time and time again. You got results that Mike and Grant could have only prayed for and you even managed to shut Grant up once or twice, and trust me, that is no easy feat. Make no mistake about it, Austin, you're special and believe me, they notice."

Austin couldn't help but smile at Geer's inspiring words. "Thanks, Geer."

Geer pulled the entrance of the tent open, ready to leave. "Now get some rest, we have a big day tomorrow."

As the sun slowly peeked up over the thick forest, the troops prepared to move out. The countless soldiers filed into several armored trucks and, in a matter of minutes, they were on their way to the compound. Austin popped a single pill and readied himself. As the trucks bounced down the snow-covered roads, the memories of Austin's journey suddenly flooded his mind once more.

"Spending a night in jail just to be recruited by a covert government agency tasked with the duty of hunting down unknown and untouchable threats," Austin said aloud.

"Sounds totally fucking ridiculous, doesn't it?" Geer laughed.

"We're approaching the compound, safeties off!" the driver of their truck announced.

Their truck screeched to a halt outside the front gates of the compound as the other trucks covered the three other sides.

"Let's move!"

The back door opened and Geer jumped out, leading the soldiers straight into the compound. Immediately, gunfire echoed through the forest as bullets filled the four walls of the property. Austin and Geer sprinted across the front yard as allied agents and Damien's private army exchanged gunfire.

"Keep going, we'll cover you!" one of the agents yelled over the orchestra of assault rifles.

They obliged and kept running toward the mansion. Two guards stepped in their way, hoping to stop them. Geer knocked one to the ground and sent two bullets into his chest. Austin stabbed the other in the gut, dragging the knife through the man's sternum.

"Damn, I didn't teach you that one!" Geer exclaimed.

Austin slipped his knife back into the holder on his chest. "No, Alexei did."

Damien slowly enjoyed a glass of red wine in his office while Boris read a book in the nearby armchair.

"So this is what you do here? Absolutely nothing?" Alyssa mocked, her hands tied helplessly behind the chair she was bound to.

Damien chuckled. "You have no idea the empire I've created here. I'm respected, feared, and soon, I will put the entire world on notice."

"Wow, someone is self-conscious. Must feel pretty small to need so much reassurance."

"Shut your mouth!" Damien screamed as he leapt from his chair.

He slowly made his way toward Alyssa.

"I gave you everything you've ever wanted! I put a roof over your head, a quite astounding roof for that matter! You were always fed, clothed, protected, you never wanted for anything! I made sure you could defend yourself and always kept you close to make sure you were safe! And this! This is how you repay my love?"

Damien knelt down and hovered over Alyssa.

"You chose that rotten, disloyal traitor, Austin, over your own father," he snarled in her ear.

As he moved away from her, Alyssa stared at him with nothing but disdain and, without warning, spit in his face.

"How dare you!" Boris erupted from his chair, the book he was reading dropping to the floor.

"You disgust me. You're nothing but a selfish, sadistic monster. You may have Mom and Sean fooled but not me. I've known about the devil in my house for a long time," Alyssa growled.

Damien stayed silent until his mouth subtly bent into a smile.

"I don't hate you, sweetheart, I don't even blame you," Damien revealed. "Your hatred of me simply stems from misunderstanding and that is my fault. I should have brought you into this life a long time ago."

Damien turned and headed back towards his desk.

"If you only knew the extraordinary work we've been doing here and the possibilities we've created. But I'm ready to rectify that mistake right now. I brought you here so you can stand by my side when the state of the world changes. I'm giving you a front row seat to the future and one day, you'll be grateful I did."

"Go fuck yourself," Alyssa barked.

"He is your father!" Boris shouted.

"It's all right, Boris. Soon, nothing she says will matter. My soldiers will be ready and we'll be standing at the forefront of a new link in the evolutionary chain. Nothing can stop us now, especially not Austin."

Alyssa stared at Damien with hatred but tears began to form in her eyes.

"Did you really care that much for him? He was nothing! He was a lost soul, clinging on to any semblance of a family he could find! He was just as lost now as he was when I found him in that train yard!" Damien lifted his wine glass once more. "And now, thanks to Agent Lancer, Austin has been put out of his pathetic misery."

"Speaking of which, Sir, Lancer was supposed to report in after disposing of Austin. Shouldn't we be more alarmed about his silence?" Boris questioned with worry.

"Nonsense, Boris. What on Earth could I possibly have to

worry about?"

Suddenly, the gunfire erupted from outside causing Damien to jolt, the red wine spilling freely onto his shirt.

"What the fuck is going on out there?" Damien growled.

The door swung open as a guard rushed into the room.

"Sir, a small military force has stormed the compound. They have heavy fire power and it has been confirmed that Austin Michaels is among them."

Alyssa perked up in her chair with hope while Damien's eyes bulged from his skull to an uncomfortable degree.

"That's impossible, he has to be dead!"

"No, Sir, he's here, several of our men have radioed in the same sighting," the guard continued.

Alyssa laughed. "You're right, I am grateful to have this front row seat. Now I get to see you crumble."

Damien threw his cup across the room, the glass shattering into countless pieces against the wall.

"Get every available body out there! I want them all dead! Except for Austin, I want him brought to me!"

"What do we do, Sir?" Boris asked.

"We're moving and we're taking my ungrateful daughter with us." Damien cut Alyssa's binds and ripped her from her chair, storming out of the room hastily.

Austin opened the front doors to the mansion and quickly met a firing squad that was standing atop the staircase. He and Geer ducked back behind the wall to the side of the door as a handful of agents ran up to meet them, one tossing a stun grenade inside the lobby. When it detonated, they ran inside and started firing. Austin and Geer didn't waste the opportunity, ducking through the mayhem and running along the side of the staircase. A guard popped out from a door on the side but Austin quickly disposed of him. Austin turned and saw four guards standing firmly with their rifles aimed high.

In an instant, all four men were gunned down with deadly precision, a single bullet to each of their skulls. Geer walked up to Austin with his pistol still raised.

"Thanks."

Geer nodded. "Keep moving."

As the two came to the back door, a knife suddenly whisked by their faces, imbedding itself in the adjacent wall. They turned, seeing Alexei standing before them.

"We have unfinished business to attend to, Austin. Allow me to teach you one more lesson." He grinned sinisterly.

Before Austin could reply, Geer placed his hand on Austin's chest and held him back.

"I got this. Get to that lab and complete the objective."

"Geer, are you sure? We can take him together."

"No, we don't have time to waste. You need to destroy that lab as soon as possible. I'll handle Alexei."

Austin stared at Geer somberly, debating his options. "All right, good luck."

Austin blasted through the backdoor and into the courtyard while Geer lowered his gun and pulled out his combat knife, Alexei doing the same.

"Do you have any idea how many people I've killed?" Alexei asked, a deranged smile crawling onto his face.

Geer adjusted his grip on the handle of his knife, making sure to hold it tight. "Only cowards brag about their number."

The two skilled soldiers leapt at each other. Both tried effortlessly to end the fight quickly but the other was too skilled, blocking or dodging with ease. Their fight made it back toward the lobby which was now void of any life.

"Do you honestly believe you can best me?" Alexei asked.

"Trust me, it's just a matter of time." Geer snuck in a quick jab straight into Alexei's face.

Alexei backed up as the blood trickled from his nose. When he wiped the blood from his face and examined it, he looked up at Geer and smiled, as if enjoying the challenging fight. Alexei sprung back into action not allowing Geer a moment of reprieve.

Austin ran through the snow behind the mansion and made it safely to the laboratory entrance. Upon entering the building, he could hear the explosions, gunfire, and screams coming from around the compound.

He made his way to the elevator and down to the main lab. As the doors opened, he raised his gun and walked out diligently onto the catwalk though it didn't take long to realize that no one was there. The main power was off but an orange glow covered the lab as the emergency systems blared to life.

Without wasting a single second, Austin began planting the explosive charges on every point of interest. As he finished planting the final charge, he regrouped in the center of the lab. He looked over to the rows of pods, most of them still occupied with a body.

"So many casualties in this war against Damien. Innocent people who didn't deserve this kind of hell, I'm sorry."

Austin found himself apologizing to the unconscious men and women slumbering inside the pods as if it were his fault they were there.

"Austin Michaels!"

Austin heard his name called out dramatically. He stopped. Before even turning around, Austin's mind told him he knew the voice, just not from where. Someone he met during his time working for Damien? No. Another agent from D.A.R.C. who made their way down to the lab? No. Then it hit him. The voice's familiarity was cancelled out by the sheer impossibility of who the voice belonged to. Austin turned around slowly, the entire time hoping he was mistaken but, as he locked eyes with the man before him, the frightening truth washed over him like a violent wave.

"Jeff?" Austin deflated in awe.

"In the flesh, brother. Did you miss me?"

In that single reply, Austin could tell there was something different about him. He had an air about him, arrogant, superior, much more than before.

"How?"

"It's actually a great story. When I first started working for Damien, it didn't take long for him to peg me as a D.A.R.C. agent. He called me into his office, just me and him, and immediately put a gun to my head. I was five seconds away from being executed and realized that I would be dying for nothing. I begged him to spare me and even offered to be one of his test subjects. Anything would be better than being six feet under. Damien couldn't pass up the chance to have a D.A.R.C. agent as one of his supers so he faked my death and threw me in a pod." Jeff paused in thought momentarily. "Well, that's not entirely true. He didn't just fake my death. There was definitely an O'Neal in that box, it just wasn't me. Dear old Dad was very apologetic at the end, just a bit too late though."

"You killed your own father? You turned on D.A.R.C.? And aligned yourself with Damien?" Austin questioned with pure disgust.

"Don't act like you're above me, Austin. You know nothing," Jeff snarled.

"I've been everywhere on this compound for months. How

come I never saw you?"

"Turns out my blood was actually quite useful for Project: Hercules. Apparently, it counterattacked specific anomalies in the serum: the mental and emotional instability, all of it solved with my blood. I'm the reason the Hercules formula was perfected. Damien kept me in a secret pod that only he and Dr. Arushka knew about. Not even Boris knew about my allegiance; you were no exception."

"So, I guess I can thank you for blowing my cover."

"Oh, that was the best part. When I woke up, Damien immediately started blabbering about how you joined. To be honest, he was genuinely excited and proud. The second I heard that, I told him everything. How you were supposed to be my partner because of your connection to him and how my 'death' forced Mike and Grant to use you."

"Mike and Grant thought the world of you. They believed in you!"

"Oh, spare me the sermon! Mike and Grant care only about themselves. Give it time, you'll come to see them in the same light."

"You betrayed your agency and your friends!"

"They were never my friends! They were my employers, my superiors, and I was just their little soldier. You may have been thrown into the spotlight for now but that's only temporary. Soon, you'll become an expendable number just like the rest of us."

Austin gripped his rifle and readied himself. "I'm done talking to a piece of shit traitor like you."

Jeff smiled playfully like a child. "Oh good, the killing can start."

Austin pulled the trigger on his rifle but Jeff grabbed the

nearby table and hurled it at him. The bullets that managed to leave the barrel of Austin's gun collided with the table, none of them reaching Jeff. Austin jumped aside as the table smashed into the floor. He quickly popped up onto his feet but even his quick reaction time was too slow for Jeff, who was already standing over him.

A single strike to the chest was enough to send Austin flying across the lab and into the wall, his body sliding down and smacking the floor with a thud. Jeff grabbed the strap of Austin's rifle and tugged on it, forcibly pulling Austin to his feet, and heaved him through the air.

Austin hit the floor and slid into the siding of a long workstation. Before Austin could even catch his breath, Jeff grabbed him by the throat and lifted him into the air, slamming him down onto the top of the station and dragging him across the entire length of it.

Glass equipment, wooden stands and holders, laptops and desktops, Austin crashed through all of it before being tossed off the opposite side and smacking into a door leading to a small munitions storage. Austin panted heavily as he pushed himself to his hands and knees.

"This could work." Austin quickly formulated a last-ditch plot in his mind.

He pulled himself to a vertical base, his body screaming in pain despite the pill he had swallowed.

"You were so determined to destroy Damien's empire because of what it did to your family, because of how he took your father away from his responsibilities at home."

"Oh, don't worry. Before I was incubated, I had that heart to heart with my old man I was looking for... right before I put a bullet in his head." Jeff cackled.

"Have you really become this sadistic? How could you just turn against everything you were?"

"I didn't want to die. It was as simple as that. Do you think Mike or Grant cared that I was dead? They mourned me for all of thirty seconds before contacting you. I was just a pawn knocked off the chess board, a pawn they easily replaced with another." Jeff gestured to Austin.

"You're just a coward."

"Don't bullshit me, Austin! If you were in my position and had your back against the wall, you would beg to join too. Nobody wants to die especially for two assholes sitting safely behind a desk."

"I've lived my whole life with my back against the wall but I never gave up and I certainly never gave in! I surrender myself to Damien and then what? What's my life after that if I sold my soul to have it? You treated me like I was just some street punk with nothing but two fists to my name but now I see that was only an act because the truth is, you knew I was better than you. It wasn't just my skill outshining you that you feared, it was my determination, my will, my drive. You saw the potential I had and you knew you would be nothing next to it. And even now, nothing's changed. You're still nothing," Austin exclaimed with fiery passion.

Jeff growled with anger as he charged at Austin in a fury. Without a chance of defense, Jeff ran into Austin, crashing through the door of the storage room and into the shelving unit on the back wall. Jeff held Austin up by the throat.

"If your goal was to infuriate me, then you succeeded. I could snap your neck like a twig right between my fingers but I'd rather make you suffer."

"Sorry, I'm on the clock," Austin replied and kicked Jeff in his knee with as much force as he could muster.

Jeff dropped to one knee as it involuntarily buckled from the impact and loosened his grip enough for Austin to escape his clutches and sprint out of the room.

"You can't run from me, Austin!" Jeff shouted but something quickly caught his eye.

He looked down and saw two grenades clattering together beneath his feet, the safety pin missing from both. Jeff simply scoffed before the grenades exploded, triggering the rest of the munitions in the room to follow. The massive, fiery explosion roared out of the storage room, the sheer pressure knocking Austin to the floor. As silence fell upon the lab, the sprinkler system activated, water now raining down from the overhead spouts.

Austin pushed himself to his feet, pain-filled grunts unwillingly exiting his mouth. He slowly shuffled towards the stairs of the catwalk to make his exit when, suddenly, a spray of bullets crashed next to him. Austin turned around and saw his prime target standing before him. Damien, Boris, Alyssa, and four armed soldiers now stood across from a battered and beaten Austin.

"Even after everything that's transpired, I still feel the need to be honest with you. What you've accomplished is tremendously impressive and if I wasn't so blindly enraged, I would be proud. I assume this means Lancer was a failure through and through."

Austin ignored Damien's ramblings as his eyes fixated on Alyssa.

"I'm going to get you out of here," he declared.

"Get her out of here?" Damien began to laugh. "You're not leaving this lab alive, so my daughter isn't going anywhere."

"Your own daughter, Damien. I guess no one is sacred to you. No one is safe," Austin debated.

"Nothing and no one is going to stand in my way of achieving my goal and that includes you and my nuisance of a daughter. To you, it might seem like lunacy to treat her this way but, to me, her betrayal hurt that deep. I'm taking necessary action," Damien explained, still calm and collected.

"I can't believe I ever saw you as a father, you sick son of a bitch!"

Damien stared at Austin with a stern gaze.

"Hold him down."

"No!" Alyssa yelled as she tried unsuccessfully to wriggle away from the guard holding her.

Two guards rushed Austin, his body already too weak to defend himself. They each grabbed an arm and forced him down to his knees. As Austin knelt before Damien, completely open and vulnerable, he simply stared at him.

"Let me ask you something, Austin. Have you ever taken a life before?" he asked abruptly.

"Give me a gun and I'll show you," Austin replied with full sincerity in his voice.

Damien chuckled. "No, no, anyone can simply *end* a life." Suddenly, he wrapped his hands around Austin's throat and began to squeeze. "But have you ever *taken* a life? Have you ever killed someone with your bare hands and stolen the life from them? Watched as their very soul left their eyes?" Damien seethed with fury.

"Stop it!" Alyssa pleaded.

"Here's another front row opportunity, sweetheart. You get to watch Austin die right before your very eyes." Damien bubbled with a crazed stare.

Austin couldn't grab an ounce of air as Damien closed his throat with his hands. With no way to defend himself, Austin sat helplessly as Damien slowly strangled him to death.

Just then, as if by some act of miracle, the set charges finally ran out of their five minute timers. Explosions detonated all around the lab, devastating eruptions of fire and massive shockwaves of pressure wreaking havoc throughout the facility. Even with the already activated sprinkler system, the abundance of water couldn't contain the raging fires.

Austin slowly opened his eyes, not being able to comprehend that he was still alive. Though his vision was blurry and still readjusting, he could still make out the overwhelming carnage before him. The lab was in ruins, unfixable and unrecoverable. Across from Austin, Damien pushed himself to his feet, staggering to keep himself steady. He looked around in awe at the annihilation before him. He screamed something aggressively though Austin couldn't make out what it was, a constant ringing occupying his eardrums.

Damien stood over the corpse of the guard who was holding on to his daughter and shoved it aside, revealing a still breathing Alyssa underneath. Damien pulled Alyssa to her feet and looked around one last time before limping his way in the opposite direction to the main elevator. With every bit of strength he could gather, Austin stumbled to his feet and began to follow Damien's path. He didn't make it far before his arm was grabbed from the side. Austin turned in a panic only to see Boris barely standing on two feet, severe burns covering the majority of his body.

"I will end your life. Kill you and take your corpse to Damien. Then he will see *me* as his right-hand man! I will be the son he never had! I will be—"

Without listening to another word, Austin shoved the already fragile Boris with great force, his body falling back helplessly into a large, jagged piece of metal that easily skewered him at the sternum. Boris took his last, labored breath as his eyes glazed over in a blank stare.

Not wanting to lose track of Damien and Alyssa, Austin hurried to catch up. His chase brought him to a wall panel on the far side of the lab which led to a secret hallway. At the end of this newly discovered path was a ladder which led directly to the surface. As Austin made it to the foot of the ladder, he looked up and saw Damien already almost out of view, constantly pushing Alyssa up every rung. He prepared himself to climb, hand on one rung and foot on another, when suddenly, the entire building began to rattle.

Knowing that the structure was mere seconds away from imploding on itself, Austin began to climb vigorously. Another strong rumble caused Austin to lose his footing halfway up, barely holding on with one hand. He quickly regrouped and continued to the top where he pulled himself out of a snow-covered hill in the opposite corner of the compound from the lab shed.

Bullets could still be heard in the distance but it was clear that most of the fighting had subsided. Austin continued following behind Damien who made his way to the small parking section. Damien walked up to the nearest car and tossed Alyssa into the passenger seat. Damien jumped into the driver's seat and started the car, peeling his tires as he raced out of the compound. Austin followed close behind, jumping into the next available car and quickly turning out of the compound as well.

From within the second floor of the mansion, Geer and Alexei were fighting with everything they had to see who could best the other. Having both been disarmed of their knives, devastating fists and lethal kicks were delivered but neither backed down.

"You are an impressive fighter; it has been an honor to fight someone so skilled." Alexei smirked.

Geer matched his smile as he wiped blood from his mouth. "The honor is all yours."

Alexei growled and jumped back into the physical mayhem. Geer easily deflected his desperate swings and delivered a stiff kick into Alexei's chest. The double glass doors behind him shattered as Alexei's body crashed through them. He crawled to the railing of the balcony and pulled himself up enough to get to a sitting base. Geer stood over him, ready to do what was necessary.

"Do it, claim your victory." Alexei spat a glob of blood from his mouth.

Suddenly, the shed as well as the ground surrounding it caved in on itself, the damage finally taking its toll. Geer's attention perked to the destruction for only a moment but it was enough for Alexei to gain the advantage. He produced a switchblade from his boot and instantly stabbed it into Geer's side. Geer winced, letting out a slight grunt. Alexei tossed Geer to the floor and, by the time Geer removed the knife and regrouped, Alexei was gone.

Geer pressed his hands firmly against the wound as he laid his head back against the railing in disappointment.

"Fuck."

The two cars raced down the snowy road, barely keeping their tires firmly against the asphalt. Unless something drastic was done, Austin was never going to catch Damien.

"Sorry, Alyssa."

Austin inhaled deeply and slammed his foot down on the gas

pedal, shooting his car forward and into the side of Damien's.

The sudden and forceful contact caused Damien to lose control of his vehicle, the two cars now pinned together, spiraling uncontrollably off the road. An impactful collision with a large, imbedded rock in the ground stopped both cars' motion instantly. The frigid air silenced as everything seemed to stand still, both cars heavily damaged, thick, black smoke pluming from their hoods. No one made a move. No one made a sound.

Chapter 23

Final Showdown

The driver side door to Austin's car fell off the body, smashing into the ground as Austin dragged himself from the car. He tried desperately to regain his composure, distracted by the feeling of a trail of blood streaming down the side of his face. As he stumbled to his feet, Damien pushed himself out of his wreckage as well, the two men now standing across one another on a cliff overlooking the vast blanket of thick forest nearly sixty feet below.

"It's over, Damien!" Austin shouted.

"Nothing is over! As long as I'm still breathing, I can rebuild! I can start over! You may have ruined everything for now but I'll just continue my work even faster than before!" Damien barked.

Austin's firm stare locked eyes with Damien. "You won't be breathing much longer."

"You think you can kill me?" Damien laughed. "You fought Lancer, O'Neal, survived that explosion and this crash. As surprising as it is that you're still standing, you must be held together with duct tape and paper clips at this point. Face it, son, you're standing on your own burial site."

Austin's lip quivered in anger. "I'm not your son."

The two men charged towards each other like two raging bulls, Austin attacking high but Damien attacking low. Damien quickly took Austin to the ground, throwing fists relentlessly into him. Within seconds, Damien's fists were covered in Austin's blood but the assault did not stop there. Damien tossed Austin's limp body into the side of one of the cars, his head bouncing off the mangled frame. As Austin leaned back helplessly against the car, Damien stalked him like a hardened predator.

"Physical combat is such a beautiful thing. It allows us as humans to express our emotions in the most primal of ways."

Austin tried to create distance between them, crawling slowly away from Damien, a trail of red snow beneath him. Damien kicked Austin onto his back and climbed on top of him, gripping his throat once more.

Alyssa slowly pulled herself from the wreckage of the car, falling out of the shattered window frame and onto the ground. As she turned over, she saw her father on top of Austin.

"I should have just let you die in the trainyard that night. You have brought me nothing but pain!" Damien fumed through his gritted teeth.

Austin could feel himself fading fast, only seconds away from losing consciousness and his life. Damien stared at Austin anxiously waiting for the life to leave his eyes when he was suddenly attacked from the side, Alyssa throwing her own body into his. As the two toppled onto the ground, Austin coughed violently as he tried to regain any oxygen he could. Damien got to his feet a moment sooner than Alyssa and quickly shoved his daughter back to the ground.

"Even now you still help him! Why?" Damien screamed.

"Because a long time ago, I realized that the man who claimed to raise me was an irredeemable monster who did unforgivable things. Right here, right now, Austin is the only one who can end a sick bastard like you," Alyssa cried.

"End me? No one can end me! I'm unkill—"

Austin sent a strong right hook into Damien's mouth, shutting down his proclamation. A flurry of fists instantly put Damien on the defensive, Austin finishing it off with a solid uppercut. The punch landed squarely under his jaw, Damien hitting the ground hard. He stumbled to his feet, widening his stance just to hold his balance but, as Austin approached, Damien pulled a small pocket pistol from a holster concealed on his ankle. Austin and Alyssa froze, not making any sudden movements.

"That's it, that's the look of pure fear that I was looking for. You've lost, Austin, and I've won." Damien grinned proudly as he brushed his finger against the trigger.

Austin turned to Alyssa and stared at her, hopelessly waiting for the inevitable when he began to hear a loud fluttering sound. He turned back and a smile involuntarily crept onto his face as a chopper rose from beneath the cliff, Vlad in the pilot's seat, and Mike and Grant standing by the open side door. Damien turned, shielding himself from the sudden rush of wind that blew through him.

Taking advantage of the distraction, Austin quickly and easily disarmed Damien, now holding the gun in his hand. Damien looked down the barrel of the small gun and scoffed.

"So that's it then? You're just going to kill me? After everything we've been through? After everything we've experienced together?" Damien proclaimed. "You were like a son to me! I treated you like my own blood! And this is how it ends between us? That's it?"

Austin held the gun firmly in his hand as he looked at the man before him, the man he once considered a father. Austin tilted his head slightly to the side.

"That's it."

Austin pulled the trigger, firing a single shot into Damien's chest. Austin could see the look of shock on Damien's face but only for a moment as Damien toppled backwards, stepping off the cliff and down into the dense forest below. The pistol landed on the ground, imbedding itself in the snow as Austin collapsed to his knees. As Alyssa knelt down next to him, wrapping her arms around him, he stared at his bloody and wounded hands, tears pooling in his eyes.

"It's okay."

Austin's head jerked up, Mike and Grant now standing right in front of him.

"It's over." Mike smiled.

Grant extended his hand. "Let's go home."

Chapter 24

Back to Normal

The loud thud of knocks at the door radiated throughout the apartment, Josh nearly collapsing onto the floor once it opened.

"Calm down, Josh, we're not gonna be late." Austin chuckled as he headed back towards his kitchen.

"You don't know that, there could be traffic. There could be an accident. There could be a super soldier rampaging downtown, anything's possible." Josh's eyes expanded with crazed excitement.

"I don't think that last one is happening anytime soon." Nick punched Josh playfully in the arm as he walked past him.

"Where are you guys headed tonight?" Debbie inquired, walking out of the second bedroom with an empty box in her hand.

"We're just going out to dinner," Austin answered.

"But Josh is anxious because it's the first time Rebecca is meeting everyone," Nick included.

"Come on, Josh, it's gonna be fine. She's going to love everyone and everyone is going to love her," Debbie reassured.

"I know, I just want the introductions to be over." Josh bit his nail nervously.

Austin patted Josh on the back. "Come on, we still have to pick up Demi on the way."

"Are you sure you don't want to call Alyssa?" Nick inquired.

"Yeah, maybe she'll want to join us," Josh added.

"No, that's okay. We haven't spoken much since the raid. I think it's best if I just give her space. What happened is a lot to process," Austin admitted.

"True, I mean you did kill her father right in front of her. That has to be a lot, even if she did hate the guy," Josh thought aloud.

Austin's eyes widened slightly. "Yeah, so I'm giving her *a lot* of space."

Christian walked out of the room and dumped a stuffed garbage bag onto the floor.

"Man, Austin, when you said you kept storage in here, I didn't know you meant junk storage."

"Stop complaining and put your shoes on." Austin smiled. "Take the night off and come out with us. You won't finish moving in overnight."

Christian's face contorted in deliberation. "I don't know, I'm sure I could find better people than you guys to hang out with."

Austin laughed. "Shut up and let's go."

Christian obliged and threw on his shoes, running to the front door to catch up.

"You'll be good here on your own?" Austin asked as he looked at Debbie.

"Of course, you guys have fun. I'll just clean up a little bit more and head home for the night. You're right, this definitely won't be finished in one day," Debbie explained.

Debbie watched as the four young man left with smiles on their faces. She couldn't help but smile herself, knowing what had truly transpired over the last few months.

"Have a great time, you deserve it."

As expected, the night was perfect, everyone instantly

getting along and laughing over dinner. As dinner ended and the large group strolled by the water's edge, Austin caught sight of someone he didn't expect to see. Alyssa slowly walked towards the oncoming group, a slight smile on her face.

"Catch up when you're done," Christian whispered to Austin with a smile.

The group continued on as Austin walked up to Alyssa.

"Alyssa... hi," Austin greeted, sounding like he could barely string those two words together.

"Hi." She smiled.

"What — um, what are you doing here? How'd you find me?"

"I went to your apartment but your mother said you already left. She said you were grabbing dinner around here. She's a very sweet woman."

"Oh, okay. How — um, how are your mom and Sean doing?" Austin inquired awkwardly.

"My mom's trying to stay strong but she's obsessed with finding him. Technically, my father's considered missing as of now. And Sean's handling it in his own way, at least I think he is," Alyssa explained.

Austin looked at Alyssa worriedly. "And how are you?"

"I'm okay, better than I thought I'd be to be honest. I guess I hated him even more than I realized."

"Even if you hated him, it's still okay to be sad he's gone. When it happened, even though I was the one who caused it, I felt sad. Sad that he was gone, sad that what I thought we once had was ruined," Austin confessed.

"Tormenting us even after death, he really was a bastard, wasn't he?" Alyssa chuckled half-heartedly. "Listen, there was something I wanted to talk to you about and I didn't want any more time to pass."

"Sure, anything."

Austin listened intently.

"You know how I feel about you, it's no secret that I'm crazy about you," she began.

"After what we've been through, yeah, I'd say that's a safe bet," Austin teased. "You know I'm crazy about you too."

"I do." Alyssa paused. "But I was giving it some thought and I think right now, after everything that happened, it would be a mistake to be together again."

The hurt was apparent on Austin's face.

He swallowed the lump in his throat. "I understand."

"Austin, you don't have to do that. You can hate me for this, I wouldn't blame you."

Austin scoffed, "I could never hate you."

She smiled, her eyes beginning to glisten with tears. "Are you sure you're okay with this?"

Austin held back his own and nodded slightly.

"Hard to believe two strangers who used to jog past each other would end up like this."

"We've definitely been through it." She giggled lightly.

Austin simply stared into her eyes, a small smile forced onto his face. "Right people."

"Right place," Alyssa added.

"Wrong time."

Knowing that those words were the best closure they would ever get, the two embraced in a hug, holding each other tightly, as if knowing it would be the last time they would find themselves so close.

"I'm sorry," Alyssa cried from over Austin's shoulder.

"Me too," he responded simply.

"Hey, you guys coming?" Nick yelled from down the path, Demi jamming her elbow into his side.

"Can't you read body language at all? This wasn't a good talk," she murmured.

"Sorry," Nick whimpered.

"Come on, Nick, you're better than that. Josh is the clueless one," Christian joked.

"Shut it, Chris!" Josh barked.

Austin and Alyssa heard the distant banter and laughed.

"You have really great friends, Austin."

"They're more than friends, they're family."

"Evening, Austin," a voice spoke up from nearby.

Austin and Alyssa turned around, surprised to see Mike and Grant standing before them.

"What are you doing here?" Austin asked.

"Just wanted to let you know that we finally closed the file on Project: Hercules. All four locations were successfully raided, all of Damien's research was destroyed, and Damien was eliminated." Mike looked at Alyssa. "I'm sorry for your loss, this is awkward."

Alyssa giggled. "I get it, Mike, thank you."

"I appreciate the debrief but you tracked me down out here just to tell me that?" Austin asked with confusion.

"Well, if I remember correctly, there was a deal put in place when you took on that mission," Grant replied.

Austin's eyes widened as the realization dawned on him.

"You... found my father?"

Mike inhaled deeply. "Unfortunately, it's a little more complicated than that."

Grant handed a thin file to Austin. "We searched all our databases to find any record of his actions over the last decade but nothing came up."

Austin skimmed through the file, seeing that all the pages within were either blank or had the words *"no results found"* written across them.

"After we came up empty handed, we decided to track him down in real time using facial recognition software on every camera feed we have access to in the country. Then we reached out to our foreign contacts, still nothing," Mike explained further.

"I don't — I don't understand what any of this means. He's not dead but he hasn't been living either?" Austin questioned.

"We honestly don't know. It's as if the day he walked out on you and your family is the day he vanished," Mike admitted.

"No bank statements, purchase history, census report, death certificate, or digital footage exists. I have to admit, I've never seen anything like this in my entire career," Grant continued.

"So he just fell off the face of the Earth, just like that? My father was good at his job but he definitely wasn't capable of something like that."

Grant's stern stare locked with Austin's. "Unless he got mixed up with people that were."

Austin was confused, barely able to stammer his next question. "Are you telling me there's a chance my father got involved with people who have the same power as D.A.R.C.?"

"We don't want to confirm anything just yet, especially with no evidence, but to simply disappear like this is not something normal civilians are capable of, even civilians in your father's line of work," Mike replied.

"So what now?"

"Now, we keep looking." Grant smiled. "I may be a bastard but I never break my word. You delivered on Damien; we're going to make sure we deliver on this."

Austin smiled back. "Thank you, guys."

The two agents turned to walk away.

"Don't thank us, just don't be late." Mike raised his arm, giving a half-hearted wave behind him.

"Late for what?" Austin asked.

Grant looked over his shoulder. "Late for work. All D.A.R.C. field agents are expected to swipe their card no later than eight a.m.."

"Wait, this wasn't a one-time thing?"

Mike scoffed, "Not any more. Hardwick likes you too much to let you go."

Grant gave a slight salute. "See you in the morning, Agent Michaels."

Austin didn't realize it until that very moment but he enjoyed the work he had done. Though starting out on this sudden, laborious journey as an unaware civilian, he pushed himself and strived to rise to the top. The drastic changes to his life were obvious and challenging but also necessary. Austin learned things about his life and about himself that forced him to grow into a better person, all while doing genuine good for the world.

Austin smiled widely, the thought of such a glorious prospect growing broader in his mind with every passing second. He raised his hand and returned the same salute back.

"I'll be there."